INTO the SIDEWAYS WORLD

Books by Ross Welford

THE DOG WHO SAVED THE WORLD

INTO THE SIDEWAYS WORLD

THE KID WHO CAME FROM SPACE

THE 1,000-YEAR-OLD BOY

TIME TRAVELLING WITH A HAMSTER

WHAT NOT TO DO IF YOU TURN INVISIBLE

WHEN WE GOT LOST IN DREAMLAND

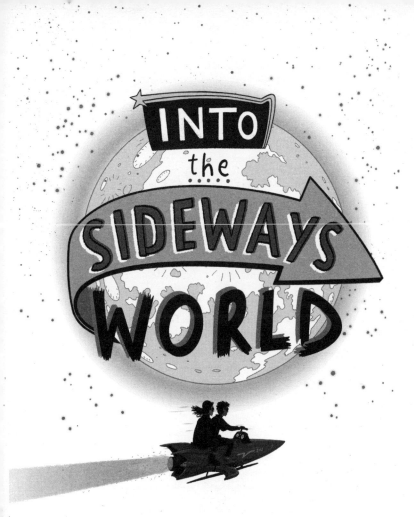

Ross Welford

HarperCollins *Children's Books*

First published in Great Britain by
HarperCollins *Children's Books* in 2022
HarperCollins *Children's Books* is a division of HarperCollins*Publishers* Ltd
1 London Bridge Street
London SE1 9GF

www.harpercollins.co.uk

HarperCollins*Publishers*
1st Floor, Watermarque Building, Ringsend Road
Dublin 4, Ireland

1

Signed Edition ISBN 978-0-00-853516-2
ISBN 978-0-00-833384-3

Ross Welford asserts the moral right to be identified as the author of the work.
A CIP catalogue record for this title is available from the British Library.

Typeset in Adobe Garamond by Palimpsest Book Production Ltd,
Falkirk, Stirlingshire

Printed and bound in the UK using 100% renewable
electricity at CPI Group (UK) Ltd

MIX
Paper from
responsible sources
FSC® C007454

This book is produced from independently certified FSC™ paper
to ensure responsible forest management.

www.harpercollins.co.uk/green

'Our problems are man-made, therefore they may be solved by man. . . . No problem of human destiny is beyond human beings.'

John F. Kennedy
US President, 1961–63

A FEW YEARS FROM NOW

The whole world was heading for war when Manny Weaver and I went through a 'grey hole' to another world.

Till then, I didn't believe in magic. Fairies, witches, magic spells, strange lands with talking animals, monsters with three heads and potions to turn you into a giant?

Even when I was very little, I knew all that stuff wasn't real. Then I encountered Manny, and the strange animal we called a 'cog', and the brother who I'd never met because he died before I was born. I rode through a lightning storm on a flying jet ski, and lived in a World Without War.

And so now, if you ask me if I believe in magic? Let's just say I'm not so sure.

PART ONE

CHAPTER 1

We watch the war on TV most nights as it grows worse and gets closer.

Dad sits there, tutting and shaking his head, calling the prime minister names. My older sister, Alex, gets angry, disagreeing with everything Dad says about it, though I don't think she understands it much better than any of us. Then they shout.

Mam gets upset with both of them, and she has even started shooing me out of the room when it comes on. She says, 'You're only twelve, Willa. You don't need to see this stuff.'

Then Dad says, 'This is history happening right now. History girl needs to see it!'

'History girl' – ha! I won the Year Six history prize last summer, and Dad hasn't stopped going on about it. He loves stuff like that. Me, I just wrote an essay about the American president John F. Kennedy (the one who was murdered in 1963), with a cool drawing that I copied from a photo and coloured in really carefully.

When it comes to what's happening now, and World

War Three being just round the corner, I'm scared. Everyone is. Well, everyone apart from Manny Weaver, but we'll come to him soon enough.

Even if I do leave the room, it makes no difference. It's there when I open my laptop or my phone: video clips of bombs falling from planes, smoking buildings, people being dug out of rubble, angry mobs throwing things at angry soldiers, and angry people posting angry messages on Kwik-e.

I hate it, but it's pretty hard not to look. You know what I mean. You've probably seen the same sort of stuff.

I'm quite good at understanding history when it's in the past. Less so when it's happening all around me.

I don't even know why they're fighting. Water, I think. And oil, probably. God? In some places, I think it's all three. One bunch of people hating another bunch of people, everyone else taking sides, and suddenly . . . boom! There's a war. That seems to be how it works. Mam says I shouldn't be scared because the war is happening miles and miles away in other countries. But it's getting closer; everyone knows that.

My school prize, by the way, was a book called *A Little History of the World*. There are a lot of wars in it. It sits on my shelf, more or less unread. Every time I go to pick it up, I remember my name being announced in the school hall and nobody cheering.

Mam and Dad couldn't be at the prize-giving because

they had a big meeting with the SunSeasons people who are going to buy our family business and merge it with the bigger (and much nicer) park nearby. They didn't see what happened – the tumbleweed moment when I walked on to the stage and only the teachers clapped – and I haven't really told them. I haven't really told anyone because there's no one to tell. I suppose I could tell old Maudie, but seeing as she helped me so much with the essay it would only upset her. I've kept it to myself.

Meanwhile, the certificate I got is still on the mantelpiece, next to Dad's air-force medals, and the photo-and-candle shrine to baby Alexander. He was my older brother who didn't make it past eight days and is now part of history himself.

Right now, they're arguing again, Mam and Dad, and their door just slammed. It's sometimes about the war, usually about work. The business is in trouble, I know that much. Mam calls Dad 'lazy and unimaginative'; he calls her 'controlling and obsessive'. I can hear them from my room, hissing at each other like angry cats.

Alex stays in her own room, headphones on, fighting a game-war on her computer with someone she's never met. It wouldn't be so bad if she would at least talk to me, but instead she just sighs and seethes like the faulty boiler in the shower block.

Conflict? It's all around me, and I hate it.

Then, before we know it, the prime minister's on

everyone's screens saying that Britain may be forced to declare war, if our allies do. Suddenly it's all anyone is talking about.

That is when I meet Manny and find the Sideways World, and nothing is the same ever again.

CHAPTER 2

I think I love Manny Weaver! Not *that* kind of love, don't worry. All right, by anyone's standards, Manny is very good-looking, but we're only twelve, and I don't get any of that heart-pounding-squishy-tummy feeling that my sister Alex says is a sure-fire sign of being in love. (She should know: it seems to happen to her about every other month. She's fifteen.)

So, I guess I just like Manny – a *lot*. What's more, he seems to like me, which marks him out as unusual among the kids in my school.

Manny has a streak of . . . *something* in him. Something I noticed this morning when he came into our classroom and stood in the doorway: tallish and skinnyish, with a slight stoop, like he's always getting ready to duck. Everyone turned to look at him: the New Kid.

You or I would probably have done the whole eyes-down-please-don't-look-at-me thing and scuttled to the place (next to me, worse luck) that Mrs Potts has created: new notebook, school-logo pencil and 'Welcome to Class 7P' card.

Not Manny. He stared back for, like, *ages*. There must have been about twenty people in the classroom. He looked at us all, one by one, his shoulders hunched, his eyes hardly blinking through his long blond fringe. He wasn't exactly scowling, but he didn't look friendly, either. Gradually, everyone in the class fell silent as this staring match went on. When his gaze had taken us all in, he gave a tiny nod and whispered, 'Hi.' Then the small crowd of Year Sevens parted for him respectfully as he made his way to our table and sat down.

It was obviously another of Mrs Potts's attempts to 'bring me out of my shell', as she once said. You know, pair up the New Kid with the Quiet Kid and see if they make friends. Or perhaps she thinks I'll be a good influence on him. I never get into trouble at school, and Manny has a look of mischief about him.

I think it's his eyes mainly: as green and as shiny as a halved kiwi fruit, and starey and sad, which is an odd combination.

There's no uniform at our school, but we're supposed to dress 'sensibly'. Manny came in wearing striped trousers, rainbow-hoop socks and a purple velvet sweatshirt. I heard Deena Malik say, 'Wow, check out Willy Wonka!'

It's all part of his streak of 'otherness'.

A streak of magic, it feels like.

At the end of the school day, I'm waiting by the gym

to walk home with Madison and Jess. It will make the walk longer, but I don't really mind. I've brought a Fry's Chocolate Cream with me to share with them, but then I see them walking off on the other side of the playing fields, too far away to shout after them. How they got there without passing the gym is a mystery. I turn my bike round and go the other way, trying to push down the thought that they're avoiding me.

Manny is at the end of the alley that leads up from the seafront to school, which everyone calls Dog Poo Lane. He's just sitting on the wall next to his scuffed yellow bicycle, seemingly minding his own business.

'Hi, Willa,' he says before I'm even level with him. I have to brake sharply not to hit him. 'I thought I'd tell you about myself. Save time, you know?'

What do you say when someone says that? Well, wittily, I go, 'Erm . . .' which he takes to mean, *Yes, go right ahead – tell me absolutely everything about yourself even though I haven't asked.*

He pushes back his long blond fringe and says, 'All right then.'

We start pushing our bikes along the pavement, past the boarded-up shopfronts with graffiti on them. It's May, but there's a cold, damp breeze blowing in off the grey North Sea; little clumps of litter snap at our feet like naughty puppies. He stops to pull an ice-lolly wrapper out of his wheel spokes.

'Don't be freaked out, Willa,' he says. 'It's just I've been in about a thousand foster families with new parents, new brothers and sisters, and I just think it's quicker this way. I'll end up telling you this stuff sooner or later, so why not make it sooner?' Then he grins as if daring me to disagree.

'Because . . . I don't really know you?'

'Exactly! And this way you will. You see, we're going to be friends, I can tell. Whoops, watch out – dog poo!'

I skip round it. 'You can?'

'Believe me, when you've been in as many schools, families, Pupil Referral Units and children's homes as I have, you get a sense about this stuff. Besides, you need a friend, so why not me?'

Prickling with shame, I stop pushing my bike and swing my leg over, ready to ride off.

'Hey, wait!' says Manny. 'What's wrong?'

'*You're* wrong. I don't need a friend.'

'So why are you coming out of school alone? Why were you hanging round the library at lunchtime on your own? Why—'

'All right, all right,' I snap back. 'Maybe I don't have *loads* of friends. What's it got to do with you?'

'Well, I don't have any. Not yet. So, you know . . .'

Manny can see that I'm a bit embarrassed, so he quickly picks up the thread of the conversation.

'Right,' he says. 'Emanuel Weaver – you know that.

Birthday: February first, presents are welcome but not required. Kidding! No brothers or sisters. Last foster family emigrated to Australia to get as far away from me as possible.'

I glance at him. He's half smiling, so I guess he's joking. He continues. 'Now living in the care of North Tyneside social services at Winston Churchill House behind the seafront. Never met me dad. Mam . . . no longer with us.'

He pauses. 'There you go. That's me.'

It's all so abrupt, especially the last bit. I say, 'Oh. Right. Good. Well, not the last bit, that's not good. Sorry. Your mam, I mean . . .' I'm babbling and embarrassed.

'Aye, well, thanks. You probably want to know what happened to her?'

'No! Well, I mean, if she's, you know, erm . . . dead, then, erm . . .'

Oh no, I hate this.

Manny jumps in. 'She's not dead, Willa.'

'Oh. It's just you said she's no longer with us, so I thought . . .'

'Mental breakdown,' he says. 'Basically, she went to the shops and never came back. It's a long story. I was very little.'

'That's horrible, Manny. Poor her. Poor you.'

He stops pushing his bike, fiddling with one of the brake wires. 'Thanks,' he says with a sigh. 'No one really knows exactly what happened. I was only four, so I was hardly told anything other than "Mummy's poorly in the head", that sort of thing. She's still a "missing person" officially. But Jakob – that's my social worker – says I should learn to live with the possibility that my mam is dead.' He shrugs. 'Only she isn't.'

It's difficult to know what to say. Nobody usually shares that much personal stuff with me, especially not straight away. We push our bikes in silence for another moment, then I say, 'How do you know?'

'I don't,' he says. 'But just because I don't know doesn't mean it's not true. I'll find her one day. I can feel it.'

I look over at him again, and he has his jaw stuck out and his mouth clamped tight shut as if he's used to telling this story and not crying about it. His eyes are shiny. It's really awkward for a few moments, then Manny says, 'Okay. That's me. What about you?'

Wow.

'Erm . . . er . . . Wilhemina Shafto, but no one calls me that. Birthday: November fourteenth. I live with my mam and dad, who run the Whitley Bay HappyLand Leisure Park.' I'm gabbling, and it all sounds far too perfect and normal compared with Manny's life history, so I add, 'I have a sister called Alex. She's fifteen and a total pain. Plus my mam and dad are forever arguing because business is so bad, and . . . well . . .'

I stop talking. It's all true, but of course I don't know

16

the details. Mam and Dad have told me not to talk about the business in case word spreads that HappyLand is in trouble. Whenever the SunSeasons people are due to come round in their shiny cars, my parents' shouting gets worse.

'. . . and the war,' I add. 'They're always arguing about the war.'

'Why?' Manny says, sounding genuinely puzzled.

'Well, you know, they have different opinions about it.'

'Can they do anything to change it?'

'Well, no – obviously. None of us can.'

'Nope. That's why I stick to worrying about things I can change.'

We're at the point where I carry on straight to go home, and Manny has to turn left to go to Winston Churchill House. He says, 'See – we're friends now? Meet you here tomorrow at eight thirty and we'll cycle in together. By the way, what's your number?'

'My . . . my *number*?'

'Yeah – you know, your phone number?'

I have to open my phone and find my number because it's not in my head. I don't think I've ever been asked before, at least not by someone my own age.

I say, 'Don't you use Kwik-es?' and he looks a bit embarrassed but covers it with a grin.

'Nah – that's for losers! I'm old-school. Check *this* out!'

He takes out his phone, which is tiny with hardly any screen. There are buttons on it, like on phones from years ago, and the logo says ERICSSON, which I have never even heard of.

'It's kind of an antique. My social worker's Swedish, and he got it for me. It makes calls and sends texts. That's all. Jakob doesn't really approve of smartphones. Reckons they "stop us talking face to face", and so on. That reminds me,' Manny says, reaching into his bag and handing over a battered book. 'I thought you'd like to read this.'

CRYPTIDS – BEYOND LOCH NESS
by
Dr E. Borbas

On the front, there's a grainy picture of something in a lake – the Loch Ness Monster, I presume. I flip the book over and scan the blurb on the back.

From ancient stories of the Loch Ness Monster, to modern tales of the Beast of Bodmin Moor, there are countless accounts worldwide of mysterious creatures. If they are real, where do they come from?

I look up and Manny is smirking. 'Jakob says that lending someone a book is the perfect way to make friends because you have to give it back, and then you can talk about it. Some of the words are a bit tricky, but it's pretty good.'

With that, he is off on his bike, and I'm left flicking through the strange book. It has pictures of big, catlike beasts and lake-dwelling giant serpents, something called a bigfoot and a Mexican monster that sucks the blood of goats . . .

It's a minute or two till I get on to my bike, and I realise that, despite how weird this all was, Manny's right. I think I have a friend.

CHAPTER 3

Weeks have passed since Manny lent me that first book. He's lent me more since, with titles like:

YETI – The Himalayan Mountain Man

and

LAKE MONSTERS OF THE WORLD!

Now it's a Saturday afternoon, and he's picked up another one from the bookstall at the school's spring fête.

MEGALODON – The Final Proof?

The megalodon is supposed to be a massive shark, like twenty metres long, which lives in the unexplored depths of the ocean. Flicking through it, I see that most of the pictures in the book are blurred, or taken from miles away.

I try to point this out to Manny as we unlock our bikes after the fête.

'The problem is,' I say, holding up the copy of *Megalodon*, 'the final proof isn't really proof, is it? Otherwise, they wouldn't have a question mark in the title.'

Manny hunches his shoulders, which he does when he's thinking. 'You know what your problem is?' he says, huffily. 'You have no imagination!'

'No imagina— Manny! That's not fair! It's just . . . there's no real evidence.'

'There you go again. Flippin' *evidence*! What about eyewitness accounts? That's what most of your precious history is about, isn't it? People who have seen stuff! Honestly, Willa . . .'

He cycles off in the direction of the seafront, and I follow him.

We stop outside the mini-supermarket, and I sigh a little when I see Deena Malik and her pathetic 'gang' approaching. She has taken to calling us 'History and Mystery'. Thankfully, it hasn't caught on with anyone else, but that doesn't stop her. I discreetly hand him the book back, and we both head into the shop.

Deena and her mates follow us in. I pick up some sweets, and while I'm paying I keep my eyes fixed on the video screen behind the counter. It's usually war news, but this time it's something else.

'. . . **to our north-east correspondent, Jamie Bates.**'

'*Thank you, Tatiana. The quiet coastal town of Whitley Bay in Tyneside has been buzzing for days now with reported sightings of what locals are calling the Whitley Cog.*'

Deena has sidled up behind Manny and goes, 'Ha! This is your sort of thing, Mystery!'

He ignores her, his attention on the screen.

'*Described as a cross between a huge dog and a wild cat, the animal has been spotted on beaches as well as on agricultural land as far north as Blyth. I spoke to a local woman, who described a recent close encounter.*'

I gasp as old Maudie, HappyLand's part-time handywoman, appears on the screen, being interviewed sitting on her favourite seafront bench. 'Manny, look – that's Maudie!'

'*It was dusk, and I was just sittin' here like I do, and that's when I saw it, down by the beach. It turned its head and looked straight at me: big yellow eyes, and I swear it had a massive fish hanging from its mouth. Great big pointy ears. And then – whoosh – it was back off into the water, quick as you like, and that was it.*'

The reporter is walking along the beach now. I can see HappyLand's ragged flag in the background.

'Sightings of large creatures like this are not unknown in Britain, although very little in the way of hard evidence has ever been produced . . .'

'That'll be because it's all made up,' sneers Deena. 'Listen to her, the silly old cow! Hey, History – isn't that your rubbish caravan park?'

The sweet packet crackles as I tighten my fist round it. I'm seething inside, although I don't say anything. For a start, it's a holiday centre, not a 'caravan park'. Also – this is Maudie! I really like her. She helps me with my homework and gives me hot chocolate and . . .

'Spring is, of course, the start of the tourist season here in Whitley Bay. It remains to be seen if the presence of a mysterious animal will draw the crowds – or scare them away. This is Jamie Bates in Tyneside for **NewsHour.***'*

'Thank you, Jamie. And you can see pictures that purport to be of the Whitley Cog on the **NewsHour** *website. Back to the worsening international situation now, and the prime minister, Mrs Boateng, has reacted quickly to reports that . . .'*

There's a hurried movement behind me and the tinkling of the shop's bell.

When I look round, Manny's gone. Deena is hooting with mocking laughter. 'He's off to catch it!'

Her friends cackle in response

I hurry out of the shop after Manny, leaving my Haribos on the counter, Deena's jeering ringing in my ears.

'History and Mystery strike again, ha ha! Hey, thanks for the sweets!'

'Ignore her,' says Manny, who's waiting a bit further down the street. He's unable to keep his voice from shaking with excitement. 'I want to see the Whitley Cog! Quick – look on your phone! Mine doesn't do websites.'

I bring up the *NewsHour* webpage. The picture is very bad. It's been taken from a huge distance away and blown up again and again so that it's very blurry. You can sort of see the big pointy ears, and a single glinting eye, but most of the body is hidden by undergrowth.

'See what I mean?' I say. 'This is not evidence, this is . . .'

I look up at Manny, expecting him to be as disappointed as I am, but instead his face is alive.

'Did you say that old lady was Maudie, your gardener?'

'Yeah – well, she helps out and mends things and . . .'

'And is she a liar?'

'No! Of course not! She's . . . she's Maudie.'

He's off, shouting back, 'Come on then! What are you waiting for?'

CHAPTER 4

We head straight to HappyLand, which is right next to our house. At least this 'Whitley Cog' is a good excuse to call in on Maudie, who lives in one of the lodges.

Manny's bike gets a puncture on the way. He wheels it behind me to Maudie's workshop-cum-hut where – rain or shine – she sits on an ancient, crooked sofa listening to the news on the radio, or stroking one of her cats, or snoozing.

Manny's been pestering me from the minute we left the shop. 'What's she like? What's she seen?'

'Just play it cool,' I tell him. 'Maudie is very . . . mellow.'

She's in her usual position when we come round the neatly clipped hedge. She looks up and smiles, which makes her glasses slip down her nose, then heaves herself off the sofa. It creaks almost as much as she does, waking Plato the tabby from his hundredth nap of the day.

Maudie's always pleased to have something to fix. She beams at the broken bicycle as though Manny's presented her with a bunch of flowers, and rubs her hands together.

She's too old to do any of the heavy work around the park, but she always has something in pieces on her workbench.

'Puncture, is it, young fella?' she says, spotting it straight away. In one swift movement, she upturns Manny's bike and gets to work detaching the wheel and then taking the tyre off. 'I like your jeans,' she says to Manny, pointing with a tyre lever. They are red-and-white checked denim (I'm not kidding). 'Had a pair like that meself once, back in the day.'

Maudie's very old, quite short and so round that she rocks when she walks in and out of her shed, fetching tools and repair kits, and so on. I don't know exactly how old she is – Mam reckons 'well into her eighties', but she looks much younger, with a shiny, round face, smooth and tanned pale copper from the weak sun and salty air. She wears an ancient navy-blue beret over long white hair, which she often braids with beads. She always has the same dungarees covered with coloured badges and sewn-on patches, with slogans on them like **PEACE** ☮, **THE POWER OF THE FLOWER**, and one she claims is worth hundreds of pounds that says **JFK FOR PRESIDENT '60**. She has it pinned on the bib of her dungarees – 'next to my heart', she says.

Maudie's a bit like an extra grandparent, I guess. Mam's parents, Gramps and Nana, live in Leeds, so I don't see them all that often. Dad's parents separated. His mam lives in London; she's okay. His dad died in the big pandemic when I was very little, so I can't really remember him.

'You're quiet, son,' Maudie says to Manny with a smile, showing gappy old teeth. 'Ah, here it is. Massive great thorn. Soon put this right.'

Quiet? It's like poor Manny's going to burst.

We stand and watch Maudie's old, gnarled fingers deftly marking the inner tube and applying the glue and the patch, and eventually Manny can't hold back any longer.

It's like a light has come on behind his eyes, and he says, 'What do you know about that animal? We saw you on the TV! Where exactly was it? Do you think it's escaped?' A cascade of questions.

Maudie looks up slowly from the upturned bike and adjusts her beret. 'Ha ha! It speaks! Aye, I certainly did see it! Massive thing it was.' She holds her hand out to indicate its size – easily up to her waist.

'When was this?' says Manny, the urgency in his voice unmistakable.

'Couple nights ago. Havin' a little drink I was, over in the birding hide, you know?'

I nod. There's a small wildlife reserve with a man-made lake between the leisure park and the beach. There's a broken-down old caravan for bird-watchers where Maudie sometimes goes with a can of beer and sits watching the birds as the sky grows darker over the shallow lake. She once told me it was 'better than anything on the telly'.

'He came out of the water. It was getting dark, and he came up the lake shore and then into the shadows, and I lost him.'

Manny's face falls.

'Don't worry, son,' says Maudie. 'I kept looking, and then I saw him again, down that way.' She waves her hand towards the sea. 'He was heading along the beach to Culvercot, keeping in the shadows.'

'Hang on, Maudie,' I say. 'On TV, you said you saw it coming out of the sea.'

She winks at me through her smudged glasses. 'Ha! Questioning your sources, eh? Little, ah, *diversion*, that was! Don't want everyone swarmin' in here, disturbing the birds, now do we? We've got a red-backed shrike at the moment, and I haven't spotted one of them since 2026. There you go,' she says, turning Manny's bike the right way up. 'Good as new.'

'Do you really think it's some kind of creature that's never been seen before?' I say.

Maudie gives a massive shrug that makes her whole top half wobble. 'No idea, pet. But just cos we don't know doesn't mean it's not true.'

I recognise the phrase: it's like what Manny said to me about his mam being alive.

'Exactly!' he crows, then he grabs the bike and hops

on it so quickly that he's several metres away before he brakes hard and turns back. 'Thanks, Maudie. Thanks a lot!' Then he's off again, expecting me to follow.

I do.

Manny has the annoying ability – which I also kind of admire if I'm honest – to treat everywhere as if he's automatically welcome. Like that day he arrived in school: he just found his place, immediately rearranging stuff to his liking.

He's doing it again as he whizzes on his bike through HappyLand, completely ignoring the NO CYCLING signs. I would tell him not to because, well . . . because it's the rules. But it's not high season yet, and so there aren't many guests. (To be honest, even during high season it's pretty empty, which is another reason why Mam and Dad are always arguing.)

This is where I think of as 'home'. Our little house is almost on-site, and Mam and Dad run the business that's been in the family for years. There's a picture in reception of great-grandad Roger who started the whole thing as a caravan park in nineteen fifty-something, and now there's 120 pitches, and they're not even caravans – not the sort you pull behind a car anyway. Most of them are what we call 'bunga-lodges' – single-storey cottages, basically. They're getting a bit damp and run-down now, though – at least, that's what the latest one-star HaveAGoodTrip.com rating said, which really upset Dad. (He says we don't have enough money to upgrade them.)

I pedal past the open-air swimming pool. It needs a clean and some replacement tiles, but it's unheated and no one ever goes in anyway except for toddlers on the warmest days of summer. Even then, they come out as pink as Percy Pigs and have to be rubbed warm by their mums.

I've caught up with Manny at Jungle Joe's GymTastic – a kind of jungle-themed outdoor playpark with slides and stuff. It's all roped off at the moment because of missing parts and a broken carousel.

'Wow, Willa! Shame about your playground!'

'It's not mine,' I say, suddenly feeling a bit embarrassed at the run-down holiday park. He's not listening. He doesn't stop till he's at the opposite end of the park, where there's a decrepit old caravan half covered with branches a few metres from the nature reserve – basically a very large pond.

'Is this where she meant?' says Manny, and I nod. 'In that case, this is where we start our search. What time does it get dark?'

'About, erm . . . eightish?' I say. Manny has a kind of manic look about him, and I can see this whole thing might get a bit out of hand.

If only I'd known.

'Are you quite sure about this?' I say to him.

He rolls his eyes. 'Willa! If he's been spotted here once, then surely that's the best chance we have of spotting him again. Yeah? Unless Maudie's lying, of course,' he adds, slyly. 'Oh, come on – don't give me that look!'

'It's . . . Mam and Dad,' I say. 'They don't like me being out after dark.'

Manny laughs, but he's not mocking me, I don't think. It's just that he doesn't seem to see this as any sort of a problem.

'Okay – number one, you can practically *see* your house from here.'

We can't, but it's not far. I get his point.

'Two, so long as you stay on this side of the little fence, you're still on the park premises, yeah? You're still *at home*. Three, it won't be dark. Twilight maybe, but that's not "after dark". Four, it's a wildlife investigation for a school project. We're gathering evidence.'

Now this bit definitely isn't true, but, before I can say anything, he's slipped off his backpack and brought out yet another book about mysterious creatures that he waves at me.

'This is a school project, and you are my partner!' He doesn't wait for me to respond. 'See you tonight at seven! No. Make that tomorrow.'

'Why tomorrow?'

Manny turns away, looking a bit guilty. 'There's something I need.'

Then he just cycles off, a pedalling whirlwind of colours, as if his mind is already somewhere else entirely.

He stops after a few metres and looks back. I realise I have a worried face, and so I readjust it. Manny grins and pushes his fringe back.

'Relax, Willa. No one's ever remembered for the rules they followed!'

CHAPTER 5

I'm still thinking about what Manny said about rules when I pass Maudie's lodge on the way back home. It's pretty much invisible to the rest of the leisure park, hidden behind a hedge. Half of the plot is taken up with junk, laid out in neat rows, some of it covered with tarpaulins. There's a broken swing, two old car engines, half a classic motorcycle ('A Norton,' Maudie says with pride, as though I should be impressed), a sit-on lawnmower, a push-along lawnmower, a plastic playhouse in pieces. There's also her shed, the front of which opens up completely to reveal a workbench with countless tools, polished like they're new.

Maudie's wrecked sofa, plus a garden chair draped in rugs and cushions, are arranged next to a wood-burner, all beneath a corrugated-iron roof with a faded sign saying BAN THE BOMB hanging from it. She calls it her 'sitooterie' because you 'sit oot' in it.

She looks up, smiling, as I come round the hedge, and puts down a large wooden letter H that has fallen from the HappyLand sign at the entrance that she's been cleaning.

34

She's been here since Dad was a boy, when HappyLand was literally just caravans. She lives in it for free because of her job.

She doesn't have much family. There's a son called Callum who lives in Canada. I've never met him. I don't know who Callum's dad is. Maudie has cats, though: three of them, called Aristotle, Plato and Berta.

'Poor old Maudie,' said Mam once to me and Alex. 'She thinks of you two as her granddaughters.'

I reckon this freaked Alex out a bit. She hardly ever visits Maudie, but then she is very busy playing video games, falling in love and keeping up with her social-media stuff.

Me, though – I see Maudie most days after school. I like to sit on an old wooden crate, stroking one of the cats, while she makes hot chocolate on the little wood-burner and tells me the same old stories, which I don't really mind. It's all far more peaceful than being at home.

There's the story about when she was young woman in the navy and swam with a whale; or the time she visited her son in Canada and came across a grizzly bear cub; and the time in nineteen sixty-something that she met the American president and sat in his car . . .

'What do you want this evening, Willa?' Maudie asks, pointing to a stack of differently labelled chocolate bars on a shelf behind her. I indicate one at random.

She makes hot chocolate the hard way: whisking

squares of shiny dark chocolate into hot milk, but it's never the chocolate you get in regular shops. I think she has it delivered, and it's always delicious.

'Ah, good choice,' she says, taking out the red-wrapped bar. 'Hand-pressed, high-roasted Madagascan. Seventy per cent cocoa solids – smooth and dark and rich like my ex-husband wasn't. Ha!'

She's a bit obsessed with chocolate is Maudie. She reckons a great-great-great-grandfather invented chocolate bars, and she's just 'preserving the family history'.

As she unwraps it and breaks the squares into the battered pan on the stove, I say to her, 'Maudie? You wouldn't make anything up, would you? I mean – about that animal you saw?'

As you can tell, I'm still a little doubtful.

She looks at me, bewildered, and I immediately regret even asking her. 'Why would I do that?' she says, sounding a bit hurt.

'It's just . . . eyewitness accounts aren't always very reliable.'

She thinks about this and says, 'Maybe not. But the truth is the truth, whether or not you choose to believe it. Eyewitness accounts are pretty much all we have for most of history. That and the parts we managed to catch on film.'

Maudie nods towards the wall, and I spot a new picture pinned behind her workbench.

She's got a few of them in frames: two or three of Callum when he was little, and another of him grown up with another man, both of them in suits and grinning at the camera in front of a Canadian flag. But the new one is a printed copy of a newspaper article. I stand up for a closer look.

'I think I told you about that, didn't I? An old navy friend found the clipping and sent it to me.'

There's a photograph of a very young woman in a sailor's uniform shaking the hand of a handsome, grinning man in a suit.

PROUD DAY FOR YOUNG CADET
3 July 1963

US President John F. Kennedy shakes the hand of a young naval cadet during his visit to the UK this week.

'Is that you? That's nice,' I say. 'But was there no more, not even your name? Just that picture?'

Maudie replies as she whisks the steaming milk. 'Aye. That's all they printed. I told the reporters about the conversation I had with the president, but I don't think they were interested. To tell you the truth, I don't think they believed me.'

'Well, they should have,' I say, settling back down on

my cushioned crate. 'It's a brilliant story! An encounter with the great man himself.'

'Oh aye, you're right. Just a shame it came to nothing. There I was, nearly twenty minutes more or less alone with the president of the United States, and he was properly listening, you know? Listening to little seventeen-year-old me blethering on about my grand vision of the world!'

I've heard this story so many times, but I don't mind listening to it again. President Kennedy's visit to England in 1963 – just a few months before he was killed – even formed part of my prize-winning history essay. As Maudie tells it, the president was visiting a navy training base, and his car was delayed because of engine trouble, and Maudie made him laugh by saying if it was a ship's engine it would have been repaired in no time, and offering the president a back-seat ride on her Norton motorcycle instead.

'This kid's a blast!' said President Kennedy to one of his security team. 'Wanna soda, cadet?' He took a Coke from a refrigerated compartment in his car.

Maudie pours the hot chocolate into chipped mugs. 'A fridge in his car – imagine that! So I sat with President Kennedy in the back seat and told him how I joined the navy instead of continuing my education and about the dream I had of a world where people would talk instead of fight. The World Without War! A young-hearted and optimistic vision to persuade everyone in the world to stop fighting. Hee hee!'

She rolls her eyes and smacks her lips. 'If only, eh, Willa? If only! I could have changed history, sitting in the back of that car.'

'I think it's a lovely idea, Maudie!' I have told her this before, and she smiles wistfully.

'You know, I think President Kennedy did too. When he drove away in the mended car, I saw his mouth move as he spoke to his secretary. I could read his lips. And he was telling him about the World Without War. And he tapped his secretary's notepad like he was saying, "Write it down."'

Her old fingers wander to the **JFK FOR PRESIDENT** badge on her dungarees.

'Of course, we all know what happened to poor old President John F. Kennedy before the end of that year.'

I do. I could hardly not. Every year on November 22, Maudie hoists a faded American flag up the pole that usually flies a banner saying HAPPYLAND. It is her commemoration of the president that she met and who was murdered on that date in 1963 when he was only forty-six.

'See, Willa, only months before I met him, the whole world had believed a nuclear war was coming. America, Russia – there they were, eyeballing each other, their fingers on the buttons to fire the weapons that would destroy the world. And all because of what?'

I know this. 'A little island in the Caribbean.'

Maudie blows on her drink and takes a noisy sip. 'Exactly. *The Cuban Missile Crisis* they call it now. The closest we ever got to a nuclear war. The whole world was terrified, Willa.' She pauses as if wondering whether to say the next bit. 'Just like now, eh?'

Then she says it again, almost whispering. '*Just like now.*'

Maudie plays with the ends of her long white hair and stares into the flames of the little stove. 'Just think, eh? Just think what might have happened if the world *had* stopped fighting. If all that effort and brainpower and money had been devoted to solving *other* problems. What might the world be like now, eh?'

She looks older, somehow, her mouth a downward curve, her tired eyes glistening with tears. I say nothing for the longest time and watch her eyelids droop half closed.

'Thanks for the hot chocolate, Maudie,' I whisper, but she's miles away, transfixed by the fire, her mug steaming beside her, Plato and Berta snoozing at her feet.

After a while, Maudie starts to snore, but I stay; there'll just be more arguing at home. Only after my cup is empty do I get up and tiptoe away.

CHAPTER 6

The next day is a Sunday, and it's raining. I can hear it splattering on my window even before I get out of bed. My weather app says it'll rain all day. Whoopee.

My news app says a 'group of rebels' have attacked a 'government stronghold' in a country I've never even heard of. More people killed.

I think about going back to sleep, but Mam and Dad are already bickering. The back door slams, and then I hear Alex and Mam fighting. I try to listen at first, but then decide I don't even want to know what it's about.

I close my eyes, and up pops a picture of Manny's face, with his big smile and too-long fringe and green eyes. It makes me feel better for a moment, and I get out of bed.

The rest of the day passes in a haze of:

1. History homework. ('Imagine you are a soldier at the Battle of Hastings. Describe the day.') I normally love history homework; today I manage one side by enlarging my handwriting and hope Mrs Potts won't notice.

2. Chores. Alex and I are supposed to clean the bathrooms and sweep the path. Alex opts to sweep the path, but says she'll do it later cos it's raining, which means she won't do it at all. When I point this out, she shouts at me and stomps off to her room.

3. The TV in the kitchen. '*The prime minister has expressed grave concern at the escalating international situation . . .*'

'Ee, this war gets worse, pet. It's getting closer,' says Mam.

I turn the volume down, and Alex turns it up again. 'If Dad's gonna die, I want to know why,' she snaps, and Mam says angrily, 'Alex – that's enough!'

But the damage has been done. I look pleadingly between Mam and Alex for an explanation of what Alex has just said, but neither of them will meet my eye.

Eventually, Mam sighs and murmurs, 'You know your dad used to fly planes for the RAF, Willa.'

I nod. Of course I know, although he left the air force when I was a baby. Mam continues, still without looking at me, 'Well, if this war happens, there's a chance – a small chance – that he may be called back into the service. I don't think he'll be flying. He'll probably be ground staff. If it even happens.' Then she glares at Alex as if to say, '*Happy now?*'

I close the kitchen door quietly as I go to my room, and I'm not even sure they've noticed that I've gone.

All day there's been this unspoken anger between Mam and Dad that lingers in the air like the thick rainclouds outside. One of the bunga-lodge roofs has sprung a leak, and the guests have to be moved. This results in lots of tutting and huffing from Mam because Dad said he'd fixed it.

I try to cheer myself up with the prospect of getting a glimpse of the strange creature later. It doesn't really work, mainly because I don't yet believe there's anything very strange about it. Surely it's just a big dog? My cousin Zach's next-door neighbour in Consett used to have a Leonberger that was bigger than me when I was about six. Okay, so it didn't have a huge long tail, but this thing could be a mongrel?

Anyway, since learning that Dad (however small the chance) might have to go to war, every bit of enthusiasm has drained from me. I can't even be bothered to send Manny a message.

Sunday used to be Mam and Dad's 'date night'. They haven't done that for ages. Instead, Mam has gone round to her friend Emma's, and Dad has gone to the pub. Alex is 'babysitting'. She's overcooked the frozen pizza that Mam left, so I just eat the middle bit, and now I can hear her through her door down the hallway. (It's always

like this: 'OhmiGOD! No! . . . she didn't! . . .
OhmiGOD . . . what did he say? . . . OhmiGOD!')

I'm in my room, staring at the ceiling, worn out by
doing almost nothing. So, when I feel my phone buzzing
in my pocket, I yelp. It's from Manny.

Just seen it. The hunt is on. Come now.

He's *seen it*? No sooner have I read the message than
there's a tap on the window, and Manny's face is pressed
against the wet glass. My heart sort of jumps a bit, but
in a good way.

When I open the front door, Manny's eyes are even
brighter than usual. It's even a little bit scary. He can
barely contain his excitement. He hops from foot to foot.
(Purple Converses, by the way. *Purple?*)

'I saw it, man, Willa! Honestly. Exactly where Maudie
said it would be. Down by that bird-lake thingy.'

'You mean the Roger Shafto Memorial Nature
Reserve,' I say, probably way too primly, but it is my
great-grandfather. Manny doesn't notice anyway. He pats
a fat, cone-shaped pouch hanging from a strap around
his neck.

'Got the camera! Big telephoto lens as well. Just the
job.'

'Where did you . . .'

'Jakob lent it to me,' he says, too quickly.

44

Jakob, Manny's social worker? I'm suspicious. 'You asked him and he lent his camera to you just like that?'

'Well, I've not seen him today, but he definitely would've done if I'd asked him, probably. It was just in his room, not locked away or anything. So, you know . . . it's fine.'

There's an awkward pause during which I work out that this is why Manny had to wait until today.

'You're coming then,' he says, with his not-really-asking-a-question tone.

I put my finger to my lips. I'm still thinking about it as I head down the passageway to Alex's room and knock on her door. She wouldn't hear me leave. I sometimes think her headphones are superglued into her ears. I go in, tell her I'm having an early night, and she holds up her thumbs and fingers in a W to signify *whatever*. She doesn't even look up from her laptop.

I think that decides it.

Back in my room, I take out my phone and put it on the charging pad. Mam and Dad make me have a 'Family Tracker' app, which I can't turn off or they'll get an alert, so it's best if I just leave my phone here.

Before I join Manny, I take a deep breath.

Is this really me? Sneaking out behind Alex's back when it's getting dark? And that camera Manny's got: is it stealing to borrow something without asking? I'm not exactly sure. I've never been much of a rule-breaker, really. Till now.

CHAPTER 7

I'm pedalling like mad to keep up with Manny; the backpack he's tossed to me is bouncing on my back. To the south, on my right, a massive full moon is rising.

Manny's talking to me as we cycle, but his words keep getting snatched away by the wind. '. . . be famous, man, Willa! . . . out of the water . . . fish in its gob . . . shelters in the bird sanctuary . . . eats the eggs . . . probably escaped from a private collection of exotic pets . . .'

In the end, I can't keep up with him, even though it's not far. It has stopped raining, at least. The open twilight sky over the sea ahead of us means I can see him easily.

Where the road bends round to go towards the lighthouse, we stop. Manny chuckles and says, 'As I expected.'

We're not the only ones hoping to get pictures of the Whitley Cog. There are six cars in the normally-empty car park, and people are positioned at various lookout spots with binoculars, and cameras on tripods, all pointing at the beach.

'Think about it, Willa. Not only do we know where

to look and they don't, but we've also got an advantage that the rest of those suckers haven't.' A half-smile flits across his face. 'You've been carrying it.'

'I have?' I reach for the backpack that Manny gave me earlier.

Inside is a cardboard box containing three tins, the size and shape of extra-large cans of tuna. I lift one out. The label's not in English, and each tin is slightly swollen on the top and the bottom, as though it has somehow been inflated.

'Hey, steady. That one's ready to burst, and you do *not* want that to happen.'

Manny's being a bit bossy about this whole thing so I can't resist tossing him the can across the space between our bikes. I mean, it's a tin can. What's the worst that could happen?

'*Wahhh*, no!'

My throw is rubbish, to be truthful, but not as rubbish as Manny's catch. The can hits his wrist, bounces off his other hand, which had shot out to grab it, then it strikes the middle of his handlebars. It finally splits open as it lands on the ground, spraying liquid at high pressure everywhere: all over the path, his bike and his jeans.

Two seconds later, the smell hits us both – and by 'smell' I don't mean aroma, or light whiff, but a stink so completely overpowering that for a moment I'm stunned into inaction. The choking fishy stench is worse than anything I have ever smelt before, including when the whole sewage system of HappyLand blocked up last summer, and for a day there was a large, brown, stinking pool right by reception.

In my haste to get away from the smell, I slip on the can-juice and bring Manny down with me, soaking our clothes as we scramble to our feet. After a few seconds, the can stops spraying; instead, it just oozes a clear, slimy liquid on to the grass like a burst wound.

I stagger away, panting and trying to breathe through my mouth.

Meanwhile, Manny is moaning, 'Oh no, oh no, oh no . . .' as he too stands up. He turns to me. 'You complete . . .' but he stops when he sees me almost vomiting.

'What . . . in the name of . . .' I pause to cough again. 'What is *that*?'

'That, Willa, is called *surströmming*.'

I try to repeat it. 'Soor-strumming? And that is . . . ?'

I expect him to say that it's some sort of industrial cleaner, or a high-grade solvent. Or maybe one of the banned chemical weapons that have been on the news. Anything but what he says next.

'It's, erm . . . a Swedish food. Jakob eats it. He keeps it in a shed in the backyard.'

I don't need to ask. Jakob has lent this to Manny in the same way that he lent his camera.

'He . . . he *eats* it? Please tell me you're joking.'

'I know. It's a bit ripe, isn't it?'

'A . . . a bit . . . ? Manny. That is the foulest thing . . . I have ever . . .' I honestly think the stink has fuddled my brain a bit.

'It's herring that's gone rotten, or fermented or something. Then they put it in tins that can swell up because of the gas produced. And then they, erm . . . you know, eat it. Jakob says it's best with sour cream.'

I let this thought sit in my head for a moment.

'I suppose, if you're going to eat rotten fish, why not add cream that's gone off as well? But . . . w*hy*?' I wail, genuinely baffled. 'Why, how, would anyone eat that?'

Manny shrugs. 'Jakob says the same about Marmite.'

I give up. I'm still feeling too nauseous. But I have caught up with Manny's thinking.

'That's our bait?'

He nods. 'Devious, eh? The beast will find it irresistible.'

Half an hour later, we've cleaned up as best we can, with clumps of damp grass and a dried-up wet wipe from my pocket, but the smell lingers in my nostrils and on my jeans. The opened can smells less badly. It's the juice that stinks, rather than the fish itself, although just the thought of eating it is enough to make me gag again.

We have left the beach car park to the amateur cryptid-spotters, and we're now near the birding hide –

the knackered old caravan. Manny's given me a piece of chewing gum to disguise the smell of *surströmming* in my nose.

'That's fresh water, see?' says Manny. We look across the small, shallow lake that years ago my great-grandad excavated for a wildlife reserve. 'Every animal needs fresh water, right? So this thing is bound to come back at some point. I just saw the ears and the head. No wonder Maudie spotted it – they were huge. We'll entice it back with our smelly bait!'

Honestly – Manny seems so sure of himself that I'm almost beginning to believe it all. We empty most of the burst can down by the water's edge near a half-submerged supermarket trolley, and trail the remaining juice up towards the hide. There are still two other cans in the backpack that Manny carries especially carefully in case they too explode.

It is now a chilly spring evening when the cold comes through the broken caravan floor. In front of us and very low in the sky, the moon is spectacular and full and seems bigger than usual with a slight orange tinge.

Without taking his eyes off the moon, Manny offers me a sandwich from a triangular pack, but it's tuna, and I don't feel like eating at all, so I take another piece of gum instead. He's been quiet for a while now. It's making me uneasy.

'Why is it bigger tonight?' I say to break the silence. 'I mean, surely the moon doesn't change in size?'

'It's not bigger,' he mumbles with a full mouth. 'Just looks like it. It's a supermoon.'

He goes quiet again, and I have to prompt him. 'What's that then?'

It's like he has to make an effort to pull his eyes away. He swallows his mouthful and says, 'It's the world's biggest illusion, innit? For a start, it's at its nearest point to earth in its orbit. That's called the perigee. When there's a full moon at the same time as a perigee, you get a supermoon and it appears up to fourteen per cent bigger.'

He says this fluently, like he's learned it. I'm sort of suspicious. 'And you know this how?' I ask.

He sighs as if weighing up whether to tell me this. 'I . . . I sort of researched it.' He sounds almost embarrassed, and I want him to say more so I keep quiet. At last he says, 'I found out later that my mam went missing during a supermoon. That's why I'm interested.'

I feel awful now.

'That's really sad, Manny,' I say.

He nods and makes a strange gulping noise, and when I look over he has turned his head away.

'Manny? You okay?'

He takes a deep breath and turns back, his jawline set firmly like it was when he first told me about his mam. Then he nods. 'Yep. Fine. Just . . .'

I give him time. He shifts his position to look at me closely and takes a deep breath. 'If I tell you something, do you promise not to laugh?'

I nod quickly.

He closes his eyes as though he is forcing himself to say something. 'I can feel it, you know. That moon. A supermoon. Sometimes, anyway.'

I stare at him, and he stares back. I want to say, 'Don't be daft, Manny,' but it has obviously taken some courage for him to say that.

Slowly, he puts his hand out towards mine, and I feel compelled to take it, even though it's a bit odd. I'm half expecting a little static-electric shock like you get from the carpet in the school's music room, but there's nothing. Well . . . maybe the faintest, almost undetectable tingling, which could easily be my imagination because Manny's gaze is pretty intense.

In a low voice, with his face so close to mine that our breath-clouds become one, he says, 'Can you feel it too?' and I nod slightly, even though I'm not even sure I do.

'What is it?' I say with a dry mouth.

He pulls his hand away, and I realise that my palm is damp with sweat (my own, I think) and my heart is racing.

'Dunno,' he says, looking back out across the water. 'I sometimes get it, though. But this time it's more because this is an extreme perigee – the moon only gets this close to earth every few decades. Thing is, according to the experts, you're much more likely to see a cryptid during a supermoon. Something to do with the increased light and the gravitational pull of the moon on the earth increasing the tides, and affecting . . . shush.'

'Affecting what?'

Manny is staring straight ahead, eyes wide. '*Shush.*'

CHAPTER 8

I follow Manny's eyeline, but I can't see anything moving. In fact, the absolute stillness and silence of the night is mesmerising. The moon is now higher in the royal blue sky; it has moved westwards to the right over the earth and is reflected perfectly in the bird-sanctuary marsh.

I check the time: it's half past ten. I'm a bit nervous because Mam and Dad will surely be back soon. There's barely a breeze, and I can hear the waves breaking on the beach a few hundred metres to our left, though even that's pretty faint. A distant baby's cry is carried on the air from one of the bunga-lodges. Out at sea, a ship's light winks.

Manny reaches for the camera with its telephoto lens and lifts it to his face. He's seen something. I hear him swallow, then he hands the camera to me. 'Middle of the lake.'

I put it to my eye and focus on the moon's reflection in the water. And there is something, definitely *something*: a black shape moving through the water fast enough to leave a V-shaped wake behind it.

'Duck?' I whisper.

Manny tuts and snatches the camera back. 'Too big. Wrong shape.'

By now, the shape is nearly at the edge of the lake and close enough for me to see even without the camera. There's a head – shaped like a cat's or a dog's but with bigger ears – and, behind, a slight hump rising from the water with a . . . is that a *fin*? Like a *shark fin*? Finally, a tail, standing vertically like a periscope, follows at the rear.

'This is awesome!' breathes Manny, and he snaps more pictures, the quiet click of the camera's button sounding almost loud in the confined hide. 'Here he comes . . .'

The animal walks out of the water and heads straight for the tiny pile of rotten fish that we left as bait. It lowers its head and starts to eat, while Manny continues to take pictures. Neither of us dares to speak.

We now get a good look at it, from about fifty metres away. Its fin seems to have collapsed into its back and is barely visible. What we see is a huge beast, the size of a wolf or a cheetah, with a sturdy body and a cat's face, but longer. Every few seconds, it stops and lifts its head, its big triangular ears pointed outwards and its thick tail waving from side to side, flicking droplets of water.

Then it sits on its haunches like a dog and lifts a piece of fish to its mouth with a strange, hand-like paw.

'Do you see that . . . ?'

Manny nods and keeps snapping away.

It's like watching a monkey at the zoo holding food in its little hands. Then it rises on its hind legs and looks around, its eyes glinting yellow in the moonlight, before resuming its four-legged stance and coming nearer to us, following the trail of fish.

I don't think I've breathed for about a minute. This is definitely not somebody's dog. It's like no animal I've ever seen.

I'm startled when, under his breath, Manny curses. 'Oh no, oh no, oh no . . .' He's looking at the little screen on the back of the camera and pushing buttons frantically.

'What's wrong?'

'They're all hopeless, Willa! Every single one. Look.' He hands the camera to me, and I look at the screen on the back. He's right. In some of the pictures, you can just about make out a dark, distant animal shape, but that's about all. 'I must have got the settings wrong. I had to turn the flash off, obviously, but . . . oh, I don't know.'

Poor Manny's face. I don't think I've ever seen anyone look so disappointed.

I watch the cog moving through the distant shadows towards the beach and out of sight.

'We need to come back tomorrow,' I say.

'We can't wait! Jakob won't, erm . . . lend me this camera again. We need to follow it.'

The cog's path has taken it round the back of the cryptid-spotters and their cameras. None of them have seen it.

We've been pedalling like crazy for at least two kilometres, passing the big white dome of the Spanish City leisure complex on our right, riding along the pavement and the paths, catching glimpses of the strange beast as it lopes along in the shadows of the low, sandy dunes below us. There are no lights on my bike, and I've completely lost track of time. Two or three times we think we've lost it, but I'm so into the whole chase now that it never occurs to me to say, 'Come on, Manny – let's go back.' Now and then, we'll see it: a flick of its tail behind a rock, or a flash of its eye, and we keep pedalling until we're almost at the end of the beach. Here the land juts out a bit to form Brown's Point and Brown's Bay at the end of Whitley Sands, just as it becomes Culvercot.

'Look – there he is!' says Manny, and he's right. The animal is running ahead of us, almost hidden against the dark cliff wall.

There are one or two cars on the top seafront road, and a single person on the long beach throwing sticks for a dog. Manny and I have mounted the pavement, cycling furiously. We pass a couple walking arm in arm, and the man shouts, 'Oi, slow down, you little pests!', but still no one has noticed this strange animal only a few metres away in the shadows.

I want to stop someone and tell them, but that's just mad. What am I going to say? So I ride on till Manny brakes hard at the steps leading down to the promenade that forms more than half of the semicircular bay.

Brown's Bay itself isn't much to look at: there's a steep cliff with some steps from the road to the sea-lashed promenade. It's all overlooked by the abandoned Culvercot Hotel, its off-white front shedding flakes of paint like dandruff.

Manny doesn't stop to ask me or even look back, but he dismounts, hoisting his bike on to his skinny shoulders and carrying it down the steps with me following. The broad concrete walkway curves round until, at the end, there are some more steps, slimy and seaweedy with a rotten, rusting handrail, down to the tiny so-called beach. It's more like flat, grey and brown rocks and pebbles. Twice a day, it's almost submerged beneath the rising tide.

The cave is a crack shaped like a big upside-down V in the cliff, about three metres high, and there are signs warning you against going into it. When the tide's up, you could paddle a kayak inside. Or even swim, I suppose, but hardly anyone does: it's rocky, the tide's too strong and it's f-f-flippin' f-f-freezing. If you want to swim, Culvercot Bay is just round the headland.

Standing on the cracked old promenade, I feel like the rest of the world has broken away and drifted off somewhere. The dark cliff looms above us and muffles the sound of the traffic; the black sea swishes in and out, the white breakers slapping against the seawall below us, and there – about twenty metres away by the mouth of the cave – is the cog, its chest rising and falling from its long run, a rope of drool hanging from its mouth. It looks straight at us.

It can't actually be waiting for us, can it? Surely that's my imagination.

We lean our bikes on a bench and start to walk to the end of the promenade. Neither of us has said anything, and the cog hasn't even moved. It's strange: there are cars rumbling along the main road above us, yet Manny and I are stalking a mysterious creature like primitive hunters.

We are so near to the cog now, but it still hasn't moved – and my mouth is as dry as sand.

Almost inaudibly, Manny says, 'It's watching us.'

It definitely is. I knew it.

He fumbles with his bag, pulling out Jakob's huge camera. He holds it in front of him as he steps over the rusty barrier and starts down the slippery steps. I follow.

Two more steps, and there's now nowhere for the cog to go; there's hardly any beach left as the sea licks its foamy tongue further up the rocks. My heart is beating so hard I can almost feel it in my feet.

'Manny – we don't want to get too close. It could become aggress—'

'Shh,' he says and holds up his hand. There's a blur of movement, and suddenly the cog's darting into the darkness of the cave.

'Come on, Willa! We haven't followed it this far for nothing. We need to get proper pictures.'

He's already halfway along the little beach, ignoring the seawater lapping over his shoes.

I don't really have a choice, do I?

All right, I do.

I could turn round and go home. But something happened today. Something inside me dissolved in the rain and the arguments and the knowledge that Dad may be called up to fight in a war.

'By the way,' Manny says without looking back, 'do you believe me now?'

'I believe you, Manny,' I say, as much to myself as to him.

Then I take a small step forward that is, in fact, a giant leap.

CHAPTER 9

We're inside the cave when, without thinking, I grip Manny's wrist, and he grips mine back. And there it is again, almost undetectable: the faint prickling that I'd felt in the bird hide. I had dismissed it as my imagination, but now it's definitely real. Probably.

A few more steps and we're nearly at the back of the cave. Then there's a noise, a sort of high-pitched *pooshhh* from the mouth of the cave as a wave hits the narrow entrance. Seconds later, a surge of water washes over our feet. As the wave retreats, I realise that it's now knee-high.

'Come, Willa. Quick. There's dry sand here.'

'Where is it? Where has the cog gone, Manny? It's just vanished!'

I push through the water as another wave advances. The sand underfoot rises steeply, and soon my feet are out of the water. I blink hard as my eyes adjust to the dark. The cave has opened out wider, and a wall of rock stretches up above my head. There's no sign of the cog. On the ground is just sand and a few scraps of seaweed, and a mound of something that I take to be a stone. I kick it with my foot. It's soft, and disturbing it releases a strange smell of hot metal and burnt matches that is actually pretty foul.

Cog poo? Surely not.

Manny is still holding my wrist, and he pulls me away from an advancing wave that washes over the poo and pulls it back as it retreats.

'Manny! The tide's getting higher! I'm scared we're going to . . .'

'Shh!' he murmurs. 'Look. Can you see? It's dry.' He points to a strip of sand at the very back of the cave just below the dark wall of rock. 'Even at high tide, which must be right now, the water doesn't come this far. We're going to be all right,' and he slaps the dark rock with his other hand.

At that exact moment, the greyness comes at us from the cave mouth like a, like a . . .

Nothing. It's like nothing. Like *a* nothing. It *is* nothing, in fact. So let me start that again.

Nothing comes at us from the cave mouth. Except it's sort of grey. No, it's very grey. Greyer than anything I've ever seen. Can you tell how difficult I'm finding this? I don't have time to scream, and I don't know what I'd be screaming at anyway and, besides, all the breath is knocked out of me.

I'm still gripping Manny's wrist as the grey nothing engulfs us both. I look up, down, and there's just grey, and my stomach surges in the way it does when you drive over a small bridge, only ten times, a hundred times, more intense.

There's a scraping noise of metal and the tinkling of broken glass, and from somewhere I hear Manny saying, 'No! The camera . . . !' The words echo again and again.

The walls of the cave have gone, sucked into the grey fuzz. Stranger still, the sand and gravel beneath my feet have gone as well. I can't see what's supporting us, and from somewhere I find the breath to squeak, 'Mann—'

And, when I say the final syllable, the grey fades almost as quickly as it appeared.

'—neeee!'

PART TWO

CHAPTER 10

It starts slowly, and then builds and builds. It's like I'm in a tumble drier of weirdness, and – for a while at least – I don't know what is real and what is not. It turns out to be *all* real, but I don't know that at first.

I have already hit snooze twice. I'm in a fuzzy state of semi-wakefulness, and I can dimly remember the dream I'd been having of Manny and the cog and the cave.

'Mina, my love! Wake up! You'll be late!'

Mam's thumping on the door, and my first thought is, *Who's Mina?*

So, my full name – as you know – is Wilhemina. (I know: who the heck is called Wilhemina? My great-grandmother, that's who, so . . . yay. Lucky me.) Anyway, it never bothers me because I'm usually just Willa. But Mina? Hardly ever. Why on earth Mam has decided to use it this morning I have no idea. Is it a friendly thing – you know, a new, affectionate nickname that's she's trying out? That would be nice, to be honest. Mam's been a bit snappy lately. 'Mina, my love' is a pleasant change.

So, I'm lying in bed, feeling confused and dizzy. My head is swimming, I'm finding it hard to focus my eyes, and my whole body feels like my skin doesn't quite fit properly. I sit up, then I squint at the walls and think, *Were they always pale blue?* I could have sworn they were cream.

At least I don't have that sticky, morning-dry-mouth thing. I can still faintly taste the mint of the chewing gum that Manny gave me to get the smell of *surströmming* out of my nose . . .

Only that was all a dream, wasn't it? It's amazing how vivid a dream can be. You can wake up and still imagine that it was real!

Except . . . I run my tongue round my mouth and here it is: an almost flavourless, well-chewed piece of gum that I take out and stare at for a moment, before putting it on my bedside table.

Okay, that's strange. How come I had gum in my mouth if that whole thing with Manny was a dream?

I don't usually even buy chewing gum. I don't dislike it – I sometimes take one if I'm offered – but, you know, it's not my thing. I'm sure it came from Manny. And didn't he give me it right before we went to chase that cog?

Even stranger, I'm *fully clothed.* The bottom of my jeans are wet; at some point in the night, I have removed my trainers because they're next to the bed, and they're wet too.

As if in a trance, I sit on the edge of the bed and peel off my clammy clothes while a storm of thoughts explodes in my head.

If we really did chase the cog to the cave, how did I get home?

Why don't I remember?

Did I hit my head or something?

I run my hand over my skull. I can't feel any bumps or bruises.

The walls were definitely cream, I'm sure of it.

I try to get some sense of normality back into my mixed-up head by brushing my teeth in my bedroom sink. Mam's been busy with stuff: she has replaced my plastic toothbrush with one with a cool wooden handle, and my toothpaste is in a jar instead of a plastic tube. Except it's not a new jar. Someone else – probably Alex – has used some of the stuff inside, which I suppose is a bit yuck if she's sticking her own toothbrush in it, but . . .

As I brush, I'm looking for my phone that I left in my room last night so Mam couldn't track me.

Didn't I?

I can't find it. Did Alex borrow it last night? Why would she do that? I flap my duvet (new cover, when did I get that?) and look under the bed, where I find an unfamiliar pair of shoes, but no phone.

I definitely left it next to my bed. I mean, it's always there, on the charging pad, which isn't there either. Now

I've been up for five minutes, my head is getting a bit clearer, but I'm not sure that's actually a good thing: it just means more questions.

'Mam!' I call down the hallway. 'Have you seen my phone?' She doesn't hear me.

I sit on the end of my bed in my knickers and grab my school clothes from the chair to get dressed. Mam has replaced them as well. This is *all* new stuff. Well – not *new* new. They're just new to me. Perhaps it's Alex's old stuff, although none of it's familiar. There's a red T-shirt, blue jeans, a pair of yellow socks (*yellow* socks? Eww.) and a vivid lime-green hoodie. She'd never wear that.

I hear Mam shout, 'Bye!' Then, 'Love you, Ted!' to Dad.

'*Love you, Ted*'? I haven't heard *that* for a while. The front door bangs. Where's she going at this time?

I pull on the green hoodie. I think Mam's been buying stuff at the charity shop. Perhaps our money worries have been more serious than they told me?

Definitely cream. Dad painted the walls cream two summers ago with some paint left over from doing up his office.

In the kitchen, Dad has his back to me, eating toast and frying eggs.

'Dad? I've, erm . . . mislaid my phone. And my bedroom walls are the wrong colour.'

'You what, love? One egg or two? Shall I make this to

go? You're gonna be late again, Mina. What phone? The phone's in the hallway, you know – where it usually is.'

He turns round, and I gasp. 'Wow! When did you do that?'

'Do what?'

'Your . . . your beard. When did you shave it off?'

He rubs his chin and grins. 'My *beard*? I haven't had a beard since I was a student. What are you talking about?'

'Your *beard*, Dad. The one that you keep saying you'll shave off cos Mam hates it, but you never do. That beard!'

He smiles, bemused – like he's trying to work out the joke. 'Must've shaved it off then, eh?'

Okay, I get it. He's joking about the beard. And about being a student. Dad was never at university. But the phone . . .

'I can't find my phone, Dad. You know, my cellphone, mobile, "the devil's device", as you call it, "the pocket pest" . . . I've, ah . . . lost it.' I trail off because Dad is looking at me like I'm insane. Then he smiles.

'I think you have definitely lost it, love. Dunno what you're on about. Whatever you've lost, we'll find it later. And, if you don't like the colour of your walls, we'll talk about that as well. Anyway, take this with you and hurry, hurry, hurry! Big day at school today, isn't it? All the preparations for the big WWW thing.' He hands me a paper package with a fried egg sandwich in it. 'Everyone's late this morning. Your mam's only just gone, and Alex isn't even up yet. Teenagers, eh? Not far off yourself. Now go!'

Mam's just gone? Where to? They run the holiday park from the converted garage. But Dad's ushering me out of the door.

'Dad – stop! I woke up in wet clothes this morning, and . . .' I'm distracted for a moment as there's a coat on the hall rack that I don't recognise. My head hurts. 'Dad? I've had a really weird dream . . .'

'Enough, Mina – you'll be late!' Seconds later, Dad's shoved my school bag in my hand and given me a kiss on the head. The door slams behind me, and I'm standing there, holding a warm packet of food.

What.

The heck.

Is going on?

Something has definitely happened to me while I've been asleep.

The idea of getting to school on time is probably the last thing on my mind. I walk up the hedge-lined path as slowly as possible, my foggy head clearing more with each step. It's quiet, as though it's really early morning. Usually at this time, I can hear the traffic on the road at the end of the path. Come to think of it, usually I can *smell* the traffic. Today I can hear birds, and I can smell the hedge, the distant sea, the puddles evaporating in the morning sun, and . . . something else, something a bit fishy and rotten . . .

That dream. The cog, the cave . . .

Except it was NOT a dream.

With a dream, you can only remember so far back, right? You don't remember the exact details of how you got into whatever strange situation you're in. There's a point where you can't recall any further back because . . . well, because that's when the dream started, I suppose.

I trace the events as far back as I can.

The cave? The cog; me and Manny carrying our bikes down to the promenade; the bike ride in the dusk; Manny and the *surströmming* . . .

The thought of the *surströmming* brings back a memory of the smell. It was on my hands. I haven't had a shower this morning. I raise my hand to my nose and sniff and . . .

That's it! Faint as anything (thankfully), but it's the distinctive smell of fermented herring.

So that whole thing was definitely not a dream, was it?

I sniff again, just to be sure, and wince at the stink. I wrack my brains to try and remember how I got home after the cave, but come up blank.

By now, I'm at the top of the path. What I see next is . . .

Well. 'Mind-blowing' is not really an exaggeration, to be honest.

CHAPTER 11

I come out from between the high hedges on to the wide pavement on the side of the road between Whitley Bay and Seaton Sluice.

Normally, the road here is pretty busy in the morning. There's a set of traffic lights at the junction a little way up the road, and there are usually loads of cars backed up, often honking their horns or revving their engines, with motorbikes growling, cyclists weaving in and out and a cloud of fumes surrounding everything like grey porridge.

I stand there, and what I see so overloads my senses that my fingers lose their grip, and my sandwich packet falls to the ground with a plop.

There are vehicles, for sure, but fewer of them and not like any I have ever seen. Some are vaguely car-shaped, but lots of them are like huge, squat cigars with holes in the top where people sit. Most have two holes, but I see one with three, carrying its grinning passengers in a line. Here and there are tricycles with steering wheels and wide seats at the back like a rickshaw, making a little *ding-ding* sound. And still others, shaped like skinny jet skis, carry one or two riders. All of them have their wheels concealed beneath them so they look as though they're floating.

And the colours! All of them are brightly painted, many decorated with patterns and polished chrome, and all are more or less silent. There's a swishing noise from their motors, but it's quiet enough for people to chat to each other and exchange greetings as they pass. No fumes, no smell, no noise.

I look quickly up and down the street. Are they filming this? Have I just walked on to a movie set? It really is the only explanation. They're always filming that TV series with the old detective and his dog around here – I've seen them loads of times – but they have big trucks and lights and stuff, and there's none of that.

Mesmerised by the vision before me, I hardly notice when someone approaches me and says, 'Excuse me! You've dropped something!'

'Oh. Thank you.' I bend to pick up my sandwich, and the woman smiles as she passes. She's dressed in brilliant colours but seems otherwise normal. I'm on my knees, gathering up my breakfast, when I see the most astonishing thing yet.

The jet skis have no wheels! I lower my head further and look all the way underneath them.

Yes – that is definitely the other side of the road I can see.
In fact, loads of the vehicles don't have wheels! The

cigar-thingies as well. They are definitely *floating*. Not a sort of wobbly floating, but firm and steady like they're *resting on air*! They glide along unsupported by anything. I stay there on my hands and knees, just staring.

The lady has stopped and come back. I see her pink shoes first, then I look upwards past her bright orange skirt and matching jacket to her face, old and smiling but puzzled.

'Are you all right, pet?' she says. Her voice is kind, but with that slight creakiness that very old people have, although she doesn't stand like an old person. 'Are you hurt?'

'Is . . . is something happening?' I say. 'Is this a film or something?' She looks at me quizzically, so I add, 'The . . . the car-thingies.' I stammer and get to my feet. 'They're . . . f-flying!'

The lady laughs, but not meanly. 'Aw, bless you! I thought it was only us oldies that were still amazed by all of that! "Cars", eh? Now there's a word I haven't heard in a while. Ooh, it takes me back. I'm a hundred and four, you know! Anyway, so long as you're all right, pet. I hope you never lose your sense of wonder because it was wondering that got us here, wasn't it!'

With another brilliant grin, she turns and struts off, humming happily to herself.

A hundred and four? Surely not.

Now I'm scared. Not just, you know, a bit scared. I

mean, this is leg-wobbling, heart-thumping, dry-throating, head-pounding, stomach-churning and – sorry – bowel-loosening fear. I honestly feel a twitching deep in my gut that makes me think I'm going to lose control, and that would just make everything a thousand times worse. I back away from the road to a sort of grass-covered bench (again, not something I've seen before) and sit down with my head in my hands and take some deep breaths.

Breathe in for four, breathe out for six, breathe in for four, breathe out for six.

Maudie taught me this. I do it for about a minute, with my eyes shut. I hope that, when I open them, everything will be back to normal.

It isn't, obviously. But I'm no longer panicking. I lift my eyes and look once again at the scene before me. The traffic has died down for a moment, and I notice the field on the other side of the road. I say 'field' – there's nothing there normally: it's just a patch of grass leading down to the beach. I've definitely never seen cows on it before, but there are about twenty of them, and some calves, grazing peacefully on lush green grass. There's a big shed – huge – with open sides and a roof covered in more grass with little wildflowers poking through.

I'm dreaming, aren't I?

That really is the only explanation. I've even heard of things called 'lucid dreams', when you're in a dream and you know it. The realisation calms me down a bit.

I thought I'd been dreaming when I woke up. In fact, I'm dreaming right now! That's crazy, eh?

I look around a bit more and try to imagine what else might happen. I cross the road when the traffic halts for the lights, walking in front of a vivid blue, cigar-shaped thing, which I slap to check if it's real or not.

It is. The driver gives me exactly the sort of funny look that you would expect if you just randomly slapped someone's car as you went past it.

If this is a dream, the cows will talk, surely?

'Hello, cows!' I shout, trying to sound cheerful and not scared out of my wits. 'Looking good this morning, ladies! Love your milk!'

One of them looks up, lifts its tail and deposits a splattering poo on the grass without even bothering to reply.

'I said hello! It's a lovely day! Erm . . . butter too! I like that. Oh, and cheese! Yum-yum! Come on – talk to me! I don't eat meat, either, so you're totally safe!'

Two more cows look up briefly and then go back to munching the grass.

A voice behind me says, '"Cheese, yum-yum"? You're madder than I thought, Willa Shafto!'

I spin round. I don't think I've ever been so relieved to see anyone in my life.

CHAPTER 12

'Manny! Oh my word, it's so good to see you! I . . .' I'm so relieved that I fling my arms round his neck and don't let go for ages, not even noticing what he's standing next to. After a little while, I can feel him tensing up, and he starts to wriggle out of my fierce grip.

'Hey, Willa! When you're done acting like a boa constrictor and talking to the livestock, you'll need one of these,' he says, his face lighting up. He indicates a brightly painted blue-and-violet single-seater tricycle next to him, with a canopy coming over the seat.

I stand there, gawping, till Manny says, 'Are you getting one or not?'

I don't move. I'm still just staring. 'Manny, where are we? Please tell me you remember last night. The cog? The cave? Is this all real?'

He laughs. 'Yes. And I can explain! At least some of it. Come on – we're late enough as it is. I just couldn't get moving this morning. I felt like I'd been stepped on by an elephant!'

'Me too,' I say, relieved. 'What's happening, Manny? What's going on?'

'I'll tell you what I think, but you'd better get some wheels first.' He points behind me, where there's a row of similar tricycles lined up in a sort of rack. A sign above says:

FreeRides
Sponsored by the Fry Foundation
TAKE ME & RIDE ME!

'Do I really just take one?' I say. At this point, I'm still not sure whether I'm in a dream or not, but Manny seems so sure of himself that I'm just going along with him, for now at least.

'You'll need a code,' says Manny. 'Here, you can borrow mine.' He takes a pen from his pocket and grabs my arm, pushing up my sleeve and writing a string of numbers on my skin. 'Nice colour top,' he says. 'Not your normal style. Now, enter those numbers on the pad. It's like a computer password. You'll have one as well.'

'No, I don't! What are you on about? Stop acting like this is all perfectly normal. Manny, I . . . I . . . please tell me this is a dream, Manny. Take me back home, or wake me up or whatever you need to do. I want to go back to my bed then wake up again when everything is back to how it was. Have you noticed these things that are floating? I've just met someone who was a hundred and four. I don't even like lime green. That roof over there has grass on it . . .' I'm gabbling but I just can't help it.

Manny brushes his hair from his eyes and fixes me with a calming look.

'It's not a dream, though, is it, Willa? You know that too, in your heart and in your head.'

I think about this, and he's right. I know it's not a dream.

'Hey, check out that bus: that's got wheels at least!' Manny goes on. 'Something amazing has happened, Willa. Come on – put the code in.'

In a bit of a daze, I push the buttons on the box that's like a parking meter, and there's a clunk as the lock on a tricycle pops open. I wheel it out and get on it uneasily.

'Careful how hard you pedal. They're like electric bikes only a million times more effective. A tiny push is all you need.'

I've ridden electric bikes loads: we have six at the park that Maudie maintains. But these are different. As soon as I push the pedal, the trike lurches to life, and I have to brake straight away.

'See what I mean?' says Manny, zooming ahead and joining a line of traffic. 'It's unbelievable.'

'Oh really?' I call after him sarcastically. 'No kidding. It's definitely unbelievable. Flying cigars. Everything painted like a blimmin' rainbow. My dad's beard has gone. And his tattoos – I've just realised! His tattoos have all gone. Manny, slow down! I don't understand and I'm scared.'

'. . . and I don't understand it all, either. Only I woke up this morning with a banging headache, and everything's different.'

'Yes, me as well. But I'm not . . . that is, I don't . . . Manny, are you not bothered? Don't you mind? We're in a world with *flying flippin' cars*, Manny!'

'I know! Thing is, I've lost count of the number of times I've woken up in a strange bed, in a new bedroom, with new foster parents. This is . . . well, it's just kind of a more intense version. Isn't it awesome?'

Is he for real?

'*No!* No it's not! It's not even a tiny bit "awesome". How can you be so relaxed? It's horrible! I'm terrified.'

I draw level with him on my trike and look at him closely – I mean, *really* closely, staring into his brilliant eyes which are *literally* sparkling.

'It's the cog, Willa. It brought us here, I'm sure of it!'

The cog! I hadn't exactly *forgotten* the cog, but . . .

'So what happened? We followed that thing into the cave. That really happened, yeah? Thanks for nothing, by the way. Then . . . then what?'

'I don't know for sure.'

'But you said you'd explain.'

He doesn't answer. We're on the seafront, and I try to take in everything, but there's just so much to see. Apart from the strange vehicles silently swishing along with happy-looking passengers, there's the riot of colour. It's like looking at a child's picture book. On the pavement, a group of joggers pass us in the other direction in an explosion of different reds, yellows, purples, pinks. In fact, the only thing that was the same was that they all had white hair, except for one old lady and hers was dyed blue.

On the Links, the long field between the road and the beach, people are busy erecting barriers; there's a stage with lights and a row of huge crimson marquees, as though a big festival is being prepared. I steer my tricycle in front of Manny and stop, forcing him to brake sharply.

'Manny. Tell me what's going on.'

He shrugs and starts pedalling again. 'I reckon we'll find out. I don't think we can change anything, do you? So why worry? It'll probably turn out okay. Meanwhile, we might as well . . . enjoy it, I suppose. Do you have a better idea?'

I find it hard to believe he's okay with all of this. We've turned right off the seafront and arrived at the school, and Manny's still talking as we get down. '. . . but we're going to find out more.'

I look closely at my friend, and I'm hit again with that feeling that Manny is in some way different. He smiles at me, and I think that he looks taller somehow, and he's not stooping. I have never seen Manny stand up completely straight before. He's always had this slightly defensive hunch to him.

He points at his trike. 'So *that* is a FreeRide. Bonnie at Winston Churchill House explained it all. She got a bit frustrated. She thought I was just playing at being stupid.'

'So . . . you woke up in your normal bed as well then?'

'Yeah. Felt rotten in the head. Everything seems different.'

'Yes! Oh, thank God for that, I thought it was just me. But why, Manny, why? And what is all this?'

I'm looking up at the front of the school where normally, in big letters, it says WHITLEY MIDDLE SCHOOL. Now it says FRY ACADEMY.

Then, among the noise of the other kids, I hear a familiar voice.

'Good morning, Wilhemina, good morning, Emanuel. I see you made it just in time.'

'Mrs Potts!' I exclaim, and I am so relieved to see her that I run forward with my arms open to hug her. When I squeeze her, she stiffens like a shop mannequin. I let her go, suddenly feeling totally embarrassed. The look she gives me is one of amused disapproval.

'I beg your pardon, Wilhemina? I think you mean "Claire", don't you?'

I give this a moment's thought and so does Manny to judge from the look on his face. Mrs C. Potts. I never knew her name was Claire.

'Erm . . . yes! Claire?'

Mrs Potts smiles: no harm done. 'Thank you, Wilhemina. As your peace studies teacher, I'm not quite ready to be addressed by my formal name. Now, in you go.'

To be honest, all I really want to do is to go home. But, while I'm thinking of all this, I'm kind of swept into school in a wave of multicoloured clothes.

CHAPTER 13

I decide I'm going to stick as close to Manny as I can. However strange I'm feeling, it helps to have him near.

'Peace studies? What's all that about?' I say to him as we head to our class. I recognise some other kids (but not all of them) and say 'hi', but I feel like I'm swimming underwater: everything seems slowed down and a bit quieter.

People are moving around smoothly and swiftly, but not noisily. Everyone is smiling, at least. A few people say, 'Hi, Mina!' and I try to respond with a smile – when I remember they're addressing me, that is. Not only am I not used to the name, but I don't remember many kids around school saying, 'Hi, Willa!' to me, either. This must be what it's like to be popular.

Just inside our classroom door is a shelf where everyone has to put their phone as they come in, and I start to reach for mine before remembering that I don't have it. Then I see there is no shelf, and there's something else, even stranger.

I nudge Manny and say, 'Have you noticed? No one has their phones with them.'

'I don't think they have them at all,' he says. 'Have you seen anyone using one?'

Once we're sitting at our table, I properly look at all the new faces and stuff on the classroom walls. I say to Manny, 'Looks like our Planet Action poster has gone.'

It had been there, huge, to the right of the whiteboard. Manny and I had done this (pretty awesome, if I say so myself) poster in our PSHE lesson, which Mrs Potts – sorry, *Claire* – had liked so much she put it on the wall. It said:

All We Are Saying Is
Give Peace A Chance!

It's a line from a John Lennon song from ages ago in big letters. And we'd made pictures on the school printer of lots of peaceful people. There was Lennon himself, Martin Luther King, Jr, and Jesus, and Nelson Mandela, and Mother Teresa of Calcutta, and M. K. Gandhi, and loads of others. We had made tears out of silver foil, and the tears were falling from the eyes of the people on to a picture of an earth that was in flames.

Deena Malik had sneered and pretended not to understand, and actually put her hand up and said it was a 'mixed metaphor', but she was probably just jealous. Mrs Potts said she loved it, so that was good enough for me.

Anyway, in its place is another that I lean forward to look closer at. There's a picture of the earth: round and blue – at least that's similar. Standing on it are loads and loads of people of all different skin colours and hairstyles and clothing types, and they're all grinning and laughing and waving beneath a caption in colourful letters.

WE DID IT!

What did they – we – do?
In smaller letters it said:

50-year Anniversary
WWW

What does it all mean?
And then I remember that Dad had said something about WWW too, as he pushed me out of the door this morning. What could it be? Obviously, something about the World Wide Web, but I've no idea what.

I need some answers, I think as Mrs Potts bustles in. But, for every answer I get, there are a billion more questions. And it's not easy to ask questions when every time I open my mouth I sound like an idiot.

I just can't help saying the wrong thing. Like at break, everyone – not just the little kids – is given a choice of a piece of fruit or a paper packet of nuts, and I said, 'An apple? Awesome!' and everyone who heard me laughed, but in a nice way.

'It's just a flinkin' apple, Mina,' said Olly B, smiling. 'What's the big deal?'

I ignore 'flinkin' – it could be Olly's own word for all I know – and say, 'Well, since when are we given snacks at break?'

As soon as I've started the sentence, I realise that this is *yet another* thing that's different, so I try to cover it up. 'Other than, like, every day, yes, every day we get a lovely snack, and I just think it's pretty awesome when so many people in the world are starving. Aren't we lucky? Ha ha! Apples.'

Oh no. I'm cringing inside even as I say this. I sound mad. What's worse is that everyone around has gone kind of quiet to listen to my ridiculous burbling. There's a long silence, punctuated by me crunching on my apple. Then Olly says, 'Who's starving, Mina? There hasn't been a famine anywhere in the world for, like, decades. And what's happened to your teeth?'

My teeth? How rude! Yes, my teeth are a bit crooked. Okay, quite a lot crooked. I have my first appointment with the orthodontist next month, actually.

Then Olly says, quite sincerely, I think, 'Are you all right, Mina?'

'I'm fine!' I say as brightly as I can. I smile, and then I stop smiling because everyone's now looking at my teeth. 'Lovely apple!' Then I edge away as naturally as I can, and catch Olly out of the corner of my eye twisting his forefinger by his temple.

I have never experienced a day like it. A couple of minutes later, I overhear someone (a new classmate I don't recognise) say, 'What's wrong with poor Mina?' as though she genuinely cares about me.

'I know! She asked me what WWW meant!'

Everyone laughs.

'That's flinkin' crazy! Hey, Mina!' this girl calls over to me. 'What did you say WWW was? World Wide Wobble or something?'

I say nothing and glare at her instead.

She says, 'It's like she's in another world.'

Well, that's one way of putting it.

It gets worse. There are loads and loads of *little* things.

For example, the whiteboard in the classroom is black, and Mrs Potts writes on it with chalk sticks. She doesn't have a computer on her desk for showing us stuff like pictures or films or anything. And I forgot again to call her by her first name, and she now thinks I'm doing it deliberately to be rude. ('Mina,' she said, crisply, 'we are not in the twentieth century now, you know!' which made everyone except Manny laugh, and me blush.)

In the lunch queue, I find myself next to Dante,

who's usually not very nice to me. He says, 'The chicken pies have been popular, Mina. Do you want the last one?'

And I say, 'No thanks, Dante. I don't eat meat.' The way he looks at me, I might as well have said, 'No thanks, Dante. I'm a cannibal.'

'Since when? Why not?'

'Well, you know . . .'

Oh no, I realise I've said something else dumb, but I kind of have to brazen it out again.

'. . . because I don't like killing animals.' I don't think I've ever had to explain this before. Loads of kids at school don't eat meat. Dante, though, just moves off, shaking his head in confusion.

I find a seat next to Manny, who heard this exchange and is smirking. 'What's so funny?' I snap. 'I've just made a fool of myself for about the millionth time.' I glance across at where Dante has sat down, and I *know* they're talking about me. Again.

'The meat is all grown in a lab, Willa. I asked the supervisor. He thought I was being thick, but I don't care. It has never been alive, so it's never been killed! Here, try it – it's good!' He offers me a fork with a lump of sauce-covered chicken on it. I still don't fancy it, and I take a bite of my bean burger instead.

Oh, last example, and this is weird. Deena Malik *was nice to me.*

I know. She came up and offered me a sweet because, she said, 'You seem a bit upset today. I don't want to pry, but I always think a toffee improves any situation. Here!' and she practically forced me to take two. And she was being genuine, I could tell. I looked deep into her brown-black eyes for any sense of her usual snideness and instead saw nothing but . . . niceness.

By the afternoon, Mrs Potts (I'm doing it again – I mean *Claire*) has definitely got her eye on me. We stay in our form room for 'pre-peace history' with Christopher, a teacher I haven't met before, and, as Mrs Potts is leaving the room, she and Christopher have one of those conversations that only teachers can, where however hard you try to listen you can't hear a single word they say. I sometimes wonder if talking without moving your lips is part of getting a teaching degree?

Anyway, they murmur away, and Christopher's eyes keep flicking over to me, so I know Mrs Potts is saying something like, 'Keep an eye on Mina; she's having a funny day.' Then I see him nod, and I just know he's going to pick on me.

It doesn't take long.

We're doing the Tudors. It's history: what's not to like? But, to be honest, things have been so strange that by this stage it wouldn't really surprise me to learn that Henry the Eighth had changed his name to Belinda the Hundredth or something, who'd had fourteen husbands, but no – so far, it remains Henry the Eighth and he's still only got six wives.

This Christopher has got a loud, booming voice, and he's one of those teachers that likes striding up and down the classroom, waving his arms and being all 'dramatic'. He's talking about King Henry's coronation, and using words like 'magnificent' and describing the crowds who turned out to see the royal parades. I'm sort of enjoying it when he stops and waves an open hand at me, and my stomach tightens.

'Mina!' he bellows. 'What do you think might be an equivalent in modern times to a Tudor coronation? Think big, Mina! Something that lots of people have seen at the same time?'

Well, I don't mean to boast, but I'm quite good on this sort of stuff, mainly because Dad's a keen quizzer, and he's forever firing things at me like, 'Who ran the first four-minute mile?' So I pretend to think for a moment so that I don't look like a clever clogs, then I say, 'The moon landings, sir. I mean Christopher. Sir Christopher.'

There's a pause while he appreciates my brilliance. Then he says, 'Sorry. What was that?'

'The moon landings!'

'And what, pray, were the moon landings?'

Of course, he's asking so that I can demonstrate even more of my history knowledge. So I say, 'Nineteen sixty-nine. Neil Armstrong set foot on the moon, and millions of people around the world watched it on television.' A murmuring chuckle starts to spread round the room. Perhaps they don't believe me, so I go on.

I know – I should have realised by now.

'When he came down the ladder, he said, "One small step for a man, one giant leap for mankind!"'

'Are you trying to be funny, Mina?'

Olly – who *is* trying to be funny most of the time – chips in, 'He got there on his flyke, Chris! He had to pedal really hard!'

Big laugh. Someone else says, 'Did they discover if it was made of cheese or not?'

By now, everyone is hooting with laughter, and my face is flushed and hot.

'All right, thank you, class, settle down,' says Christopher with exaggerated patience. 'Mina. I'll thank you to take this a little more seriously and confine your stories about moon landings to your creative-writing lessons with Claire. The very idea!'

By now, though, I have had enough. Perhaps it's the stress of everything that's happened, but I find myself getting to my feet, knocking back my chair and shouting, 'But it's *true*! It really happened! It's one of humanity's greatest achievements! Apollo Eleven it was called. I saw the film. Neil Armstrong and Buzz . . . someone called Buzz something . . .'

'Buzzy Bee?' says Olly. He adds a *bzzzzz* sound, and everyone collapses, howling with laughter.

'You can watch it on YouTube!' I shout.

'Right! That's it!' shouts Christopher. 'Mina. You will leave the classroom right now. Go and sit in the corridor. And Class Seven – calm down this instant.'

So I get up and storm out. Sitting on the bench in the corridor, all I can think is: *I hate it here.*

CHAPTER 14

I just want my mam. I want my mam to hold me tight in her big arms and tell me that everything will be all right. That, however strange I'm feeling, it will pass. She'll explain what has gone on and hug me again, then Dad'll come in and make some daft joke, and it'll be so corny that even Alex will giggle at it, and we'll all laugh together like we used to do before Mam and Dad argued all the time, and Alex shut herself in her room with her computer.

Then I'll go and drink hot chocolate with Maudie by her fire, and she'll walk me back, and I'll have a bath, and Mam or Dad or even Alex will read to me, and there will be no news on the TV about the war, then I'll wake up and everything will be normal. Then . . .

'Willa? You okay?'

It's Manny's voice, but I don't even dare to look round in case something else has changed. I have made it through the rest of the day mainly by keeping my mouth completely shut – which is hard when most of the time it wants to hang open in astonishment. Now I'm in the school foyer that's emptying as everyone rushes past. I never thought it was possible to get tired of bright colours, but I'm just finding them annoying.

'Willa!' Manny says again, right next to me. 'Have you seen this?'

Reluctantly, I turn and follow his gaze. The crowd has thinned out, and we're more or less alone in the foyer, looking at a plaque on the wall. There's a photograph of a white-haired, important-looking woman in a smart jacket, with a Hollywood smile and inquisitive eyes.

BARONESS FRY OF WHITLEY BAY
Philanthropist & visionary
Born in Whitley Bay
Her influence is truly global

I shrug. 'So what? Who is she anyway?'

Manny is smirking. 'Can't you see?'

I look again. 'No. What are you on about, Manny? Stop messing about. I'm not in the mood. I want to get out of here . . .'

'It's her, man! Your pal – Maudie! At least it looks exactly like her, doesn't it?'

I peer closer. I have to admit there's a resemblance. This woman is thinner and smarter and *glossier* than my round and rumpled one, but still . . . I shake my head. 'It can't be,' I say.

'But why not?' Manny persists. 'I mean – so many other things have happened . . .'

'It's just not her, all right? For a start, Maudie's not called Fry,' I snap. 'She's Maudie Lawson.' He goes quiet, but I sneak another look at the picture before we shuffle out.

Five minutes later, we're on the seafront, and still neither of us has said a word. It's as though the whole strangeness has made us both unable to speak. I mean, where do you even start? I kind of walk with my eyes cast down at the super-clean, super-even pavement (no cracks to trip on, no dog poo in Dog Poo Lane) because I just do not want another surprise where I go, 'Oh wow, look at that!' or, 'Was that building always painted like that?'

The flying cigars, the FreeRides and all the other vehicles swish by, and I don't even want to look at them.

Eventually, we're on the Links, and nearby another stage is being erected. I reckon it's safe to look up because pretty much the only thing I'll see is the tawny sand on the beach below and the sea. At least that can't change. And yet . . . Perhaps it's my imagination, but even the *sea* looks different somehow, although I've no idea how it could be.

'So, Manny,' I say at last, 'what do you think has happened?'

Whatever his answer was going to be, I don't find

out because he suddenly grips my arm, gasps and says, 'I can't believe it. Look!'

A few metres away, ambling on the grass with its odd, lumpy walk, and its thick cat's tail pointing up, is the cog. An old couple have stopped to watch it from a distance, while others cycle past, completely ignoring it.

The old couple are not amazed, though. They're just standing, mildly interested, in the same way you or I would watch, say, a fox or a squirrel.

Seconds later, Manny has struck up a conversation.

The couple look very old, and I immediately recognise one as the lady in orange I had seen this morning. She smiles indulgently at Manny's question, then she spots me.

'Hello again, pet! It's a molphin, of course! Don't tell me you've never seen one of those before?'

'Oh yeah, I knew that,' says Manny, rather unconvincingly.

'Of course you did!' says the woman's husband, jovially. 'Here – do you think he's hungry?' He takes a banana from his bag and gives it to Manny, who throws it towards the cog. It flinches and backs off.

'Don't throw it, son! You'll scare him.' The old man advances slowly and retrieves the banana. 'Just hold it out to him. I can't believe you've never fed a molphin before! Now, just stand still.'

And so Manny does, and I find I'm holding my breath as if that'll help. Cautiously, the animal advances till it can reach out and grab the banana in its monkey hand. A smile spreads over Manny's face, and he says, 'Wow!' with a chuckle, while I try to remember every detail and curse myself for leaving my phone behind in . . . wherever I came from.

'Oh my!' I say. 'Do you call it a molphin because it's like a monkey and a . . . a dolphin?' I ask the woman. She looks at me with what seems like pity and nods indulgently.

'Why not a cog then? Half cat and half dog?'

The old man laughs. 'Ha! That's quite good, that is! Very clever. Cog!'

'And it couldn't be "donkey",' says Manny, '"because that name's already been taken.' He pauses, suddenly doubtful. 'Hasn't it?'

The old man gives him a funny look.

The strange creature retreats a little bit and now sits on its haunches and munches the banana without peeling it, in a pose exactly like a panda eating bamboo. The older couple are more interested in Manny and me than the cog.

'Are you new around here?' says the woman. 'Only molphins aren't that uncommon, you know?'

I say, 'No! That is, yes. I mean, sort of.' *This isn't going well.* 'They aren't very common where we come from.' Then, to avoid questions about where that may be, I say, 'Where do they live?'

The man says, 'In the dunes, mainly. In caves. I think I've seen this one before. He's a handsome fella!'

Then, the banana finished, the cog did something that made the old couple sigh in amazement. He approached Manny and lay down in front of him, like a dog demanding a tummy rub. Manny crouched down and obliged, the cog squirmed with pleasure, and the woman said, 'I have *never* seen that before. That's unbelievable!'

Then the man says, 'You're very special, son! You must have a real connection.'

Eventually, the cog/molphin gets bored of being tummy-rubbed and saunters off down to the beach, with a backward glance at Manny. The couple wander off, holding hands, with a friendly 'See ya!' and Manny and I are on our own.

'Manny. I think my head's about to explode. Are you going to tell me what you think this is all about? Because I've had enough.'

'Oh aye. Get ready for this. I reckon . . .' He pauses dramatically. 'I reckon we've travelled into the future!' He says this with a decisive nod and a satisfied smile and waits for me to acknowledge his brilliance. When I don't, he adds, 'You know: time travel and that. Like *Doctor Who* only without a TARDIS!' He says it all cheerfully, like he's just got on a bus and got off at the stop labelled 'THE FUTURE'.

I give it a moment's thought before letting him down. 'But that makes no sense, Manny. We're still in the same year at school, for one thing. And the calendar on Mrs Potts's desk had today's date: I checked. If we had travelled forward in time – that is, if such a thing was even possible, which it isn't – then everyone we know would be older, wouldn't they? Or dead, even.'

Manny looks frustrated that his theory has been blown apart so easily, and he grunts, 'Aye, s'pose so.'

'Listen. Wherever we've come to, wherever this is, I want to go back. I have to go back, Manny!'

He blinks at me slowly from beneath his fringe, and says, 'Go *back*?' It's as if he hasn't even thought of it.

'Yes, Manny. Go. Back. Something happened with the cave and . . . and . . .' I don't even know what. 'Think, Manny – what did it feel like? Before we went into the cave, you were telling me you could feel the moon,' I urge him. His eyes narrow.

'The supermoon? The high tide?' he says, quietly, as though he's making connections in his head, and I gasp.

'Well . . . that might be how we got here! Do you think that could be it?' I'm getting excited, and I think Manny's a bit freaked out. 'We've got to go now! Back to the cave. I mean – if it started there, we could finish it there, surely?'

I've grabbed his hand, and I'm already thinking about being at home with Mam and Dad and Alex when there's a little tinkling bell sound from the road, and a familiar voice says, 'Mina!'

I turn and see a man in a bright red two-seater cigar hovering at the side of the road. Without his beard, it takes me a second to recognise Dad again. He says, 'Come on – hop in!'

My head swivels between Dad and Manny. 'Dad! Erm . . . hi! I was just . . .'

What do I say? 'I was just going to pop back to my own world!'

Manny's smiling, amused at my discombobulation, and I glare at him. He says, 'One moment, Mr Sha— I mean Ted! I just need a word with Willa . . . I mean Mina.' He steps away and talks to me in a low voice so that Dad can't hear.

'I hate to admit it, Willa, but I reckon your explanation's better than mine.'

'Thanks,' I mutter, and I glance over at Dad, who's tinkling the cigar's bell impatiently.

Manny says, 'High tide's tonight at ten forty. See you there. Yeah?'

I swallow hard and croak, 'Yeah.'

Manny waves at Dad, and I clamber into the giant cigar.

CHAPTER 15

If only I could relax and enjoy my ride in a giant flying cigar! Instead, I just feel sick with fear. Not from the vehicle itself: that's cool. It's because I've decided that I'm going to try to go back.

Whatever that means . . .

I've been watching this man, my dad in this world, and he knows something isn't right. I'm trying to act totally normally, but I don't think I'm doing very well.

But how can I possibly be honest about what's going on? Dad used to be funny and everything, and I love him loads, but he's been very grumpy lately, and he hasn't been funny in ages. His new favourite expression is 'Codswallop!' – applied in any number of situations.

1. Watching the news on TV. If the prime minister, for example, says something he disagrees with (which is most days, to be honest) . . .
   She's talking codswallop!

2. If our school sends round a note or an email that requires him to give permission for something, or sign something, or attend a meeting . . .
   This is just codswallop!

Will this dad be the same? I imagine this one:

3. 'Dad? Everything's gone weird.'
   What a load of codswallop!

When we park the cigar outside our house, lowering it on top of some sort of steel recharging panel (I guess), I'm sweating and stammering, my eyes flicking everywhere. I try to climb out the same way I got in, and Dad starts laughing.

'Just open the side panel, love!' he chuckles and presses a button on the dashboard. There's a quiet hiss, and a panel slides down, allowing me to get out easily. He's still smiling when I hang back and admire the crimson vehicle. The front has a sort of black metal grille, like a car's, and I recognise the BMW symbol. On the back it says GLIDE 200. I stroke the smooth body; it's not cold like the steel of a car. I rap it with my knuckles; it doesn't sound like plastic, either. I start imagining the conversations at school:

'*Oh yeah, my dad's got a BMW Glide 200.*'

'*Sweet! We've got the Cadillac Eagle: five thousand kilometres on a single charge!*'

I catch myself thinking of Maudie's classic Norton motorcycle and wondering what she'd make of these . . .

'Back in a minute, Dad!' I shout. He's already through the front door. 'There's someone I need to see!'

There again is the thin column of smoke rising above the hedge, and my heart leaps a bit.

It's not as if I think Maudie will be able to answer all of my questions; it's just that sitting with her is always calming, and right now I could definitely use some calm. Even if I do say things that make me sound bonkers, I know I'd feel less judged by Maudie than by anyone else.

Rounding the corner, I see she has her back to me, fiddling with something at her workbench. She has a little fire going in her burner, but the wonky, bashed-up sofa isn't there.

I'm so pleased to be here, though, that it makes me a feel a bit daring and silly, and I go up to her, poke her gently in the bum and say, 'Boo!'

I should have known.

The woman turns round, and it's not Maudie. It's not even a woman. My heart sinks a little bit more. Is there *nothing* in this world that's the same?

As soon as I see him, I think, *How could I possibly*

mistake this person for Maudie? Even though he had his back to me, he's tall and broad and stands straighter and doesn't have white braids. I guess I was wanting so much for it to be her that I overlooked the obvious mismatch. The expression on the old man's face is one of total bewilderment.

'Oh. Hello, Mina.'

My embarrassment is total. In fact, I think there must be nothing in the world (in *any* world, come to that) more cringey than poking a stranger in the bum and saying, 'Boo!' Except – obviously – I'm not a stranger to him. I'm his boss's daughter, probably, so he's not going to be rude to me – but I've just been quite rude to him, so I stand there, feeling like a complete fool, and not really knowing what to do.

He puts his screwdriver down and says, 'Can I help you?'

Think, Willa, think!

I stand there, goldfishing like the idiot I am, flicking my eyes around for inspiration – anything will do – for what might have been my reason.

'I . . . I thought you were . . .' I was going to say, 'I thought you were someone else,' but that's stupid. 'I thought you might, erm . . . need some help?'

He thinks this over for a long moment. 'Nope,' he says at last. 'Thanks for asking, though. I'll have this done pretty soon.' He nods over to what looks like a two-seater jet ski, bright pink, its double seat lifted up, revealing wires and mechanical stuff inside.

I really don't want to just slink off, embarrassed, so I say, 'Oh yeah? Cool,' like I know what I'm talking about. Then, 'What is it? I mean, obviously, I know what that is. Oh yes, it's a . . .' And I realise I don't know the name of these things. Instead, I say, 'I mean, what's wrong with it?'

'Don't you remember? Sometimes it's in one ear and out the other with you, love! I told you yesterday: its speed and height limiter's faulty – way out of authorised limits. Till I get it properly adjusted, this flyke can go as high as a small aircraft and as fast as a bird!'

So that's what it is – a 'flyke'! I put my hand out and touch the deep pink body. The chrome details are sparkling and rust-free and a badge on the side says CHEVROLET SUPER FLYKE SPORT 212. The whole thing makes me think of one of those classic old American cars from years ago. There are even little shark-like fins with rear lights set in them.

'Awesome!' I say. His eyes crease up, and I remember how the kids at school reacted when I said that word. 'That is, erm . . . dangerous. Awesomely dangerous!'

His face relaxes. 'Yes, Mina. And pretty illegal too, at the moment. But classic flykes don't come more special than this! Gotta get it ready for the parade.'

I'm beginning to catch on. 'You mean the WWW parade,' I say as though I know all about it.

He laughs. 'Obviously. Unless you know of another parade?'

'And you'll be driving it yourself?'

'Mina, pet. I'm the president of the Northern Classic Flyke Club. Of course I'm *riding* it myself. Hee hee!'

(I guess 'driving' is not the word used for these things, like you wouldn't talk about 'driving' a bicycle.)

I decide that I like this big old man a lot. He's jovial, with a friendly face, and I could swear I know him from somewhere, but if I stay longer I'm sure to say something else stupid. I spot a moment to end my embarrassment. There's a hand-painted sign above the shed door that says NORMAN'S CASTLE so I decide to risk it. I mean, it couldn't get any worse, could it?

'Okay then, I'll be off . . . Norman.'

He turns back to his workbench, chuckling. 'Hee hee! Norman now, is it? Sure, Mina. And by the way – tell that son of mine I won't be round for supper tonight, or ever again, until he learns to cook.'

'Oh. Oh . . . right.'

Without knowing who his son is, of course, I don't know how I'm going to do that.

I'm still confused when I get back to the house and find Dad in the kitchen.

He looks up and says, 'Hi, love. You dashed off quickly! Did you go and see your grandad? How is the old rascal?'

I stare at him, confused. Like I said, my only grandfather lives in Leeds.

Grandad Norman Shafto, a huge cuddly bear of a man, died during the big pandemic when I was very little, and I hardly remember him.

Unless . . . Hang on.

Norman!

That's why the old man looked so familiar.

He's my *grandad.*

CHAPTER 16

I am struggling to get my words out as it sinks in that I have just met my grandad.

'Uh yes, I saw him,' I manage to reply. 'He's alive! I . . . I mean . . . he's fine . . . He says he's not coming for supper tonight and . . . and . . .'

Should I say the next bit? It seems a bit mean.

'And what?'

'And . . . that he's not coming again until you learn to cook. Sorry.'

For a moment, I'm scared I've said something really bad. Then, seconds later, Dad's face splits into a massive grin, and he starts to laugh. 'Ha ha! That old fella – what's he like? He's always winding me up.'

Relieved, I join in the laughter and say, 'So you can cook, yeah?'

Dad gives me a funny look. 'Erm . . . yeah, Mina. You know I can.'

'Right. Yeah. Of course.' I sink into a kitchen chair, still stunned by the Grandad Norman revelation.

'Mina? You've gone very pale,' says Dad. 'How about

I make you a snack? You're in a right old state. Then you can tell me everything that's worrying you, and I promise I won't interrupt?'

Dad always used to be good at reading my moods. Honestly, it was like he was psychic sometimes.

'Or tell me it's a load of codswallop?'

He laughs again. 'Where did you learn that word? Toasted red Leicester cheese with garden herbs on sourdough, okay?'

Soon I'm eating Dad's delicious cheese on toast, but I just can't help noticing more little things that aren't quite right. Like Dad pours me a glass of milk, which is ordinary enough. Except the milk is in a bottle. It's not like I've never seen milk in glass bottles before, it's just that *normally* our milk is in plastic cartons.

I swallow my mouthful with difficulty and take a deep breath. If I'm leaving tonight, this could be my last chance to understand more about this weird world. I don't even know where to start, but the flying cars seem as good a place as any.

'Dad? Those erm . . . floating vehicle things . . .' I begin and realise that I don't even know the name of them. It's like describing a car as 'a metal thing with four wheels'. Anyway, I've started now so I plough on. 'You know, that we've just ridden in . . .'

Dad's looking at me funny again. He says, 'Do you mean the ci-kar, Mina?'

So that's what they're called!

'Yes!' I'm so relieved I sound a bit too enthusiastic. 'I mean, yeah – obviously, the ci-kars. How long ago were they invented?'

Dad likes a quiz, and his eyes crinkle up in thought. He purses his lips and says, 'Hmm. Well, there were early versions around when I was a kid: the old flykes that you sat on and pedalled to get airborne. So that was the 1990s. The ci-kars, I guess, came around ten or fifteen years later.'

'I see. And the tricycle-rickshaw-thingies?'

'Do you mean . . .? Mina, love. What's all this about? FreeRides have been around for years. You've done this at school, surely? You know – pollution, global heating and the Great Renewal? The Colour Revolution? The WWW?'

The WWW – the poster at school!

'Yes. Obviously.' I know I shouldn't make myself look more ignorant than necessary, but I'm dying to know more.

Then I have a little brainwave. I know Dad loves games – at least he *used* to – so I say to him, all casual, 'Hey, Dad, d'you wanna do a quiz? I'm quizmaster!'

He laughs. 'Sure!'

This is going to take a little time so, while I think, I get a pencil and paper from the little table where we normally charge phones and tablets and stuff (and where there aren't any now, of course). I look like I'm taking the quiz dead seriously. I even add all the funny quiz bits like Dad does when he's quizmaster, down to using a wooden spoon as a microphone.

To be honest, I think I just like pretending things are normal.

I sing the tune from *MindGames* off the TV that goes *da-da-da-da-daaa-boom!*

It's time for some answers.

CHAPTER 17

I hold the microphone spoon and put on my best game-show voice.

'All righty! In the final, we have Mr Ted Shafto from Whitley Bay. Each question wins a thousand pounds.'

Dad scoffs. 'A thousand quid?'

'Yeah, perhaps that's a bit unrealistic.'

'You bet. That'll just about pay for our fish and chips on the way home, love! How about a million?'

I gulp, even though it's only imaginary money. 'A million it is.' I add 'money' to the list of things in my head that are completely different. 'Are you nervous, Ted?'

Dad stands in the kitchen and clasps his hands, his eyes darting from side to side. 'Ooh, I'm very nervous, Mina. All these people watching as well!'

I love my dad when he's being like this, and I try not to think about how long it is since he was in a playful mood.

'All right, here's your first question.' I have to think a bit because I don't want to be too obvious. I know a lot of things are different, but some things are the same, surely? 'It's an easy one. What is the name of the British monarch?'

Dad emits a bark of laughter. 'Oh, that's *sooo* hard,' he says, sarcastically. 'It's Queen, erm . . . Queen . . . ooh, it's on the tip of my tongue. Got it! Queen Anne the Second!'

Now this is tricky because . . . he's playing with me, surely? Who the heck is Queen Anne? 'Sorry, Ted. That's not the answer I was looking for. It's . . .'

'Eh? Of course it is! Who else would it be?'

I look at Dad and I don't think he's kidding.

'The answer I have here,' I say, pretending to read from the tablemat that I'm holding, 'is King Charles the Third.'

'Ha! Where is this quiz taking place, Mina? Some sort of parallel universe where Prince Charles and his brothers weren't in that ballooning accident?'

Obviously, it's a game, but I can tell from his tone and his face that Queen Anne is the right answer. I force a grin. 'Yeah, you're right. I'll mention it to the producers. Queen Anne is, of course, the correct answer!'

Dad punches the air and hisses, '*Yesss!*' Then he adds, 'Poor old Prince Charles, eh?'

I'm thinking hard because I don't want to overdo this, but I've got a good one. 'All right, Ted: question two. How old is the oldest person alive?'

He has to think about this one, and he sucks his teeth

in thought. 'Well, since the introduction of the universal vaccine in nineteen ninety . . . eight, I think, it's been getting higher. I'll say one hundred and thirty-five.'

One hundred and thirty-five? I have to stop myself from gawping. 'Oooh, bad luck, Ted. One year out! You still have a million pounds. And for two million what do the letters WWW stand for?' This is bugging me: I never found out at school. It can't be World Wide Web – I know that much.

Dad rolls his eyes a little bit at the simple questions. Me? I could go on like this for ages. He recites his answer as if it's a thing everyone knows. 'The WWW is the World Without War, first celebrated on May the fifteenth 1981 as the first day in world history without armed conflict. Oh – and soon to celebrate its fiftieth anniversary. Come on, Mina – give me a hard one, and then I have to get on with spending my winnings.'

'A World Without War'. That was Maudie's phrase, I remember with a smile. And then a strange thing happens, because I think my head is so full of what Dad has been telling me, and I can't think of any more questions. I'm about to admit this when . . .

'Oh yeah. What sort of animal is a . . . molphin?'

Dad thinks this over, clearly believing the question is harder than it sounds. 'Ooh, good one, Mina.' He taps his fingers on his lips as he considers his answer. 'Have you just done this at school or something? I'd say a molphin is a semi-feral hybrid mammal, first created by gene-manipulation in ooh, two thousand and something. Of course, we don't do that any more. Not after what happened. But quite a few molphins still survive. I saw one the other day, in fact.'

'Oh – me too!' I say, glad to have some sort of normal connection. 'And, ah . . . that is the right answer. I think. Congratulations, Ted from Whitley Bay. You are today's winner!'

'Woo-hoo!' says Dad, and he does a little jig of delight.

I'm so pleased to see my dad being funny again that I give him a big hug, and we end up doing a little dance in the kitchen, celebrating his imaginary millions.

Perhaps . . . perhaps this world isn't so bad, after all?

I head to the toilet to have a wee, and I'm sitting there, thinking about how lovely it is that Dad's being nice again, and about Grandad Norman, when I realise that, in contrast to the kitchen, the downstairs loo is exactly the same – and that is a much, *much* bigger deal than it sounds. In fact, I sit there longer than I need to, just making sure.

There's the sink: same style, same colour. The taps are the same. The soap is the brand we usually have, and I vaguely recognise the blue hand towel, not that I've ever paid it much attention. There's the little photo in a frame . . .

I wash my hands and examine my face in the mirror.

That hasn't changed. Same straight dark hair, same pale blue eyes, same wonky teeth, and I give myself a little braver-than-I-feel smile.

But then my eyes dart again towards the picture of us all on that trip to Edinburgh, standing on top of Arthur's Seat, the big hill in the middle of the city . . .

It's the same, surely? There's me and Mam and Dad. And Aunty Heather and Uncle Derek and weird cousin Zach who didn't say a *single word* all weekend, and . . .

There's someone else.

He is standing behind Mam and definitely looking at the camera and smiling. That is, it's not a random passer-by, or someone photobombing us. I'd have noticed.

I'd have *definitely* noticed.

'Dad?' I shout, stumbling out into the hallway.

But whatever I was going to say is interrupted when I hear a key in the front door. It's bound to be Mam, but when I look there's a boy, a few years older than me. A few years older than the one in the photograph as well, but it's definitely the same boy.

I stand there, mouthing silently like an idiot as Dad says, 'All right, Alex. Good day?'

Alex? That's my sister's name . . .

'Aye. Not bad.' The boy takes off his yellow jacket and hangs it up. 'What about you? Good day at work?' He, Alex, looks at me and smiles. 'All right, Mina?'

I sort of croak, 'Hi!' back, but it's all about what he says next.

'How're you doin', sis?' he says.

Sis?

Sister?

I don't have a brother. At least – not one that I ever met.

That's when I faint.

CHAPTER 18

Like I say, I never met my brother, Alexander; not many people did, actually. He died before I was born, aged only eight days.

I have seen pictures of him. A tiny purplish baby with a huge tangle of coal-black hair. It's the eyes, though, that draw me back every time. They are huge, dark and scared, as though this poor sick baby somehow knew that his life was going to be short, and that soon his life spirit would be sucked back to wherever it came from, leaving a hole that would be filled with sadness and not enough memories.

Mam and Dad have a photo album for Alex, but how many pictures can you take of a poorly baby in hospital? Most of them were taken by Dad on his phone, so they're not very good. There are some of Alex in his special cot, with a tube that goes up his nose. His eyes are shut in these. There's one of Mam holding him, but she looks terrified, as though she's scared she'll drop him.

And there's the one with his startled eyes open, looking straight at the camera. Dad's photoshopped it so that his nose tube isn't there any more, and adjusted the skin tones. It looks pretty much like a regular baby picture. There's a copy of it in a silver frame in the living room, and, every now and then, Mam and Dad light a little tealight in front of the picture, which has left a burn mark on the mantelpiece.

Little Alex died of a rare heart problem that couldn't be cured. 'Poor fella never stood a chance,' said Dad once. My sister was born a year later and was named after him: Alexandra. I came along three years after that.

The rest of the photo album's pages are empty. They're the saddest pages of all: the life that never happened. At least, not in my world . . .

When I come round from fainting, I'm being carried along the hallway by Dad.

'Shhh,' he's saying, soothingly.

Behind him is the boy, Alex, going, 'Mina, Mina, you okay?'

Dad says, 'What came over you, eh? Did you not drink enough water today? You need to sleep. Tomorrow we'll see the doctor.'

Ages ago, Mam gave me her clunky old laptop, and when you ask it to do too many things, like having too many programs open, it just shuts down. I think that's what my brain does now, and so I sleep. Very, very deeply.

One of those sleeps when you wake up in exactly the same position you fell asleep.

But now I'm awake. I look over at my clock: it's ten p.m. and dark outside. I didn't even think to set an alarm, which was dangerous because I'm meant to be meeting Manny soon.

Dad is sitting in the chair – still beardless, which answers the first question that pops into my head.

I blink hard to awaken further, and I look around the room. This morning my head had been all foggy, and I hadn't really noticed all the little things that were different, but this time I do. You would too if your bedroom was changed in countless ways. The walls I had already noticed; the lampshade is different too. The poster on the wall of Felina – the old singer who dressed like a cat that Mam and I both like – is now of someone I don't recognise.

'Hello, pet,' whispers Dad. 'How are you feeling?' He sounds genuinely concerned.

I smile back at him weakly but say nothing and continue to spot tiny changes. The *smell* of my room is different. I hadn't realised it before, but now . . . I sniff my duvet cover. It smells wrong: not bad, just not like the detergent that we usually use.

'Dad?' I say. 'I . . .'

I stop when the boy, Alex, puts his head round my door. 'Is she all right?' he says, with a face that looks like it's spent the last few hours worrying.

'I dunno,' says Dad. Turning to me, he asks, 'Are you?'

I pause for the longest time. Am I okay? I really don't know. I look at Dad and the boy, both of them staring at me like their whole happiness depends on me being okay. It's a bit unnerving as well as reassuring.

Eventually, I nod.

It's a lie. I am definitely not okay. But what else am I going to say? 'No, I'm going mad,' is not an appealing option. Nor is, 'Get out of my room, I don't have a brother.' I need to seem fine if I'm going to manage to sneak out of here and get back to the cave.

'That's my girl!' says Dad, getting to his feet. 'You've been working hard at school, according to your teachers . . .'

I have?

'. . . and you're pretty popular with your classmates . . .'

I am?

'. . . but I daresay school stress can affect anyone. Why don't you stay in bed? I'll send Mam in when she gets back from seeing your Aunty Trish.'

'But . . . doesn't Aunty Trish live in New Zealand?'

Dad gives me his puzzled look again. 'Yeah? What of it? It's only a two-hour journey on the SP, isn't it?'

'The SP . . .? Yeah. Yeah, of course. How is she? Aunty Trish?'

It's kind of an automatic question to ask about Aunty Trish, who has been poorly for years with something beginning with P that gets worse and worse and means she uses a wheelchair.

'Trish? She's fine as far as I know. Why?'

'No, I mean the, erm . . .'

I wish I could remember the name of it . . .

'PPR Syndrome! That's it. How is it?'

Dad's eyes narrow and I think, *Oh no, here we go again.*

He says, slowly and carefully, 'She doesn't have that, Mina. What are you on about?'

'Sorry. I must be mistaken.'

Dad looks at me for a long moment, then he leaves the room, and Alex takes his vacated seat. He looks at me, stretching out his long legs, just like my sister does.

'Alex?' I say, trying to sound normal and not nervous. 'What does, erm . . . remind me what SP stands for, will you?'

'Super Plane, obviously. Dad mentioned you were a bit out of it earlier, asking weird questions. Crikey . . .'

'No, no. Of course I know. I just forgot for a moment, that's all.'

'Mina – are you sure you're all right? I have to say you're not yourself.'

I look at this boy Alex. Is he really the baby from the photos on our mantelpiece at home? His thick black hair is a clue, and his big dark eyes share a similar suspicious look, but I could be imagining that. He gets up and comes over to where I'm sitting up in bed, then just stops, arms folded, looking at me intently with an expression that's difficult to read. He tips his head a little, then nods as if confirming an inner thought.

I'm getting uncomfortable under this silent examination. Then he says, 'Show me your teeth, Mina. Please.'

I don't understand. 'What do you mean?'

I don't like the way he says it, and I kind of instinctively curl my lips inwards round my teeth. He repeats the command. After he says it for the third time, I slowly bare my teeth at him. I hold my mouth like that for a few seconds before drawing my lips closed and watching him as he backs away to his chair and sits down again. He folds his arms and looks at me for the longest time, like he's thinking really hard, till eventually I say, 'What?'

'*Hmmp*,' he grunts. 'This is gonna sound flinkin' ripped, but here goes. What have you done with my sister?'

CHAPTER 19

Well, it's a good question.

I haven't, of course, 'done' anything with Alex's sister. I *am* his sister, supposedly. But it makes me think. Where is his *other* sister? The Wilhemina who calls herself Mina, who's popular in school, who likes whoever the singer is on the poster on the wall, but who also went to Edinburgh that time with weird cousin Zach?

I can't answer.

Why does boy-Alex exist here, but *my* sister – grumpy girl-Alex – doesn't?

I can't answer that, either. I find my head is overflowing, like a fizzy drink poured too quickly into a glass, and I leap out of bed.

'Wait! Where are you going?' the boy-Alex says as I push past him, shuffling my feet into my shoes and grabbing my bright green top as I run out of my room towards the front door. 'I was only kidding! What's wrong with you?'

He doesn't really try to stop me, though; I don't know what he must be thinking.

As I go past his room – or what used to be my sister Alex's room – instead of the usual sight of her clothes all over the floor, I glimpse shelves of books, and two massive telescopes with wires coming off them. There's no laptop or computer on his desk.

In seconds, I'm out of the house and on a FreeRide tricycle, unlocked using Manny's code on my arm, pedalling as hard as I can to Brown's Bay, the wind whistling past my ears. It is all too much for me, and I keep looking back to see if anyone's following me.

My legs pump harder on the pedals, the bike's motor-assistance cranked to the max, till I'm whizzing along, helmetless, at the speed of a car.

Had he been 'only kidding'? See, I don't think he had. That's the second time someone mentioned my wonky teeth. 'Mina' obviously has straighter teeth than me. He must have thought . . .

. . . I don't know what he must have thought, but it felt like he was getting very close to the truth, and it scared me. It scared me so much that I felt I had no choice but to run, right there and then. Because what if they tried to stop me leaving? What if, I don't know, they *called the police* or something?

I'm exhausted, I'm scared and I've definitely had enough.

Whatever it is that's happened to me, I want it to . . . to . . .

Unhappen? Is that even a word?

As I cycle in the dark, it seems as though everything that has been a confused blur for the last twenty-four hours is becoming sharper in my mind, like a camera slowly focusing. The ci-kars on the quiet roads, the colours everywhere, the sea that was bluer!

This is not time travel. It's something else . . .

The long seafront road leading towards Culvercot and Brown's Bay is lit by ghostly yellow strip lights set into the raised kerb, leaving the pavement dimmer. It's a strange effect at first, but it makes the stars and the moon seem brighter. Ahead, I can see the big white Culvercot Hotel that looks over Brown's Bay – now gleaming white, its windows all repaired and sparkling with light and life.

By the time I get to the bay where it all started – was it really just twenty-four hours ago? – I'm panting hard, despite the tricycle's added power.

I hop off the trike and descend the concrete steps to the promenade three at a time. The moon, partially obscured by clouds, is still bright, although a tiny slice has been carved from the top-left edge.

Manny is waiting for me down on the concrete walkway, leaning against the railings, and he turns when he hears my footsteps.

'I know what's happened, Manny,' I say as calmly as I can manage through my panting, so as not to alarm him.

'Oh aye?' says Manny. 'You've worked it out then?'

'Yes! That is . . . hang on. You sound like you know.'

He grins a little sadly and turns back to staring at the moon. 'Nope. It's just . . . I'm not sure if I *want* to know.'

'What do you mean you don't want to know?' I don't like the tone in Manny's voice. 'Why not?'

He straightens up, and I notice again that the hunch in his shoulders has gone. 'I think I could like it here, Willa – you know? I feel like I belong. Don't you?'

'Are you . . . are you joking? I had a sister, now I've got a brother!'

His eyes widen in astonishment.

'Yes, Manny! Still called Alex, but definitely a boy. This is not the world I belong to. It's not yours, either, whatever you might think. We went into that cave last night and, when we woke up, everything was different. My Grandad Norman is alive, Manny! He died years ago. I've just met him.'

Manny's eyes widen further. 'What was he like?'

'He . . . he was lovely and . . . and grandaddy and everything – but it's just not right. Does all this not bother you? Even a little bit?'

He shrugs one shoulder and brushes a lock of hair from his face. 'Course it does. It's weirded me out. But I think I'll get used to it. You said you know what's happened, though. What do you mean?'

I walk a little bit further to look at the entrance to

the cave, unchanged by the wave of otherness that has swept over everything else, with the tide slurping round the entrance just as it had when we first went in. Already the tide is higher, and I realise I may lose my chance. It's risky enough already.

'Listen, Manny,' I say. 'You said before that you thought we'd time-travelled. To the future.'

He shrugs again and makes a *pffft* sound. 'Well, yeah. But we haven't, have we?' He leans with his back on the yellow-painted railings.

I go on. 'Exactly. Of course not. We're obviously not in the future or the past. But what if – and I know this is going to sound daft – what if you can't go forwards or backwards in time, but you can go . . . sideways?'

He puffs out his cheeks and expels the air as he takes this in. 'Sideways in time, eh?'

'Yeah. Like this is a world that *could* have existed, if things were done differently,' I say. 'Something happened in this world's history that has made everything different. Fairly recent history, I mean. What's the name of your children's home?'

'Eh? Well, it's still Winston Churchill House.'

'Exactly. They must have had World War Two, and things are named after Churchill. But we know they didn't have the moon landings or invent the internet. Sideways in time, see?'

I take a few steps further along the promenade and

lift my leg over the railings to the steps towards the cave. 'And, right now, I'm going back. Sideways back. If that's even possible.'

'How?'

'How else? By doing the same as we did last night. You coming?'

For once, Manny follows me. I wade into the cave, the water already up to my knees, till the ground slopes upwards beneath my feet. I turn back and see the entrance to the cave: a crooked dark blue triangle dotted with stars. The sea level in the cave keeps rising; together, Manny and I wade nervously up the two metres of dry sand at the back of the cave where the water doesn't reach. The smell of metal and burnt matches is familiar.

'Are you ready?' I say to Manny, my voice echoing around the cave and disturbing a seagull that flaps above our heads, making us both yell out.

Neither of us has a light, of course. It's almost completely black, but Manny's eyes catch the starlight and glint as he peers at me.

'Can you feel anything?' I ask him, nervously, and I see him nod.

'It doesn't feel as strong as last night, though.'

I hesitate. Will this work? I'm not even sure I know what to expect. Will I be taken back to my bed?

If I am, will it mean I won't ever see my brother again, or Grandad Norman, or my old-style joking dad?

'Ha'way then,' Manny says as though he's talked himself into it. 'Take my hand.'

I reach out in the dark and grip his palm in mine. I hear his other hand hit the back wall. Immediately, I feel the fizzing sensation up my arm, and I see the greyness rush towards us again from the mouth of the cave.

Just as a wave advances up the dry sand and knocks me off my feet, the grey mist engulfs us both in emptiness.

PART THREE

CHAPTER 20

'I've got you, pet!'

'I've got one of them, skipper!'

'Are you all right, son?'

'Hold on to me, love!'

The cave is full of criss-crossing torch beams flashing over the stone roof and walls, and a pair of strong arms are round me, hauling me through the cold water towards the cave mouth. Someone else has got Manny, I think.

My head is sore and foggy just like it was last time, and I can't work out everything that is going on, but there's a boat – one of those rigid inflatables used by the police and the coastguard – and someone is shining another light on me; the man who's holding me is wearing bright yellow, chest-high waders, standing waist-deep in the sea.

But even though my thoughts are clogged up, I can tell that it hasn't worked. Surely I should be waking up with wet clothes in my bed? Isn't that what happened last time?

There's a discussion about whether to take us to the boat or to the steps leading up to the promenade.

'It's all right, I've got her. I can get to the steps okay.' The owner of the voice hoists me up in his arms and wades to the seawall, which isn't far, and Manny and I are led up the slimy steps to the promenade and then up more steps to the seafront.

There's a van with TYNEMOUTH RNLI on the side – the local lifeboats – and all I can think is, *It hasn't worked*, and, *I'm going to be in so much trouble*, so I end up saying, 'I'm fine, I'm fine. You didn't need to do all this . . .'

Sitting on the back step of the van, there's only one thing that I want and that's my mam. Closely followed by my dad, and maybe Alex.

Girl-Alex, that is.

But it's my mam that I ask for, and Manny and I are both doing all the name, address, phone number stuff and telling them who we are, and they do all the phoning up, and they tell me that my mam's coming in the car to get me.

'He can come with me,' I say, and Manny nods in thanks.

Someone pours me tea from a flask into a plastic cup, and, as I sip it, I look around and slowly things come into focus. A car swishes past on the road: a normal car, on wheels, with a throaty engine and exhaust fumes. I look across the road and there it is: the tatty Culvercot Hotel with its broken windows. Then I see a man pushing two bicycles towards the van, one in each hand. Not

FreeRides, but Manny's yellow bike and my black-and-red one.

That's when I know for sure that I'm back – back in my world.

We made it, I think.

CHAPTER 21

'These yours, kids?' the man says. He props our bikes up against the side of the coastguard van, then crouches down in front of us. It's the man that carried me out of the cave. 'What the blazes were you thinking, going into there?'

The feeling that this is going to be difficult begins to bubble up inside me and I hang my head.

'Didn't you see the signs?'

I think about telling them about the cog, and about going sideways in time, and ci-kars, but I feel my cup slipping from my fingers, and I kind of watch it in slow motion as it bounces on the hard ground, an eruption of tea arcing out on to the road, and I end up crying instead – then sobbing and gasping for air.

Then two big arms are around me, and I hear Mam's voice . . .

Questions. So many questions.

Mam has brought me and Manny back home, and there is Dad (beard restored) and my sister, Alex.

Dad calls Winston Churchill House and tells them we've got Manny.

I'm thrown straight back into how I felt when I woke up this morning.

Where am I?

Am I dreaming?

Is this world real, and, if it is, how can I be sure?

And so I start checking stuff. Dad's beard and tattoos – check. Plastic milk cartons – check. I mean – *everything*. My bedroom walls are the right colour. The Edinburgh photo in the loo: there's me, Mam, Dad. Cousin Zach. Girl-Alex. Everything's right.

'We've been so worried,' Mam keeps saying, in between hugs. 'Oh, I blame myself. Me and your dad have been at each other's throats . . .'

'What were you thinking of, Willa?' says Dad, but he's looking at Manny when he says this. It's obvious that everyone's blaming him.

Still the questions keep coming. Why did I go into the cave with him? Was it his idea?

I discover that Alex – for about the only time in her life – opened my bedroom door to check on me. Seeing that I wasn't there, she tried calling me, but of course I'd left my phone beside my bed. She called Mam and Dad, who both rushed back, and the search started. Mam and Dad went north towards Blyth; Alex cycled south towards Tynemouth.

Alex saw us go into the cave as the tide was rising. She shouted at us. I didn't hear. They then raised the alarm by calling the volunteer coastguard, who were doing a night exercise by St Mary's Lighthouse and were on the scene in minutes, otherwise . . .

I had already been told parts of this, in bits and pieces, when I was sitting on the rear step of the van, but I didn't take it all in. When Dad tells me it again, it's like moonlight breaking through a cloud.

'Hang on,' I say. 'They came in . . . minutes?'

We're in the front room: me, Manny, Mam, Dad and Alex. I'm out of my wet clothes and wearing Alex's old fluffy onesie and drinking hot milk from my favourite mug. They've found some dry clothes for Manny from somewhere.

I'm still thinking, *Minutes?*

'Yes,' says Mam, dabbing her eyes. 'You were very lucky. You were picked up quickly. That tide in the bay is so dangerous . . .'

'But . . . but how long have we been gone? What day is it?'

'Willa, this has all happened in, well – the last hour or so,' says Dad, frowning. Then he says again, 'What were you *thinking* of?'

I catch Manny's eye, and it's obvious that he's thinking the same as me.

But we've been gone a whole day.

Exactly how I explain all this isn't immediately clear. I take a gulp of milk. Poor Mam is scared just thinking of what might have happened; Dad is taking phone calls from the coastguard and now the police. My sister has hardly said a word. My eyes drift from her to the photo on the mantelpiece: our little shrine to my lost brother.

Should I tell everyone about him? About what happened?

But no one would believe me, would they? To be honest, I'm not even sure I believe myself.

Have I just suffered some . . . I don't know what you'd call it? Some sort of madness?

Has something happened in my head that made me *imagine* all of this? I've heard of people having hallucinations, when they see or hear things that aren't real. Is that what happened to me?

I lower my head and look at the backs of my hands. I see the remnant of smudged ink on my arm. Much of it has been washed off by the seawater, but it's not my imagination. There, unmistakably written in blue ink, are the remains of some numbers – the code for the FreeRides. I hold it up to show Manny. I don't even need to say anything. He gives the tiniest nod, and I know he gets it.

That's when I realise things are stranger than my brain could possibly dream up.

CHAPTER 22

A bit later, Jakob, the social worker from Winston Churchill House, turns up in a car to collect Manny, who has been very quiet, hunched over his warm milk on the sofa, saying absolutely nothing.

He leaves quietly too, muttering, 'Thank you.' He's following Jakob to the car when he turns to me. He can't say much, but his green eyes meet mine and he says, 'It really happened, yeah?'

'Yeah.'

Jakob hears us. 'Too right it flamin' happened. Honestly, Manny, you won't believe the number of forms I'm going to have to fill in. Get in the car. Oh, and by the way, I don't suppose you know anything about my camera, do you . . .?'

I give Manny a sympathetic smile and close the door.

From inside comes the sound of a hissy fight between Mam and Dad.

'. . . I only went to the pub to get some peace and quiet . . .'

'. . . don't you start, Ted. How you can go to the pub with the state the accounts are in is beyond me . . .'

I hate hearing them rowing. I sometimes wish they would shout at each other, but they seldom do: it's always hushed voices and snapped comments. Poor Alex looks like she's been dipped in a huge bucket of sadness. I assume she's been hissed at because she was meant to be looking after me.

I can't stand it. By the time Mam and Dad come back into the lounge, I've decided I'm going to tell them everything.

And I mean everything. It can't make things worse, can it? Maudie has this framed picture on her workshop wall that says, 'Three things cannot be long hidden: the sun, the moon and the truth.'

So I think of that and say, 'Mam, Dad – I need to explain.'

And I tell them the truth about Manny and the cog, then the cave.

I tell them about waking up in my room and how everything in the new world is the same but slightly different. The flying ci-kars, the FreeRides, the Fry Academy . . .

'And they don't fight wars, either!' I say. 'They've devoted human ingenuity to solving problems rather than creating them. Surely that's wonderful, isn't it?'

They're looking at me pityingly.

'See?' I say, holding up my inked-on arm. 'This was the code that Manny used to operate the FreeRides. He wrote it on my arm so I wouldn't forget it.'

I can see the glances going between them. Obviously, Manny or I could have written this stuff on my hand anywhere, any time. Still, I'm pleased when Alex leans over for a closer look. She stares at the writing for a while and then just says, '*Hmmp.*' Just that: *hmmp*, which doesn't give anything away, but sounds exactly like the other Alex, the boy-Alex.

'My clothes!' I say. 'That lime-green hoodie. I didn't have that before!' Even as I say it, I know they're thinking I could have got it from anywhere: probably Manny. It's his sort of thing to wear, after all.

And then I tell them about school; and the bluer-than-blue sea; and how Deena Malik was suddenly not mean any more; and the cog eating the banana; and the World Without War; about me and Manny's trip back to the cave. There's one thing I don't mention – the one thing that I can't find the words to say – until I've finished everything else. Then I sort of blurt it out.

'And I met my brother,' I say.

I tell you, talk about a change in the atmosphere. Till that moment, everyone had been looking at me with confusion, but in a kind of warm, gentle way, and I realise what it was.

They were all pretending to believe me.

You know: 'Let Willa say what she needs to say, and we won't judge her. That way, she'll calm down, and we might uncover the truth which – quite obviously – is that bad lad Manny lured her into the cave on some crazy danger-dare.'

And then I go and mention boy-Alex, and it's like someone has opened a window and a cold breeze has swirled in.

First Mam's, then Dad's and Alex's eyes drift to the mantelpiece and the little silver-framed photo of baby Alexander. They start to talk at once.

'Willa, love . . .' says Dad with a sad tone.

'What are you on about?' sneers Alex.

'I met him. He was alive – a teenager, like he should've been by now.'

'I think you've said enough, Willa,' says Mam coldly. 'That's quite a cruel thing to make up . . .'

'I'm not making it up. It's the truth . . .'

I'm about to add, 'I also met Grandad Norman,' but I stop myself just in time. It would just make things worse. I can see from their faces that they won't believe me.

What I have done – so far as my family is concerned – is something recklessly dangerous with a new kid from school, requiring a rescue by the lifeboat crew. Then, to cover my tracks, I have made up a stupid lie about a whole day in another world, like some four-year-old.

Honestly, it's beginning to sound untrue even to me.

Still, before I dissolve into more sobs, I tell them what Maudie told me: 'The truth is the truth, whether or not you choose to believe it.'

CHAPTER 23

It's been a day now. I've hardly been out. It's Monday and Mam and Dad have asked school to give me time off to cope with the 'trauma' of being in a supposed life-or-death rescue, but I know what's really going on.

It's the 'delusion' thing. No one believes me. I'm being given time to 'come to my senses' before going back to school, otherwise my story will be ripped apart by the likes of Deena Malik. Manny and I will be mocked mercilessly, and the school will have a major bullying incident on its hands.

All right, truth be told – because 'the truth' is becoming increasingly important here – I didn't arrive at that conclusion completely alone. It's what Alex told me 'for my own good'.

'I don't want to be mean or anything . . .' she began. This – in my experience – is always the lead-in to someone being mean. 'But you'd better not say any of that steaming pile of lies outside of these four walls. You might not care what people think of you, but I care about what people think of *me*. I'm pretty sure Finlay McQueen is about to ask me out and, if my little sister's going around with tales of flying cars in magical caves or whatever, it won't reflect well on me. You're twelve, for heaven's sake, not six!'

Trouble is, I can see her point.

Meanwhile, the text messages from Manny have been pinging all day.

We're not mad, are we, Willa? It all really happened?

Yes, it definitely did. They think we're just lying like little kids.

You're lucky. Jakob thinks it's a sine of something serious and because of my mam he wants to take me to a psychiatrist, but they are pretending it's just a regular doctor for a check-up. I wood come round but i'm not aloud out.

Manny's spelling is bad, and the automatic spellcheck doesn't always spot it. I reply.

Not a good idea anyway. My parents blame you for taking me into the cave.

Their write. I did.

At least he's honest. A few moments later, my phone buzzes again.

We'll back each other up, yeah?

Straight away, I reply: **TOTALLY**

I've tried to talk to Mam and Dad and Alex about what happened. I've tried to sound as calm and reasonable as I can, but they won't have it. Mam keeps telling me that I'll feel better if I just admit that I was led astray. Dad keeps saying I don't need to cover for Manny.

Nana and Gramps are supposed to be driving up from Leeds tomorrow. After dinner, Mam says to me: 'Willa, just do me a favour, eh? Don't mention the stuff about . . . you know, what you say happened . . . to your nana. She'll just worry.'

That's when I snap, like a rubber band that has been stretched and stretched. 'Do you mean the thing that *actually happened*?'

Mam sighs.

'Don't sigh like that, Mam!' I sob, and yet again I say, 'I'm telling you the truth!'

I get to my feet and stride over to the mantelpiece, picking up the picture of baby Alexander. 'It's this, isn't it? You can't bear the fact that I've seen him! That I know he's alive *somewhere else*! You're jealous!'

There's a beat of silence. Then, as Mam sinks on to the sofa, her face crumples.

Dad has heard this and storms in from his study. 'Willa, that's enough of that! You're being cruel, and the time to give up this ridiculous story is *right now*, do you understand?'

We stand facing each other, both of our chests heaving with emotion. He presses his lips together into a thin white line, closes his eyes and takes a deep breath to calm himself. With a lowered, deliberately calm voice, he says, 'I think you should apologise to your mam. We're all under enough stress with the HappyLand business and you nearly drowning without adding more.'

I look over at where she sits, her chin wobbling and her eyes moist.

I immediately regret being so harsh. I don't think anyone likes making their mam cry. But still I wonder: how can the truth hurt so much?

I sit next to her and hug her. 'Sorry, Mam,' I say.

She sniffs and hugs me back. 'I know, pet. Things have been tough for you,' she says, and she kisses the top of my head. 'It's just all that talk of baby Alexander, you know? If I could believe it was true, it would be all right. I honestly think that, if it *was* true, then I'd like it, you know? It would be nice and comforting to know that my poor baby lived on in some . . . other world or something. But pretending? That doesn't help at all, Willa. Not at all.'

She gives me a final squeeze and I know what the squeeze means: *I don't want to hear any more about it.*

Still, an idea has begun to form in my head.

A thin wisp of smoke rises over Maudie's high hedge – a sure sign that her fire's going, and that usually means hot chocolate.

'Got summin' special today,' says Maudie, without turning round. I suddenly remember the last time I greeted her by poking her in the bum and for a split-second I wonder if it's really her, but I needn't have worried. She's standing over a pan of milk in her open-fronted shed. 'Just received a delivery. Eighty per cent organic Ecuadorian. Might be a little on the bitter side for you, my love, but we'll add some sugar if you like.' She breaks a few pieces into the milk, moves the pan nearer to the flame and hands me the wooden whisk.

Before I can even say anything, she says, 'That's a heck of an adventure you've had, Willa, you an' that wee fella you were with. It's . . .'

I stop whisking. 'So you know about it?'

Maudie folds her arms under her boobs and hoists them up. 'Oh aye. Your dad mentioned it when we were fixing that faulty boiler this morning. It was pretty clear to me that he didn't have much time for your story, but I only got it second-hand. Thought I might like to hear it first-hand myself – you know, get the eyewitness account. You might want to watch that milk there – don't want to burn it.'

I pull the pan away from the flames and give it another whisk. The rich aroma of chocolate mixes with the woodsmoke. I pour two frothy mugs and then settle down on to my usual cushion-covered crate with Aristotle wrapping himself round my ankles.

I tell Maudie the same thing that I've told everyone else, while stroking the cat and sipping my drink.

Unlike everyone else, Maudie doesn't interrupt, not once. She just sits there, drinking her hot chocolate, letting me take as long as I like, and pause, and correct myself if I've said something wrong, and she nods and listens and takes everything in as if she has all the time in the world.

When I get to the bit about the World Without War, her white eyebrows lift slowly above the rim of her glasses, but still she doesn't say anything.

'. . . and now everyone thinks I'm mad. Suffering from delusions. Or just lying for fun, I don't know. And crazy for going in there in the first place, and they blame Manny for leading me astray . . .'

Maudie drains her cup with a satisfied slurp. She gets to her feet. 'Are you coming then?'

CHAPTER 24

Somehow I never imagined dear old Maudie even owning a computer, let alone being completely comfortable using one. And by 'comfortable' I mean her thick, grime-ingrained fingers are dancing over the keyboard as fast as anyone's I've seen.

She sees the look on my face and chuckles. 'Ha! You thought I spent my evenings listening to the "wireless" and reading seed catalogues, or knitting socks like a little old lady, didn't you?'

'Well, no . . . it's just . . .'

She's right, of course. I know she doesn't have a television; she's told me that before. She's also told me that she doesn't bother much with stories and has not been to the cinema since she was a girl. So I guess I imagined her listening to old-fashioned music and doing practical stuff when she wasn't working.

She stops typing and tells me to pull up a chair, which I do, waking up Plato, who gives me a dark look as he hops down.

We're in her living room, which is pretty much the

same as her crammed and cluttered shed. It's dusty, for a start, with a comforting smell of old books, cat litter and incense. The walls are lined from floor to ceiling with books of every kind: old leather-bound volumes, newer paperbacks, and piles of yellowing magazines with titles like *Mysterious World* and *Fortean Times*.

I have been in Maudie's living room maybe once or twice before, but this is the first time I've really noticed it. A rainbow of patterned cushions is scattered over a dark red sofa, and it looks as though she's reading about six books at once, as there are at least that many turned over to keep the page open.

'I thought you didn't like books,' I say as I sit down.

'When did I say that?' she says. 'Can't say I'm all that keen on *made-up* stuff. To be honest, I don't exactly see the point in making up stories when there's so many real things to discover. I suppose you love all that? That young wizard fella at school, whatever his name is. He still popular?'

I laugh. 'Do you mean Harry Potter? Of course. Everyone still loves Harry Potter!'

'That's the one.' Maudie stops for a moment and turns to me. She takes off her glasses and fixes me with an intense gaze. It's clear that she wants me to pay attention because she says nothing, not shifting her eyes from mine even while she huffs on her specs to steam the lenses and polishes them slowly on her tie-dyed T-shirt. Finally, she places them back on her nose and settles them with both hands. Then she blinks hard and says, 'What is it, Willa? You look like you've seen a ghost.'

I shake my head, 'No, no . . . it's just, I . . . I haven't seen you without your glasses before.' There's something about her without them that I can't put my finger on.

Maudie turns back to her computer. 'I'll tell you what, young lady, there are more mysteries in the real world than you'll find in any story. Not only that, but because they're real they're far *more* mysterious. People have tried to explain it all since the dawn of time. Humans have fought each other, killed each other in their millions – billions probably – all because someone was convinced they knew the answer. Religions, sciences – they've all been used as reasons for us to knock the stuffing out of one another. Now give me a minute . . .'

While she concentrates on finding something on her computer, I force myself to stop staring at her by looking at her rows of books. There are labels on the shelves:

Eastern Mystics
Christianity and Gnosticism
The Philosophy of Science
Earth's Natural Energies

Honestly – I don't know what half of them mean. I look back at Maudie, with her weathered outdoor face and long white hair, thinking that she doesn't *look* at all 'clever'; she doesn't sound it, either: she doesn't use long words, or quote Shakespeare, or have a posh accent . . .

'Here we go,' says Maudie, hitting the keyboard with a satisfied thump. 'Get yer noggin round that!'

I nudge my chair forward and start to read the words on the screen. Slowly. You'll see why.

A QUANTUM AND MULTIDIMENSIONAL APPROACH TO HYPERSENSORY LUNAR PERCEPTION

I have to read it again. And again. Then I'm on to the next bit:

Dr Amara Kholi
Newcastle University School of Neurology

Just getting this far has taken me at least a minute. Maudie is drumming her fingers on the desktop.

A teleological assessment, accounting for geography and chronology, of . . .

Hang on, hang on, hang on.
Stop.
Right.
There.

All I've read is the title and the first two lines and already my head is swimming. Tele-what? Chrono-what? Maudie has seen my face, and I'm a bit worried that she'll think I'm stupid, so I pretend to read on, but none of it makes any sense. I mean none at all. I may as well be reading Japanese.

Maudie takes pity on me. 'Sorry, love. Didn't mean to put you off. It's a bit technical, eh?'

'Hmm, yes – a bit. Can you, erm . . . simplify it for me?'

'Perhaps this might make it clearer.' She scrolls down page after page of this dense, difficult text. Meanwhile, she says, 'Amara Kholi – the author of this study – was ridiculed for her work. It finished her academic career more or less. She ended up working for the government in some capacity or other. I knew her, you know?'

She seemed quite proud of the fact, and I feel I should be impressed. 'Oh really?'

'Well, not me so much as my son, Callum. They studied together. They're still in touch so far as I know. I get a birthday card from her every year. Very thoughtful woman is Amara Kholi. Ah, this is it.'

Maudie finishes scrolling, and the screen shows a film of a baby bird in a nest. 'You've heard of cuckoos, haven't you?'

I nod – although that's where my knowledge ends.

Well, that and the fact that their call sounds like their name – *cuck-oo*.

'I filmed this myself, years ago, by the wildlife reserve. See this fella here?' She points at the screen with a stubby finger. 'His mam has laid her egg in another bird's nest. That's what cuckoos do. They get someone else to raise their kids for them, cheeky blighters.'

The picture changes to the little fledgling leaving the nest. 'Now this is the curious bit,' says Maudie. 'This bird's mam is long gone by the time he hatches. Yet he knows he has to fly back home to Africa at the end of the summer. And he knows the way! No one's told him. How does he do that then?'

The film cuts to a picture of a full moon. 'There! We've kind of known for years that the moon had something to do with it. Gravity, you know. The tides. Also, the magnetism of the poles. They're all connected, according to Amara Kholi. But there's something else as well.'

I shrug, and then try to turn it into a nod. She clicks on the film and the screen goes back to the dense, difficult text that made no sense. She turns to me. 'This Dr Amara Kholi is a north-easterner and a very deep thinker. What she wrote here – and paid for with her career – suggests that some humans – so-called "super-sensors" – can sense these things as well. A form of perception – feeling, if you like – that could, under the right circumstances, have some very profound consequences.'

'Wait, what?'

'She suggested that with the right conditions – moon, tides, star alignment – these people could – *could*, mind you, not *would* – unlock a force that would allow them to interact with infinite other dimensions.'

I'm still staring at the screen, and I say, 'Uh-huh.' Then I blink hard. 'Can you say that again, Maudie . . . only in, you know, *normal*?'

Maudie clicks the mouse to shut down the screen, and suddenly her room is darker with only the blue twilight from outside lighting up her face.

She takes a deep breath. 'For all sorts of reasons, Willa, I never got to go to university. And I reckon I'm far too old now . . .'

I begin to protest. 'You're never too—' but she holds up a finger to stop me.

'But that doesn't mean I've ever lost my desire to learn things, to try to *understand* things. To try to know what makes the whole thing, you know . . . work. Me and Amara Kholi – we used to have grand old chats!'

She pauses, choosing her next words carefully, I think. 'You've heard of time travel, Willa?'

'Yeah, *Doctor Who* and all that!'

'Doctor *who*?'

'Yeah.'

Maudie gives me a funny look and then says, 'Well, it's not possible. Certainly not in the sense that you can go back in time to meet Henry the Eighth, or go forward in time to find out the winner of a horse race. But I wonder if you've considered another possibility?'

I nod but say nothing. I find my throat is too dry, anticipating what she might say next.

'Willa, I think it's quite possible – not probable, mind you, only possible – that you and your wee friend have gone sideways in time. Perhaps with the help of that so-called "cog" of ours.'

Sideways in time. Hearing the exact phrase I had said to Manny makes me gulp.

CHAPTER 25

'How was Maudie?' says Dad when I get home.

'Fine.' My mind is reeling, and I've walked back in a sort of daze.

Manny has a super-sense? Like cuckoos? And the gravity of the moon does something? Maudie and I spoke till it was dark. She mentioned something called the 'many-worlds theory' and quantum mechanics and a guy called Schrödinger who had a cat that was alive and dead at the same time, and, although I tried to understand it, I don't think I did, not really.

Eventually, Maudie said, 'You'd better get off or yer mam'll have me guts for garters,' which is a thing she says that I've never really understood. But, compared with understanding this sideways-in-time business, it makes perfect sense.

As I left, Maudie popped a chocolate bar in my jacket pocket and said, 'A little family heirloom for you,' but I was so tired and my brain was so full that I barely even noticed.

'Where's Mam?' I say to Dad.

'Out at Emma's. Honestly, your mother . . .' he begins.

'I don't want to know,' I snap as I leave the room. I find I'm already missing the happy-go-lucky version of Dad.

Why can't my family *here* be more like my family *there*? If only I could somehow show them how things could be.

I'm back at school the next day and so is Manny, and during registration he sits next to me. For a moment, we just look at each other, grinning in a sort of disbelief, without needing to speak – until Deena Malik says, 'Oi, oi! History and Mystery are back!'

Manny rolls his eyes at her as Mrs Potts comes in, but under the desk he grabs my pinkie finger with his and squeezes – a squeeze that says, *We're in this together*, and it's such a relief.

Manny's off on special catch-up lessons for the first period so I don't get a chance to speak to him again. I've no idea what he has been told to say by Jakob or anyone else. He's probably as keen as I am not to look like an idiot.

Anyway, compared with the school in what I'm starting to think of as 'the Sideways World', things are so wonderfully normal that already what happened to me is beginning to feel a bit like a strange dream. The noisy traffic on the way to school is as it should be, the boarded-up shops, the field without cows in it, the slalom cycle up Dog Poo Lane . . . Me and Manny's Give Peace

A Chance poster is back in its place on the wall. Mrs Potts is Mrs Potts and not Claire, and no one's wearing mismatching colours apart from Manny, which is, of course, quite normal.

Obviously, word has got around about our rescue from the cave. Hardly surprising, really, seeing as Deena's dad was one of the rescuers. But if either of us thought it would bring us any sort of hero status we are soon disappointed.

'You do know,' Deena says, sitting primly on the edge of our table, 'that you endanger other people's lives with impetuous stunts like that?'

She actually says that. 'Impetuous stunts'. I bet she got it from her dad. Now, I was just going to suck it up, figuring that's all you can do with people like Deena Malik. But Manny, who has walked in during this, is simply not the kind to suck anything up. I groan inside when he uncurls himself from his hunched position to respond.

'Well, you didn't see what we saw,' he says, and straight away I think, *No, Manny, no*. But it's too late. We're in the form room after lunch, and there's plenty of people there to hear him. Mrs Potts hasn't come in yet, and a sort of hush descends on the room. I've known Deena for much longer than Manny has, and I know she's going to get all nicey-snide, when she says mean things with a smile. Sure enough, she turns her head and looks down her nose at him.

'Oh, but I know what's in caves, Emanuel. Did you see some nice shells? Some interesting seaweed? Some *bladderwrack*? That must have been *so* fascinating! And all in the dark. Aren't you brave!'

There are a dozen people smirking at Deena's sarcasm. She goes on. 'Let me guess. Was there a dead seagull? And a rotten fishy smell?' People have started to laugh now. 'Honestly, Emanuel, you do know how to treat a girl, don't you? Some boys write their girlfriend a poem, or buy them flowers, but you take yours into a dangerous, dark, stinking cave. I hope you made it worth his while, Willa. I hope you kissed him. I hope . . .'

People are openly hooting with laughter now, and I raise my voice. 'It wasn't like that, Deena! You're completely wrong.'

'Oh well, what *was* it like? Eh? My dad says . . .'

'I don't care what your dad says!' Manny's almost shouting now, and his face is flushed with anger. 'He didn't see what we saw. There's this animal, right? It was on the news. The Whitley Cog!'

'Oh *puh*-lease! Don't tell me you believe all *that*?' says Deena. She flicks her wrist as though she's batting away a fly. 'It's just someone's dog! My dad says you've got to be soft in the head to think anything else.'

Don't say anything more, Manny! Stop digging yourself further in . . .

'Well, we followed it. And at the back of the cave

there's a rock and when you touch it the greyness comes, and then you're somewhere else . . . and everything is totally different. They have clean energy. And this school's got a different name. And everything's in super-bright colours, and there's no war!'

Deena's right on to this. 'No war? That's nice but a bit unrealistic.' She points at our poster. 'I think all you're saying is "Give Peace a Chance", eh, Emanuel?'

Whatever you do, Manny, I think, *don't mention the flying cars, just don't mention . . .*

'. . . and they have *flying cars!*'

The laughter has stopped. Everyone is just staring at Manny and his mad-sounding outburst. Then their eyes turn on me, and I find my courage melting away.

Deena sniffs and shakes her head sadly. 'Such a shame you didn't take any pictures, guys. I mean, I'm sure we'd all love to see a flying car. What was it like? Was it Chitty Chitty Bang Bang?'

'I had a camera,' says Manny, sullenly. 'But it broke.'

'Yeah, sure it did,' scoffs Deena. 'What about your phone? Oh sorry, it's an antique, isn't it?'

Manny realises what's happened, and he turns to me and says, 'It's true, isn't it, Willa? Isn't it?'

I look at Deena sneering at us both. I look at everyone else gathered round us. I screw my face up in an expression of doubt and I say, 'Well, Manny, you know, I'm not so sure . . .'

And everything else I say is drowned out in a wave of jeering laughter, while Deena snorts with contempt at Manny's ridiculous lies and shakes her head in mock-pity.

Manny runs out of the class, looking as though he's about to cry.

'Manny! Come back! I'm sorry!' I yell, and I follow him out of the class, colliding with Mrs Potts as she comes in.

I don't see him for the rest of the day. I imagine that I can still feel where we squeezed pinkies earlier in the day. I have betrayed my best friend. All right, let's be honest, my *only* friend.

I hate myself. I really do.

CHAPTER 26

I try texting Manny, even calling him. I go round to Winston Churchill House after school, and they haven't seen him, either. I'm desperate to tell him what Maudie told me last night about the moon and his super-sense powers . . .

Does he even know?

He told me he could 'feel' the moon! I could definitely feel it myself when I held his wrist – probably.

The lady stands in the doorway of Winston Churchill House while all this goes through my mind. 'He'll be back later, love,' she says with a smile. 'He's probably just down on the beach. Shall I tell him you called?'

I stand on the Links, scanning the long beach for a tall, hunched blond boy in a turquoise jacket and red jeans, and think, *Perhaps he's gone back without me?*

Back home, things are even worse. For a start, when I come through the main gate of HappyLand – which for weeks has been 'appyLand' thanks to the missing H on the sign

– I see that someone has graffitied the letters CR in front of it.

What a place to call home.

Plus, everyone seems to think I've had some sort of mental breakdown.

'In other words,' I say to Mam, 'you reckon I've gone nuts.'

We're in the kitchen. Mam's eyes are red from crying. It could be another row with Dad, but I'm now thinking they both might just be upset with me.

Mam sniffs. '"Gone nuts" is not really a helpful phrase, Willa. It can make people think less of those with mental-health difficulties. It's quite unkind and . . .'

Alex walks in on this and emits a scoffing, '*Pshh!* Willa's gone nuts, and you're worried about saying how nuts. That what I call nuts . . .'

Dad cuts her off with a sharp, 'Alex! That's enough!'

I say, as calmly as I can manage, 'I know you don't believe that I really went to this better place, but I *definitely* did. Not definitely probably, but *definitely* definitely.'

Mam and Dad exchange a look. Not a glance, but a long, thoughtful look as if each is daring the other to say something. Eventually, Dad says, 'Willa, I'm not an expert in stuff like this, but I've looked up some information on the internet. Self-deception can be very powerful. It means you lose the ability to know what's real and what isn't. Me and Mam both think that you really believe it all happened.'

Mam says, 'This is not your fault. We've all been under a lot of strain lately.' She flicks a look at Dad and purses her lips.

'Why don't you ask Maudie then?' I say, suddenly not calm any more. 'She believes me! She knows what happened.'

'Willa, I don't think . . .'

I'm shouting now, and desperate. 'You don't *want* to believe me, do you? Your minds are closed to any explanation other than me imagining it. Well, how come me and Manny imagined the exact same thing, eh?'

Mam is tapping her phone. 'Look, Willa, if it makes you happier, we'll see what Maudie has to say.'

'Sideways in time? Is this some sort of joke?'

I haven't moved from the kitchen. I'm sitting at the counter, and Maudie stands in her thick socks, her workboots by the back door, holding her beret in her hands.

Dad is not impressed by what Maudie has just told him, but I've never seen him be angry with her before, and I hate it.

'Listen, Ted, it's only a theory, and . . .'

'Only a theory?' he repeats. 'You bet it's only a theory. Sophie! Have you heard this?'

Mam comes through from the study. 'Yes, I heard. And, Ted, calm down. Maudie, I'm sorry, but this is nonsense. Surely you can see that? Willa has had a difficult time, and we're all still quite upset. I'm really not sure if this talk of going "sideways in time" is helpful.'

'Helpful?' Dad practically squeaks. 'Listen to me, Maudie Lawson. I don't know what sort of old books you've been reading, or websites or online forums you've been involved with or . . . or anything, all right? But I'd really appreciate it if you kept it to yourself or to whatever bunch of sad old hippies invent all this . . . *codswallop*.'

'Ted, steady . . .' murmurs Mam.

'Steady? No, I won't "steady"! Willa – I want you to completely forget about this crazy idea. It's just going to upset you. Maudie . . .' Dad shakes his head as though he's got a bee in his ear. 'Maudie, I'm surprised at you. I really wanted us to part on friendly terms, but this is just ridiculous. She's only twelve, for heaven's sake! What on earth are you thinking of, putting ideas like this into her head?'

'Ted, if I could explain a bit . . .'

'Enough, Maudie. I don't want to hear any more about it. Sideways in time, indeed! It's the flaming internet, isn't it? Equal access to the smartest and stupidest ideas and no way of knowing the difference.'

Maudie's pulling her boots on, and her face is bright pink – either through anger or embarrassment.

'I'm sorry you feel that way, Ted. I was just trying to help.'

'Yes, well . . . just don't, all right, Maudie?'

I'm trying desperately to catch Maudie's eye, but she keeps her head turned down as she puts on her beret. She closes the door very carefully and quietly as she leaves.

Dad, Mam and I remain silent for ages till Alex puts her head round the kitchen door and takes one headphone out. 'Did I miss something?'

'You missed Dad being horrible to Maudie.' It probably isn't the right thing to say.

'I was *not* being horrible to her. I'm trying to protect you,' he says. He goes to put his arm round me, but I shrug it off.

'She's cleverer than you think,' I say. 'At least she believes me! It's all because of . . . because of gravity and hypersensory, erm . . . other dimensional things.'

Alex scoffs. 'That's not clever, Willa. That's gullible. Kind of the opposite of clever.'

There's something else bothering me. I turn to Dad.

'What did you mean when you said you "wanted us to part on friendly terms"?'

I see Dad look at Mam, asking her to explain. She says, 'It doesn't really involve you, pet. It's just your dad's going to have to let Maudie go.'

'Oh, it's me now, is it?' Dad spits out. 'I thought we'd both agreed.'

'Let her go? Let her go where? What do you mean?' I wail.

Alex says, 'They're sacking her and selling HappyLand. Aren't you?'

Dad shoots Alex such a filthy look. 'No, I – we – are not sacking her. It's more like enforced retirement. She's eighty-five and, when the SunSeasons deal goes ahead, then that lodge she lives in for free has to be available for paying guests. Besides, SunSeasons have their own maintenance and gardening team that services all their parks.'

'But . . . but you can't do that!' I protest.

'Watch them,' says Alex, getting a drink from the fridge and shutting it with her foot as she leaves. 'It's carnage around here.'

I ignore her. 'Where's she going to live? Where are *we* going to live?'

Dad closes his eyes as if to demonstrate how calm he is. It doesn't work. 'I don't really know. I daresay SunSeasons will work out something for her. Maudie'll be okay. Don't you worry, love. As for us . . .'

I'm off my stool and heading to the kitchen door. I don't want Mam and Dad to see me crying any more, but I can't resist shouting, 'I'll prove to you I'm not lying!' before I slam the door and head to my room.

I collapse on my bed and bury my face in my pillow.

I end up spending the rest of the evening in my room. Mam and Dad don't seem to notice. They are having another ongoing row which rumbles on and comes through my bedroom door. It's like the noise of traffic with one or the other of them shouting things like the sound of car horns.

'*You've lost all your drive, Ted! Where's your imagination?*'

'*It's a good deal, Sophie! You're just being sentimental!*'

'*Sentimental? It's your family business, Ted, not mine! You left the air force to do this.*'

'*SunSeasons . . .*'

'*. . . whole place is a wreck . . .*'

. . . have you seen the sign at the front?'

Then the front door slams, and I hear Dad driving away. I know it's him because he revs the engine angrily and Mam never does. I can hear her crying in her room, and I really want to go and give her a hug, but I'm worried that I might just make things worse. Instead, I creep down the hallway and raise my hand to knock on Alex's door. Before I can, she shouts, 'Is that you, Willa? Go away till you've stopped making up lies!'

So I give up and go back to my room. Nana and Gramps have cancelled their visit, which is probably just as well, but I was looking forward to seeing them.

Every time I look at my laptop or my phone, there's another scary war story.

Prime minister says, 'Prepare for Total War.'

Situation in Pacific 'critical' as drone strikes increase.

Eastern water conflict: hundreds more dead.

I snap the laptop shut.

Mam hasn't even made us supper. I find some bread and cheese, and, while I'm making a sandwich, I see an opened brown envelope marked Ministry of Defence on the worktop.

With a trembling hand, I take out the letter, addressed to Flight Lieutenant E. R. Shafto (Retired).

I only read the first lines. It's all I need to know.

Recall of RAF Reserve Staff

Dear Mr Shafto,

In accordance with the law, as set out in the Defence Act 2030, I am writing to give you advance warning of a recall to service of former officers in the Royal Air Force . . .

I don't read the rest. I can't read it anyway as my eyes have misted over.

Leaving my sandwich untouched, I hurry back to my room, my heart racing. There, I send another 'sorry' text to Manny and spend much of the next hour checking for a reply, which doesn't come.

I can't bear it. Really I can't. Wearily, I lie on my back and stare at the ceiling, counting the reasons why I'm so unhappy.

1. Maudie is the only person apart from Manny who doesn't think I'm lying, and she has just been told to stay away from me.
2. Not only that but she's going to be kicked out of her house after working for our family for something like fifty years.
3. HappyLand is going to be sold, which means moving somewhere else. Where will *that* be?
4. Mam and Dad's arguing is definitely getting worse.
5. Alex hasn't said a single kind word to me for weeks.
6. My best – sorry, *only* – friend is not talking to me for the very good reason that I didn't stand up for him when I should have.
7. There's almost certainly going to be a war, and I have no idea what that will be like other than horrible.
8. Dad's going to be called back to the air force to fight.

It wasn't like this in the Sideways World. True, a few people thought I was crazy, but no wonder, really. Even decades later, the moon landings are so amazing that some people still don't believe *they* really happened.

And there was Grandad Norman. He was great.

A thought creeps into my head. Would it be so bad to go back? I swallow it back down.

Suddenly my phone buzzes – it's a message from Manny.

My heart leaps, but still I hesitate. At least he's okay. At least he's still *here*. But is he going to say something horrible to me about earlier on? I don't want to feel any worse than I already do. Nervously, I click open on the text message.

It's a high tide again at 11.30 p.m.

I know where this is going, and I swallow hard.

I'm going sideways in time to proove that i'm telling the truth.

My finger is trembling as I type.

Can I come too?

He doesn't reply, which is perhaps the worst torture of all. He's making me suffer for my weakness, and I can't say I blame him.

I'm just going to have to go. I'm not spending the rest of my life being called a liar.

PART FOUR

CHAPTER 27

Getting away was the easy bit.

I've got my phone, fully charged this time, its memory emptied to maximise space. With Dad still out in the car, I'm betting that Mam is asleep already (exhausted by their bickering, probably), and that she won't wake up and suddenly want to check my whereabouts.

Don't misunderstand me, though. It's not like I'm going, 'Hey-ho, what an easy and very un-dangerous trip into a cave and a different dimension this is going to be!' No, I'm actually terrified.

I've pedalled hard. It's a cold spring night, and I've got my lime-green hoodie on, zipped up to my throat. Still, I shiver a bit when I see Manny on the big stone promenade overlooking the bay.

Has he forgiven me? He doesn't look round when I come down the steps, carrying my bike, even though my feet are making plenty of noise. As I approach him, he glances at me, then looks back out at the sea, his shoulders hunched even more than usual.

When I draw level, I say, 'Look, I'm sorry about before.'

He shrugs one shoulder.

It's not exactly forgiveness, I don't think, but it will have to do for now.

Still he says nothing, though. Eventually, he clears his throat and nods to himself. It's as though he's drawing a line under what has gone before. Then he pulls out a sheet of paper, a printout of a webpage. There's a graph showing some lines and a column of numbers.

'Look,' he says. 'Tide tables plotted against the moon's gravitational pull.'

It's difficult to see it properly in the dark, so I just nod as if it means something to me.

He goes on. 'Now, I don't understand it . . .'

I start to say, 'That's reassuring, with our lives in the balance,' but I stop before the words come out. It's not the time for sarcasm.

'That is, I don't understand it *all*,' he says. 'But I know enough to think that this –' he indicates the cave – 'is able to create some sort of interdimensional shift thing . . . which is what they call it on the web forums. The serious ones. Anyway, if what they say is true, then there's a few days during a perigee, when the moon is closest to the earth, that are the ideal conditions for . . . well, for going sideways in time. There needs to be a high tide as well, and a confined space, and that –' he jerks his thumb at the cave again – 'is exactly what we have here.'

I pause for a moment to take this in. 'This is like what Maudie said. I think.'

'*Maudie* said this? When? What did she say?'

'Oh, Manny – I can't remember it all. It just sounded like what you've just told me. I didn't understand most of it. But let's say you're right: how long have we got?'

He turns his whole body to look at me now for the first time. I take this to mean I'm properly forgiven. He glances down at the triangular cave entrance looming black and forbidding at the bottom of the 'no entry' steps.

'About three minutes. You were kinda late.'

I sigh and gulp. 'Let's go then. And just to be clear, Manny – we go, we collect evidence, and we come back at the next high tide, twelve hours and twenty-five minutes later, yeah? I have my camera fully charged. What about you?'

He shakes his head ruefully. I guess one stolen-and-smashed camera is enough in anyone's life.

'But . . . how were you going to get evidence without a camera?'

He half smiles, a bit shyly, and hunches his shoulders again. 'I trusted you would come. That's what friends do, eh? Trust each other?'

There's a moment when the moon comes out from behind a cloud, and the promenade is washed with a creamy light, and it catches Manny's eyes. We hold each other's gaze for a few seconds, then a few seconds more, and it's getting embarrassing, actually, but I don't want to be the one who breaks it because that would mean we have to do what we came here to do.

Below us, a wave slaps noisily on the seawall, splashing droplets over the railing. This gives us both the excuse we need to look away, and we see that the tide is at the mouth of the cave. Soon we're over the barrier and on to the slimy steps again.

'The high tide seems lower than the last time,' says Manny, who's several metres ahead of me and already splashing through the deepening pool at the entrance.

'Is that a good thing? I mean, if it doesn't work, I don't fancy being trapped at the back of the cave till the tide turns.'

'Don't worry. If it works, we'll meet tomorrow morning at the corner by the cows. It's definitely going to be okay, probably.'

We're inside now, and his voice echoes against the damp cave walls.

'Probably? I don't like this "probably", Manny. What do you— Hang on, *shhh*! Do you hear that?'

We're ten or fifteen metres into the cave, at the bit where the roof starts to slope downwards, and I could swear I heard someone's voice shouting my name. There it is again.

'. . . *il . . . aaa!*'

'Oh, surely not. It . . . it's Alex!' I say to Manny. 'I'm certain.'

'Look, we're nearly there. Assuming the time-compression thingummy is the same now, then she'll be here when we get back! Hold my hand. It worked before.'

He doesn't wait for me to hold my hand out but grabs it instead and pulls. In the shifting beam from my flashlight app, I see the layer of dark sandstone at the back of the cave wall: a thick reddish strip like the filling in a sandwich. We're at the back wall, and too far in to hear anything but the wind outside.

At that point, a strong, low surge of seawater catches me by surprise and makes me squeal. 'Hey! I thought you said the tide wasn't going to come up this far?' I say as the water retreats. But Manny doesn't answer; instead, he pulls me closer.

'You ready?' he says, and when I don't answer he says it again, more forcefully. 'You *ready*, Willa?'

I'm too nervous to speak. I shove my phone deep in my pocket then I reply by squeezing his hand hard. In the dim light I see his other hand slap on to the darker layer of stone.

Then it's grey again – the same greyness and nothingness that I recognise from last time. Only it's coming much slower, and I don't know why that is. I'm even more scared *because I know what's about to happen.* It's like the 'going up' bit on a rollercoaster: it's actually scarier than going down. You squeak with the fear of what's to come (at least I do) as much as scream with terrified delight as the car plummets downwards . . .

And now I'm sitting upright in my bed again, my shoes soaked through, and fighting a strong desire to vomit.

If I lie flat, it's better, so I take my shoes and clothes off and crawl back under the different-smelling duvet, which is still warm from . . .

Me.

That's the bit I still don't understand.

What happened to the 'me' that was sleeping peacefully in this bed and leaving it warm? Where is she now? Then I think of Manny.

It's almost instinctive. I reach for my phone in my jeans pocket on the floor and turn it on. The screen lights up and displays the app icons, but there are no bars showing phone reception, or Wi-Fi connection, or Bluetooth or Connix or even clunky old 11G. I want to send a message to Manny – you know, check he's okay.

How did people cope before instant messaging?

I don't want to sleep. The bone-wearying tiredness that I experienced last time hasn't yet taken me over. Now my brain feels alive, like a load of Christmas lights are flashing inside my head.

See, last time I was here, it was all too confusing. Everything came at once, and I had no time, really, to work out what was happening.

Am I the same person here? I mean, I look the same, apart from the teeth thing that my brother Alex spotted.

I put the light on, pull on a dressing gown (different from mine) and look more closely around my bedroom, trying to work out just how different this world is, and how I am going to record it to show people back . . . well, *home*, I suppose.

My desk in the corner looks the same, but I usually have schoolwork arranged in coloured plastic folders, and they've gone. My books too: there's a shelf above the desk, and some of the titles are different. My Harry Potters that used to be Mam's have gone. There's a whole set of something else – *The Peace Chronicles* – all obviously well read, by an author I've never heard of.

This is evidence! I should be recording it.

I switch on my phone again and breathe a sigh of relief that the camera app works. I take a picture of the bookshelf, and my desk, and the new duvet, and the poster of the singer I don't know on the wall.

Who *is* she, this other version of Wilhemina Shafto? Is she like me?

I'm so absorbed that I don't hear my bedroom door open. But I spin round in shock when I hear the voice.

'Mina, what the flink are you . . . oh. It's you again. Just what is going on?'

CHAPTER 28

My brother does not sound happy to see me – which is hardly surprising because the last time he did I'd pushed past him and cycled a FreeRide back to Brown's Cave rather than explain to him why – so far as he could see – his sister's teeth had gone wonky overnight.

There was no way I could run away this time. 'Look, erm . . . Alex. I can explain everything.'

Well, *that's* not true, but I had to say something, didn't I?

He looks at me with a combination of puzzlement and fear. 'I hope so. I'm going to get Mam and Dad.'

I grab his arm in desperation. 'No, no! Don't do that! Please! They'll be really upset.' I'm frantic and terrified and cursing myself for not having thought of this in advance.

He takes the key from my bedroom door and backs out, pulling the door behind him and locking me in.

I would yell, but that won't do any good. I dash to the window, wondering if I can climb out for the second time in about an hour, but that's another thing that's different. Our smart new windows have gone; instead, there's an old-fashioned sash window that's jammed shut with layers of paint. My shoulders sag, and I sink back on to the bed, wondering what I'm going to say to Mam and Dad and whether the truth will work.

A moment later, the key in the bedroom door turns again.

Alex stands in the doorway alone. I glance behind him for Mam or Dad. For a moment, I'm just mesmerised once again by this older brother who's replaced my sister. His dark hair's a bit shorter, but Alex – girl-Alex, that is – has fairly short hair anyway. They have the same slightly sleepy, long-lashed eyes, and they even wear similar nightstuff: cotton shorts and a baggy T-shirt, although my sister favours blacks and greys, and this boy's are – guess what? – coloured and patterned like a wall of Lego. Despite that, there are things about him – a sharper jawline, a broader chest – that definitely suggest 'boy'. Even his voice, although a bit deeper, sounds like hers.

'You . . . you didn't tell them?' I say.

'Not yet. But, whatever your explanation is, it had better be good.' He steps into my room and closes the door softly behind him. He pulls out the desk chair and sits expectantly.

So I tell him. There, in my room-that's-not-my-room, I give him my explanation, as far as I can. And he listens – properly listens. I tell him about my sister, Alex, about my world, about Manny, about the cave and the cog, about . . . everything. I try – not very successfully – to explain about the supermoon and the tides and what Manny called the interdimensional shift.

(Well, nearly everything. I don't tell him about our little photo-and-candle shrine on the mantelpiece. I just tell him that I have a sister called Alex. That, I reckon, is freaky enough to be going on with.)

He says, 'What's she like? Girl-Alex?' and I don't know what to say. Moody? Bad-tempered? Boy-mad? Just not very nice overall? None of it sounds right.

So I say, 'You look similar. She's . . . pretty.' Which Alex is, usually. When she's not scowling.

He says, 'Can you give me one good reason why I should believe you?'

I think about this for a moment, and I notice again the books I saw before: *The Peace Chronicles*. 'Because, if you don't, then no one else will. And, if that happens, I won't get the chance to prove to everyone back home that a World Without War is possible.'

It's not strictly true, of course. The World Without War thing is not the only reason I came back. But I'm beginning to think that people here take it really seriously, and that it might be the very thing to persuade the boy in front of me to keep my secret for a few more hours so that I can do what I need to do.

He ponders this for a moment; I'm not even sure he

properly understands. Then he murmurs, 'This cave you mentioned?'

It's the way he says it: softly, questioning. I'm wary, but ask, 'Yes? What of it?'

'It explains a lot.'

'It does?'

He nods and takes a deep breath. 'Mina – that is, the real Mina – has been really freaked out by a nightmare she says she had a couple of weeks ago. But she says it wasn't *like* a dream. She was really there – she woke up in a cave with another boy, trapped in the dark by the tide, for maybe half an hour? And then she found herself back in bed. She's been flinkin' upset. She insisted it had really happened, but she couldn't explain it. And she said she had sand from the cave in her fingernails, but Mam and Dad didn't believe her.'

He's about to say more, but I hold up my hand to stop him while I process what he has just said.

'You're saying . . . I have swapped places with my other self? She – Mina – was in Brown's Cave? That's . . . that's . . .'

I trail off as waves of sorrow and astonishment pass over me. I think how horrible it must have been to be trapped in a cave, even for a short time, thinking it was a nightmare. Poor Mina! And I know perfectly well what it feels like not to be believed. It's almost as though it has happened to me.

'And you?' I ask. 'Did you believe her?'

He tuts and shakes his head. 'Not really. I just couldn't. It was . . . unbelievable. The sand thing made me wonder, but I thought it was just her messing about. It has caused a bunchacation, you know . . .'

'Hang on, what?'

Alex looks at me, surprised. 'Bunchacation? You know a lot of . . . altercation. Arguments. We totally fell out about it. She's furious with me, with all of us. And now . . . well, it seems it's happened again.'

So the two of us sit there – Alex on the chair, me on the end of my bed – just trying to get our heads round it all. And failing.

Then I have an idea.

'Check this out,' I say. 'This is from my world.' I hand him my phone.

Alex takes it cautiously, like he's handling an egg, and turns it over in his hands: a silver-backed rectangle with a matte-black screen.

'What's this then?' he says.

'A phone. A mobile telephone. Or a cell. Short for cellphone, though I don't know what the *cell* bit means. Here, I'll turn it on.'

'This . . . is a *telephone*?' He stares at the home screen (which is just a picture of Maudie's cat Plato looking cute), then the little app icons pop up. 'Oh yeah – look. It's a picture of a telephone receiver.'

He's pointing to the app for making calls, and there's a little symbol on it of one of those things from old-style phones that you speak and listen with. I'd never really noticed it before. Nor did I know that it was called a 'receiver'.

'Where's the dial? What do you speak into? Can I make a call?' He smiles cheekily, just like my sister used to do.

'Won't work,' I say, and his face falls. 'Look.' I point to where the little icon indicates there's no reception. 'Probably cos there's no signal and no, erm . . .' I dry up. I don't know how phones work, do I?

'No what? Do you have to plug it into the wall or something?' says Alex, suddenly looking much younger than his sixteen years. He has the enthusiastic eyes of an eight-year-old with a new toy that needs batteries. I feel a bit ashamed not knowing, so I make something up.

'No, erm . . . network of . . . transmitter . . . satellite signals.'

He nods as if he understands. 'Satellites, eh?' he says. 'Groovy!'

Groovy?!

I feel like showing off a bit, so I say, 'It's not *just* a phone, though. It's a camera as well.' I get a little pulse of satisfaction when his eyes widen with astonishment.

I open the camera app and show him the pictures I've just taken, which he thinks are amazing, especially the way you swipe with your finger, and he keeps doing it, and suddenly I regret uploading all the pictures that were on the memory on to my laptop. I had wanted to create as much space on my phone as possible, but I wish I'd left a few of my 'real' family.

'Do you want to see the best bit? Click on that one. I love this site!'

'Click?'

'Tap on it. Not as hard as that, blimey!'

I was hoping to show him hAppie – the one with all the funny jokes and dances. Instead – I should have known – the screen is filled with a message.

He reads it out: '*No network connection. To connect to this app, use Wi-Fi or a broadband cellular network such as 11G.* I have no idea what any of that means, Mina.'

'Me and Alex and her friend Jeanette did an awesome hAppie when I was in Year Six. It got four thousand, two hundred stars, and we thought it would go viral.'

Poor Alex. He's just blinking, slack-jawed, at almost everything I say, and I'm beginning to feel quite good about this. He's proving very easy to impress. 'Yeah, so Dad says they were only invented when he was a kid, and he's always complaining that young people are addicted to them: you know, always on social media, listening to music and stuff and watching the war . . .'

Alex's face screws up, and I immediately wish I could

take back those last few words. 'You watch the *war*? What war? World War One? Two?'

I swallow hard. 'No. Three. No, no, no – not *yet*.' He looks so terrified, and I sigh. 'It's just . . . That's where it's headed. At least that's what everyone says. If Britain joins in, then our allies will as well, and my dad will have to fight . . . Well, who knows, eh?'

Alex slumps down in the chair. 'So that's why you came? To show them there's a better world?' and I nod. It's not a complete lie.

There's a long silence between us, and he turns the phone round in his hands, examining it as if it holds some secret.

'Is it a record player as well?' he says, pointing to the Songz app, and I nod. 'Go on then – play me some of your music. Music from the future!'

'It's not the future, Alex. It's right now. But still . . .'

I take back the phone. I hadn't cleared the memory completely. There's some chart tracks that I can play, and two or three have videos attached, so I choose the one by Felina (who you probably know) that goes:

> *You've made my world a better place!*
> *Na na na na na!*

Alex just sits there with my phone in his hand, transfixed. Then he plays it again. Then another and another.

After a while, I notice with a sinking heart that all this fiddling with my phone has drained the battery down to half. I quickly snatch the phone back and switch it off, furious with myself for being so stupid and for showing off. I didn't even bring a charger.

Stupid, stupid, stupid Willa.

Alex's eyes, though, have not lost their fascinated shine, and it's nice that he seems to be trusting me. Then he says, 'So – what about Mina? What have you done with her? Where is she?'

This time I'm calmer and I say, 'I really don't know, Alex. I haven't *done* anything. It's not like I've captured her, I mean, me. Her, me, whatever. I don't understand how this works, but I think what happens is that while I am here Mina can't be, otherwise there'd be two of us, and that would be too strange. I mean, imagine two of me sitting on this bed now, each claiming to be the real me.'

Alex thinks this over, then he pinches his chin hard between his thumb and forefinger and squeezes the skin. When I see this action of my sister's, I start to laugh.

'What?' he says. 'What's so funny?'

And then I get up and give him the biggest hug, which startles him, but he hugs me back. I start sobbing a little bit, with relief as much as anything, and he pats my back slightly awkwardly. When I pull away, he's smiling.

'This has to be . . . between us?' I say. 'You can't tell Mam and Dad. Not till I've gone. Please?'

'But . . . but why not?'

'Think about it: the fuss, the questions, the . . . the police? It could all put me and Manny in real danger. I am going back, I promise. Well, if not exactly *back*, then I'm returning . . . sideways.'

We look at each other for the longest time.

'Please,' I say. 'Brother?'

As I speak the words, I get a feeling of something like regret. Promising to go back means promising to leave this Alex behind for good. What's more, I think I actually *like* it here.

At last he says, 'Stick with me, Mina, I mean Willa – gosh, that sounds flinkin' ripped!'

'Sounds what?'

'Ripped. You know: strange, odd.'

I smile. 'Yeah. Definitely . . . flinkin' ripped.'

Alex starts to nod, as though he's been struggling with his conscience and decided on a course of action.

'So, next high tide, eh? When's that, then?'

I tell him. 'Five minutes to midday.'

'Shame you can't stay for longer. The WWW Night celebrations are tomorrow.'

'Tomorrow?' I repeat, astonished. The WWW celebrations were meant to be days away when Manny and I were last here. But, then again, time really doesn't seem to work in a predictable way when we travel to and from this dimension.

Alex shrugs. 'Besides, I want to meet this Manny character too. So – school tomorrow?'

'School?' I say, feeling a bit alarmed. I hadn't had time to form much of a plan, but whatever I *had* thought about did not include school.

'Don't you have to collect evidence? You can leave when you've got what you need.'

I think about this for a moment. 'The gates'll be locked, Alex. I can't just walk out.'

Alex narrows his eyes. 'You lock your school gates? Why?'

'No idea. To keep us in? To keep bad people out? Dunno.'

He says, '*Hmmp*,' as if he doesn't really understand, and I don't blame him.

So, school tomorrow. And back home by midday.

What could possibly go wrong?

CHAPTER 29

Unlike the last time, I don't sleep for a single second. Would you? I still don't even know if Manny arrived all right, and I'm tormenting myself with feeling bad about the other me – Mina. She, I now understand, is experiencing the same nightmare again: trapped in the cave in my world.

What if she's rescued? What will that mean?

It could happen. She could wade out of the cave, or even be swept out to sea and drown. Would that make a difference to my return? What if I've made a massive, catastrophic mistake in coming here?

The 'what-ifs' are endless. So I'm up and ready and dressed when Alex puts his head round my bedroom door the next morning and gives me a big wink and a thumbs up, which kind of cheers me up, even though my stomach is churning with nerves. I give him a nervous grin in return.

'Hey, er . . . Mina. Oh, you're ready. You may want to smile with your mouth shut today. I won't be the only one to notice your teeth. Mina – that is, the real Mina, sorry – she has very even teeth. After you left last time, I mentioned it to Mam and Dad, but they hadn't noticed. They thought I was nuts and, by then, Mina was back anyway, talking about that weird cave nightmare she'd had. I began to think I'd been imagining it.'

The mention of Mina's cave nightmare twists my stomach more. I look in the mirror and bare my teeth. Honestly, they aren't *that* bad. Still, I practise smiling with my lips clamped together. I look like an idiot. Worse, I look like Deena Malik when she's being insincerely nice. I decide to keep my head down and hope that Mam and Dad don't notice.

'By the way, this might help you take your pictures with that . . . phone thing.' He hands me a black box made of stiff card with a back that opens on a hinge of cloth tape. On the front is glued (a bit messily, but still . . .) a camera-type lens, and there's a hole for my phone's lenses to see out of.

'You . . . you made this? For me?' I say, slotting my phone into it. It fits pretty well. 'It's awesome! Where did you get this lens?' I turn it round, admiring it and loving my brother for doing it. It's actually really good, and Alex has stayed up making it. It's nice of him, and, if you don't inspect it too carefully, it looks just like an old-fashioned camera. Well, almost . . .

'It's part of my telescope set-up,' he says, a bit shyly. 'It's pretty old. I never use that bit very much, and you're going to need it more than me. Oh, and don't say "awesome". It sounds ripped.'

I think this through, nodding. I hear Mam calling, 'Breakfast! Come on!' and Alex leaves.

I swallow hard and do the breathing thing that Maudie taught me: *in for four, out for six.*

Finally, turning to the mirror again, I actually talk out loud. 'You're here now, Willa. Make the most of it.'

I have to set to work straight away, gathering evidence, and get back to the cave as soon as possible, risking nothing in my determination to catch the next high tide at nearly midday.

Sometimes pretending to be brave is as good as actually being brave. I march into the kitchen with a new-found purpose. Holding up my phone-disguised-as-a-camera and being careful to keep it moving so no one gets a good look at it, I declare, 'Okay, picture time!'

As the fridge door closes, it reveals Mam and Dad actually *snogging* as I take the picture.

'Oh no! Oh, I'm really sorry!'

They both collapse in giggles, as if they have no idea at all that seeing your parents full-on kissing is just about the grossest thing ever.

'Ha ha!' chuckles Dad. 'Caught in the act!'

'Ooh, what's that?' says Mam, pointing at my cardboard camera, and I say my prepared line.

'It's a photographic project for school. "Me and My

World . . . s".' I add the 's' just as a joke to myself, and no one notices.

'Oh, Mina. I haven't done my hair. I look a mess,' she says, and, even though this is not what I think of as my real mam, I have to smile because it's exactly the sort of thing Real Mam would say. Then I remember I'm smiling, and I quickly hide my teeth.

'You look gorgeous to me, my sweet,' says Dad, and I have to resist the urge to gag as she blows him another kiss. To be honest, it's better than them arguing all the time, but still . . .

I lift up the camera for another picture. 'Okay, look this way. I mean . . . on second thoughts, don't look at the camera! Look away, look away – it's much more natural!'

I snap Alex and Mam, then Mam and Dad in his chef's apron, then all three of them. My phone makes the sound of an old-style camera, and no one asks any more questions.

A few minutes later, and Alex and I are left alone at the kitchen table. Mam has bustled out, blowing kisses and telling us to be good, while Dad said he was off to Culvercot and departed, singing some song about 'When the Boat Comes In', which made Alex laugh so I laughed along too.

Alex hands me a piece of toast and a jar of spread. I think it's jam, and it tastes okay. Sort of sweetish.

As we eat, Alex tells me about so many things that my head spins. Not fighting wars is just the start of it. Everyone has enough to eat. The air and the oceans are clean. People are free to worship whichever god they like – or none at all, if they prefer. They can live how they like, and love who they like. People live for a long time and usually die peacefully and old . . .

'You don't have diseases?' I say, incredulously, and he thinks about this.

'Yes. Yes, we do. But most of them we know how to deal with. Cancer used to be a big thing, but not so much now. I mean . . . I nearly died when I was a baby.'

'Y-you did?'

'Yeah. I mean – hurray for modern medicine!'

'What were you sick with?'

'Oh, some heart disorder. Can't remember the name of it. I got better.'

'Was it . . . Fallot's Tetralogy?' I have heard Mam and Dad say it so often that the long name trips off my tongue.

Alex says, 'That's it!' Then his brow furrows. 'How do you know?'

And so I take a deep breath and tell him. I tell him about the photo-and-candle shrine on the mantelpiece, and how Mam and Dad still think about him and his short life, and how doctors couldn't save him. When I've finished, he says nothing, but sits, eyes cast down, hands clasped together as if praying, and, for all I know, he is. When he eventually looks up, his eyes are shining with tears, and he wipes them away with his sleeve.

'That's ripped,' he says with a short laugh. 'Don't suppose many people get to cry over their own death.'

There's still more I want to ask him. 'Do you have . . . pandemics?' I say, thinking of Mam and Dad, and all the grown-ups I know. They're forever talking about the big pandemic that happened when I was very little, and I tell Alex about it, and I was going to tell him that it had killed Grandad Norman, but he looks so shocked already that I don't. Pandemics, it turns out, are unknown here.

'And the colours?' I ask him. 'What's all that about?'

He grins. 'You don't like it?'

'It takes a bit of getting used to . . .'

'I don't even notice it, but older people remember when everything was grey and brown. They called it the Colour Revolution, or the Rainbow Uprising. It just . . . caught on, you know? All at once, we were living in full colour!'

I take another piece of toast and spread the jam thickly. 'What is this anyway?' I say, sniffing the reddish-brown jelly.

'You like? That's Barichara pâté. Good, eh?'

'And what's Barichara pâté when it's at home?' I take a big bite.

'Ants. They breed them, a special type. Then they . . . oh. You don't want that? Can I have it?'

I'm not very hungry any more.

We're heading off to school, Alex and I, when I remember that I have never even seen the holiday park here, and I persuade him to go the other way. Last time, I came and went through the rear entrance. You can do that and hardly see the rest of the park, which is concealed behind massive trees.

As we turn back, a cog drops from the nearest tree to the ground near my feet, and I squeal. It gives me a long, curious look and, when it turns away, I see the flash of reddish hair on its back, and I am pretty sure it's the one from before. Alex laughs as I fumble for my camera.

'Oh, the molphin's back! Haven't seen him for a while.'

I manage a quick snatch of video on my phone as the cog/molphin patiently wanders from the tree over to a bush, where it stands up to pee, looking from the back like a very hairy little boy, and then it's gone, into the undergrowth.

'What do they eat?' I ask Alex as we walk up to the entrance and the main road. 'Bananas?'

'Well, they'll eat a banana if you give it to them. But it's fish mainly – they're excellent swimmers, thanks to the retractable fin on their backs. They can hold their breath for, like, minutes. There's not many of them left in the wild. It was a controversial experiment, and they don't reproduce very well, so they're dying out.'

I remember what Dad had said when I'd played *MindGames* in the kitchen with him. 'Yes. It's a semi-feral hybrid mammal,' and Alex's eyebrows shoot up.

'How do you know that?' he says, and I just smirk in response.

By now, we've come round the barrier of trees and bushes, and I just stand there, gawping at the holiday park.

'Different, is it?' murmurs Alex at my shoulder.

CHAPTER 30

Different? I'm almost speechless.

Where the freezing, cracked open-air pool should be there is a covered spa with mini palm trees visible through the huge glass dome. I glimpse a warm-looking pool with a waterfall. Everywhere outside, trees and bushes have replaced the cheap plastic fencing, and instead of tatty caravans and tired little lodges with leaky roofs there are cosy-looking wooden cabins, all of their doors painted different colours. It's like I'm gazing at an artist's impression of what a perfect holiday park is, and, as we walk to the entrance, it just gets better. A sign above a small shack says EGGY MEGGIE'S BRILLIANT BREAKFASTS, and some families are sitting in the morning sunshine, laughing and eating at striped tables. Everywhere there are beds of big spring daisies and yellow marigolds and blue . . . well, small blue flowers. Poor old Maudie does her best, but this is gardening on a whole different level.

Jungle Joe's GymTastic looks amazing: coloured rope swings, monkey bars, bright pink mini-trampolines and a curving water slide down the back of a massive crocodile.

I love it, and keep snapping away, trying not to draw attention to myself. This must be what happens with 'investment', I think. Perhaps it's all down to SunSeasons. I look out for the SunSeasons eye-catching logo of a bright yellow sun, but I can't spot it. Instead, at the entrance, is a huge sign.

Welcome to Roger Shafto's Heritage Holiday Park

'Great-grandad Roger!' I say, pointing out the smiling picture of him looking like the man from the KFC logo, and I take another photo.

'Oh yeah! He's a character all right,' says Alex. 'He lives in Florida. He's a hundred and fifteen, still takes the SP everywhere. He was here just last month.'

And then we're out on the main road, and once again I see the brightly coloured FreeRide tricycles – a jumbled-up rainbow of painted steel – and the flying ci-kars, with everyone smiling and waving at one another. It's all so wonderful, and I take more pictures and bits of video, making sure I get one looking *under* the ci-kars as they float only a few centimetres off the ground. The people in it grin at me before they move off with that slight swishing noise, and a trail of clear liquid droplets comes from a little opening at the back, where petrol cars have an exhaust pipe.

I hadn't noticed last time, but there's a channel, a little gutter, at the side of the road, where the liquid trickles. I point to it and ask Alex, 'What is that coming from the back of the cars?'

He looks at me like I'm daft. 'Water. Obviously.' He sees my awestruck face and says, 'Please don't tell me you still use gasoline?'

'Gas . . . erm, petrol? Yes. Yes, we do.' This is awful. It's like I'm being judged. 'It's not my fault! We do have electric cars as well! They're very popular!'

'Where does your electricity come from?'

We're walking towards the corner opposite the cows where I agreed to meet Manny, and I feel almost embarrassed. 'Most of it comes from, erm, you know . . . fossil fuels. And a growing portion from renewable sources.' I find I'm remembering stuff told to us at school.

Alex thinks this over, then says, 'Wow. I guess we were wrong.'

'Wrong how?' I want to know this, but I'm also a bit distracted, looking round for Manny and worried that he's not here.

'We did this in modern history class. Back in the 1970s, I think, we spotted massive problems with pollution from earth energy – coal and oil, yeah? Not only that, but they were making the world warm up. So, you know, we stopped and fixed it. Perhaps we were wrong. Perhaps we didn't need to. Where's your friend, by the way?'

'No,' I say. 'No. You were right. The world is heating up, I mean . . . ours is. But – go back. You "stopped and fixed it"? Just like that?'

'Hey, calm down! No, it wasn't "just like that", I don't think, but I wasn't there, was I? I think it took a while. Years, in fact. But, you know, we turned things around. "No problem of human destiny is beyond human beings," as the great man said.'

'Which great man?' I say, a little distracted. I keep looking up and down the road, fascinated by the vehicles.

'John F. Kennedy, of course,' says Alex.

I blink. Just hearing the name of the dead president sends a tiny thrill through me, as though something from my world is connecting with this world. But I pull my attention back to Alex. 'So – what is the secret then? How do these engines work? What powers everything?'

Alex smiles, a little bit sheepishly. 'You'll have to ask Jamaal. He's our engineering teacher. I think it's mainly nuclear energy.'

'Oh, we have that!' I say, brightly, pleased to have found another connection. 'But isn't it a bit . . . risky?'

'I guess everything's risky if you don't do it properly. The vehicles aren't nuclear, though. Most of them use an HCD engine. That stands for, erm . . . hyper-charging dynamo, that's it! A tiny effort from the driver and passengers is converted into something, and then something else happens with oxygen and hydrogen and something else, which becomes expelled water. That's it, I'm afraid. I got a Grade Fifteen last year.' He glances at me. 'That's not good. I'm better at physics than chemistry.'

'How does it float then?' I'm trying not to sound annoyed, but I wish Alex was a bit cleverer, especially when he just shrugs in response to my question.

'How can you not *know*?' I say.

'What do you mean? I can't know everything. I thought I was doing pretty well with HCD engines! You don't know how that . . . that mobility telephone thingy works, do you? And, besides, if your pal isn't here very soon, we're going to be late.'

I've been so absorbed in taking pictures and listening to Alex that I had almost forgotten Manny. Now, though, we're at the corner where we had agreed to meet. I get the first tingling of unease.

He wouldn't forget, would he? Of course not.

Would he go into school without me? No to that as well.

I'm pacing up and down the pavement, looking at every ci-kar and FreeRide with a desperate hope that it contains Manny. None of them do, of course.

Ordinarily, I'd send him a text, or even call him, and I find myself cursing both Manny for not turning up and this wonderful world that doesn't have instant communication.

How do they cope? How can a world come into existence with flying cars and some sort of non-polluting energy that I don't even understand, and cogs, and no wars, and not have mobile phones? Or computers, even?

'You all right, Mina – I mean Willa?' says Alex with genuine concern. 'I can't wait any longer. One more late this term and I get a detention.'

'I can't leave without him, Alex. What if he's in danger? What if . . . he didn't arrive? You've got to help me!'

I feel sick with worry. *Where is Manny?*

Alex thinks for a moment, pulling his chin in that familiar way. Then he says, 'You know what? I reckon that one detention is definitely worth it to spend a morning with a sister I never knew I had from another dimension in space-time!'

Is that what I am? I smile, weakly. 'Thanks, bro!'

'I kind of like detention anyway!' he says.

CHAPTER 31

'It's fine,' I say to Alex, trying to keep the rising panic from my voice. 'He's probably just gone to school by himself, or bunked off. This is Manny Weaver, after all. Bunking off school comes totally naturally to him.'

Alex shoots me a glance and – just like my sister – he can tell that this is more to convince myself, but, kindly, he doesn't point it out. Instead, he says, 'I'm sure you're right. If you made it through your cave-whatsit, then there's no reason that he didn't as well. Everything's going to be mass groovy.'

Just hearing those words makes me giggle a bit, despite feeling very uneasy.

'But still,' he goes on, 'perhaps we should check. Just, you know, to be cert.'

'Yes. It'll be, erm… mass groovy to be cert.'

I'm nervous as Alex and I pedal the few minutes to Manny's home. In fact, it's only at the last moment that I remember to film stuff, especially the houses on the seafront, which are normally the off-white colour of rainclouds and are now painted in pastel shades, each contrasting with the one next door. Not even the road is black – instead, the surface is a burnt red colour with markings in pale blue.

Meanwhile, I'm running through all the things that might have happened to Manny. From that, I start thinking of all the things that might happen to *me*, and I end up wondering whether I should have come back at all.

Why did I trust Manny of all people? Manny, the kid from the children's home with no family and nothing to lose! Manny with the spooky, hypnotic green eyes who can charm a cog to have its tummy tickled, Manny who . . .

'Where is this place, Willa?' calls Alex from behind me.

We turn off the main road and cycle through rows of pale pink and lavender-blue houses, and, even though the streets are laid out exactly as I expect, it's a while before I realise why I'm having difficulty recognising them, and it's not just the colours. It's because there are no cars. Think about it: pretty much every street in any town is lined on one or both sides with parked cars. But here there are hardly any vehicles at all, and it makes the streets look different. Four or five per street maybe, mainly ci-kars, not floating but resting on the ground on the dull metallic charging plates. I see a man come out of his house and stand next to one of them. He takes something from his pocket, just like taking out a car key, and points it at the ci-kar whose lights flash, then it rises up slowly to sort of car-height, the man gets in and it hisses off.

Outside Manny's home, I look up at the sign. For once, everything is pretty much exactly the same.

WINSTON CHURCHILL HOUSE

NORTHUMBERLAND COUNTY COUNCIL

RESIDENTIAL UNIT 44

I ring the doorbell while Alex waits on the pavement until a tall, friendly-looking lady with white hair and big glasses comes down the hallway, visible through the glass.

'Hello, hinny,' she says, smiling warmly. 'What can I do for you?'

'Hinny'! I've never heard anyone say that other than in the old Geordie songs that Nana knows.

'Is . . . is Manny here? Manny Weaver? Erm . . . Emanuel?'

'No, hinny. He isn't.'

I feel as though my stomach has hit the ground.

The lady lifts her glasses and looks under them at me. 'Are you Willa?' she says.

'Yes! Yes, I am.'

'I see. You'd better come in.'

I look back nervously at Alex, who smiles and gets off his FreeRide to come in with me. 'This is my brother,' I say, the words feeling a bit strange in my mouth.

We follow her into the clean-smelling hallway with pale yellow walls and an orange carpet. 'I'm Bonnie, by the way. I'm the "house aunty".' She sees me looking quizzical. 'Well – it sounds better than Senior Domestic Social Worker, doesn't it? Shouldn't you be at school, by the way?'

Her manner sounds strangely giggly and excited, with a little smile flickering on to her face.

'I got permission to come and check,' I say, surprising myself with how fluently and effortlessly I lied. She doesn't seem at all suspicious of my easy deception.

'Ha ha! Typical. I telephoned an hour ago and spoke to the receptionist. The message must not have been passed on.' Then she giggles again.

What on earth is going on?

'I thought you didn't have telephones,' I blurt out without thinking. Straight away, I wish I hadn't. 'That is, I, erm . . .'

You idiot, Willa.

I needn't have worried. Bonnie smiles. 'What? Here at Churchill House? We have two! One in my office and one right there.' She sounds very proud of the fact, and points behind me, where there is a box attached to the wall. Resting across the top is one of the curved handle things that they call a receiver, and there's a little round wheel with numbers on it below.

'Oh yes, we're quite up to date here, Willa. Now . . .' She gives another little laugh. 'Emanuel Weaver.'

Alex and I sit in her small office, and Bonnie sits at her desk, her hands clasped in her lap.

'Emanuel left early this morning, as was planned.' She sees my shocked face and says, 'Oh. He didn't tell you? I'm surprised. He'd been looking forward to this for a long time. Mind you, he's not been quite himself for a little while. In fact, we've been rather worried about him. I daresay it was the excitement. He's been so looking forward to today.'

'Looking forward to . . . what?' I say, nervous about what I'm going to find out.

'Well, I shouldn't really be telling anyone this. It's all been such a secret, you see. Confidentiality and all that . . .'

Honestly, it's like she's going to burst.

'Anyway, we have found Emanuel's mother!'

CHAPTER 32

They've found Manny's mam?

I find myself suddenly short of breath, and Bonnie laughs. 'Oh, bless you! Are you excited too? The odd thing is, when I woke him this morning, he seemed to have forgotten all about it. As I say, he has been very stressed lately, poor boy. For days, he's been talking about a very vivid dream he had where he was trapped in a cave – with you, as it happens. I think it's the excitement of meeting his mam.'

Alex and I catch each other's eye, and Bonnie sees us. 'Do you know about this?' she asks.

'No,' I say quickly. 'Well . . . only that Manny often talked about vivid dreams. In caves.' It sounds lame, but it seems to do the trick.

'Oh, I see,' she says. 'Anyway, after years of searching, we have managed to track down Emanuel's mother. She has had a . . . difficult life, shall we say? But she's now almost completely well, and they're scheduled to meet today for the first time since he was tiny. Isn't that marvellous?'

'So . . . she . . . she's *alive*?' I say, uncertainly. Then, seeing Bonnie's face, and realising how ridiculous this sounds, I add, 'Yes, of course she is, and it's all, erm . . . groovy! Where are they meeting up?'

I'm hoping it's not too far, and Manny will be back soon.

'Emanuel and Jakob caught the first train this morning. His mam has been in hospital for quite some time, and then living in social care. She's making a marvellous recovery, I'm told, and this is just the cherry on the cake. Oh, I'm saying far too much, but I'm just so excited for Emanuel! Not only that, but I don't think he's been to Edinburgh before.'

'E . . . E . . . Edinburgh? In *Scotland*?' I croak.

Bonnie smiles. 'Of course in Scotland.' It's as if she wants to say, *Where else, dummy?*

My stomach twists.

'He wanted to telephone you at home, but it was far too early, and I wouldn't let him. Instead, he was very anxious that I give you this.'

Bonnie hands me a sealed envelope with WILLA written on the front in Manny's scrawly handwriting and I tear it open.

Deer Willa,
  I'm meting my mam!
  My mam, Willa!!! I am leeving

soon with Jakob the soshial worker. Mam is in a home in Edimborouh and no boddy new she was my mam becos she had mentle illness, but now she is better and I am very exited to see her. If she is well enouf, then I will live with her and I am not coming back you-know-where.

I think this is why I came here althow I dint know it. THank you for helping me. I am staying in Royle hotle in Edinb. witch is posh and I should be back soon.

IMPORTANT: I felt the 'thing' getting weeker (but I dint say cos it wood fryten you). It's the moon, ~~deffin defnit~~ for sure.

IF I AM NOT BACK IN TWO DAYS, THEN YOU MUST GO BY YOURSELF.

Manny

x (on the cheek, dont get idears)

'Are you all right, hinny?' asks Bonnie, gently.

'Hmm? What? Yeah, yeah.' I read the note for a third time and hand it to Alex, who reads it like he doesn't understand it. When he holds it up, I see that on the other side is a colour photograph of a lady with a striking resemblance to Manny, including the green eyes and long blonde fringe. There's lots of tiny printing as well: her birth name, various addresses, ID numbers and so on.

'Isn't it marvellous?' Bonnie reaches across me and points at the picture. 'His poor mam never gave up hope, apparently, but her illness got in the way. Jakob has done a marvellous job of tracking her down. All of the records were destroyed in a fire a few years back; made it all very hard. Jakob didn't give up, though. Look at all the information he tracked down, piece by piece.'

I'm only taking half of this in, of course, because my mind is racing ahead with countless problems and possibilities. I fold up Manny's letter and shove it in my pocket.

Go by yourself, he said. How could I do that? There's something about Manny that makes the whole thing possible. That tingling up my arm when he grabs my hand and touches the darker sandstone at the rear of the cave . . .

The light in his eyes when, well . . . whenever really.

The magic that is Manny.

And now am I going to be stuck here? Here in this weird world of super-modern flying cars and ancient telephones?

He said the 'thing' is getting weaker.

'Willa? Willa? Here have a tissue, hinny. I know – it's very emotional.'

I hadn't even realised I was crying as I ran out of her office, followed by Alex.

'Willa? Willa, come back, love! Are you all right? Willa!'

CHAPTER 33

The door of Winston Churchill House thuds shut behind us. I'm down the steps and back on my FreeRide, and soon I'm speeding along the seafront with the bike's booster motor whirring beneath me, and Alex pedalling to catch up. I overtake a couple of ci-kars, each making a different cheery bell-sound as I pass, but cheery is the last thing I'm feeling.

'Mina! Stop!' calls Alex. I don't.

In fact, I don't stop till I'm at the steps leading down to Brown's Bay, where I leap off the FreeRide. Alex comes up behind me and grabs my arm, spinning me round so I can see his face, red and scared.

'Mina – I mean Willa. What's this all about?' he says, panting. 'I don't understand.'

'Just go without me, he said! Like I'm getting the school bus! He doesn't realise that I can't!' I'm yelling and upset, and Alex looks alarmed.

I'm panting too, as much from panic as from the hard cycling. When I get my breath back, I say, 'Come with me,' and we descend the steps to the promenade and sit on one of the wooden prom benches. Haltingly, I try to explain what I think has happened.

'Somehow – don't ask me how – I have swapped places with your sister, Mina,' I say, and I hold up my hand to stop him interrupting. I'm staring blankly at the flat blue sea, working this out as I'm saying it. 'So, if I find myself in her bed, she must find herself where I was – that is, in the cave. That one – right there.'

Alex blinks rapidly, and his lips twitch as if he's repeating my words to himself, trying to understand.

'Last time, the high tide meant she couldn't get out of the cave. She thought exactly what I thought at first – that it was a dream. They weren't dreams, Alex. She was actually there with Manny – the Manny from this world. They were completely terrified for the short time they were in there. Poor Mina. Poor Manny.'

I start to cry again, just thinking of the terror they must have experienced, and Alex puts his arm round me, which is nice of him. He says, 'But you were here for ages – how come they didn't come out when the tide retreated?'

I sniff and wipe my eyes on my sleeve. 'I don't know, Alex. Manny called it the "time-compression thingummy".' I sniff again and laugh. 'I know – dead scientific. It means time must pass differently here than . . . than there, I guess. Or the cave warps time or something.'

He nods slowly. 'That makes sense.'

'It does?'

'Yes. Sort of. Einstein. Relativity. We did it in physics.' He sees my puzzled look. 'How do I put this? Time isn't the same everywhere or for everyone. And, if you've done something like, I dunno, travel to another dimension, then I guess time might get . . . bent out of shape? It must do, otherwise how come there is a supermoon here as well?'

I say nothing. It makes as much sense as anything else, to be honest.

'Look,' I say, pointing at the incoming tide. 'We know the moon causes the tides, yeah?'

I half expect Alex to contradict me, as though in this world there's been some fabulous new discovery, and the two are not connected at all, so I'm relieved when he says, 'Of course.'

'So . . . it turns out that some people are affected by the moon as well. Like cuckoos.' I realise that I'm not explaining this well, and I sigh. 'Manny is a "super-sensor" – he's the key to it all. I can't do it without him. Unless he's with me, I'm stuck here. I don't even know how long we have left to catch this supermoon.'

Alex reaches into his backpack and pulls out a schoolbook, which he hands to me. The cover shows a photograph of a smiling woman in front of a starry night sky.

Cosmic Resonance – An Introduction
by
Amara Kholi

I blink in astonishment at the cover. Amara Kholi? Isn't that the woman Maudie mentioned?

Alex sees my face. 'You know this person?' he asks.

'Well . . . I think . . . that is . . . I've heard of her.'

'Groovy. She's quite well known. She does stuff on TV and the wireless. She reckons our lives are affected by the movements of the planets and stars.'

I think about this for a moment. 'Is this . . . is this the idea that everything is connected, and there are forces that we can't see that affect us, like cuckoos flying south?'

Alex shrugs. 'I guess so. Look at you, sitting here. There must be something in it.'

He gets to his feet. 'Come on,' he says. 'I want to see inside this magical cave.'

I start to tell him it's not magical, but he's already off, climbing over the barrier and down to the pebbly sand. I call after him, 'Your backpack – you've left it!'

Alex stops and looks back. 'I know. So what?'

'So . . . someone might steal it.'

I immediately feel slightly ashamed of my own world, where leaving things unattended is pretty much never done. After a moment, I take off my own backpack and place it next to Alex's on the stripy wooden bench in full view of anyone who might happen to walk past, then I hurry towards the steps before I can change my mind.

The tide is still way out, and Brown's Cave looks somehow different in the sharp spring daylight – less mysterious and more like just a wide crack in the cliff. The rock pool at the entrance is shallower and easy to hop across, and even the fishy, seaweedy smell seems less intense. I can almost see to the back wall of the cave.

Alex and I walk in confidently.

'So this is it?' he says. He doesn't sound disbelieving, just a bit disappointed.

We go in further, to where the sand, which is finer now, less gravelly, gradually banks up towards the rear rock face with its broad horizontal strip of darker stone.

Alex says, 'Seems the molphins like it here,' and he points to tiny hand-shaped prints in the sand.

'But look,' I say, going further in. The prints, slightly scuffed, go right up to the back wall and then stop. 'There are no prints leading away!'

Alex says, 'It's as though a molphin has just walked up to the wall and passed straight through it.'

I stare at the sand and the wall, and then back out towards the cave entrance.

'So this is the bit that you touch?' says Alex, and he slaps the wedge of reddish sandstone.

Nothing happens. Of course nothing happens. Holding my breath, I do it myself. Again, nothing.

I say, 'It has to be high tide. And it's obviously Manny that makes the difference.'

No Manny. My heart is still racing as I turn and head back towards the beach.

Back at the striped bench, our 'backies' as Alex calls them are undisturbed, of course, and we sit for a while. I'm trying to calm my nerves. High tide is coming, I can't do this without Manny, and Manny's not here.

Alex knows I'm a bit freaked out by Manny's letter, but he doesn't push me into talking about it, letting me take my own time, just watching the incoming tide.

Slowly but inevitably, the rock pools below us fill up, and little rivulets of seawater encroach on the sparse strip of sand where there is often some discarded fishing net or plastic bottles or other litter. Today there's nothing but seaweed and shells and a group of sandpipers hopping by the shore.

You're going to think I'm daft, but here goes. The sea is a different blue. I know I mentioned it before, but now, as I sit on the wooden bench and stare out at it, I'm convinced. How can that be? I know the sea isn't always the same colour, but this is the North Sea, and it's hardly ever as blue as it is today. The sky is that typical British whitey-grey, with some darker rainclouds building on the horizon, but still the sea sparkles a rich, deep indigo.

And then the water is lapping round the mouth of the cave. I check the time on my phone. It's midday; the tide will soon be retreating.

Alex goes, 'Wow!' when he sees the digital clock-face, which makes me laugh, until I see that I'm now down to ten per cent battery.

I pat my jacket and feel something hard. I take out the bar of chocolate that Maudie had put there when I'd last seen her. I offer it to Alex, and he points at the wrapper. 'I like the name!'

Fry's Chocolate Cream. That name: Fry. What was it that Maudie had said? It was one of her stories. Her great-great-someone-or-other invented solid chocolate bars! And his name was . . .

Fry.

'You've gone quiet again,' says Alex.

'Oh my word!' I breathe. 'What's the name of the school founder? You know – the Fry Academy?'

'Lady Maud Fry. Everyone knows that.'

I'm on my feet and racing to the steps. 'It makes sense now! People change their names when they marry, Alex!'

'Yeah. So what?' Alex comes after me, and we stop at the bottom of the steps.

I say, as patiently as I can, 'Maud Fry became Maudie Lawson! Don't you see?'

'No, I don't see at all. Who the flink is Maudie Lawson?'

Who the . . . ? I think something changes inside me at that moment. It's almost like I can feel something clicking into place. I sit down on the concrete step and rest my head on my folded arms for a moment. Then I look up at Alex, who's still standing over me.

'I love your world, Alex. But it's *your* world. I just . . . don't belong here. Everything's right for you, but everything's wrong for me.'

Alex sits down next to me. 'So why did you come back, Willa?'

'I wanted to show people at home that a better world was possible.'

'*Hmmp*,' he says. 'Is that all? I think you were wanting to prove something else. That you weren't lying. Thing is, Willa, I reckon the truth can often look after itself. It remains the truth, whether . . .'

'. . . whether or not you choose to believe it. I know. And now . . .' I lower my head again and force the words out of my tightened throat. 'And I've put everything at risk. Right now, Mina and the other Manny are in that cave there. And it's all my fault.'

A worried look passes over Alex's face. 'My sister,' he says. 'I want her back.'

CHAPTER 34

We don't bother with the FreeRides. We walk home, my head down and my hands deep in my pockets. I don't want to have to look at anything else.

I stride through a group of people without apologising. They shuffle aside, but instead of tutting they smile, and one says, 'In a hurry, love?'

I ignore a cat on a wall in a weak patch of sunshine, which is kind of breaking a personal rule.

All the while, Alex walks a couple of paces behind me, not judging, not saying anything, but it makes me feel a bit less alone. I like him for that.

I hadn't even noticed before, but the strip of shops on the seafront that has been shuttered up since as long as I can remember has opened. Or perhaps it never closed here. Where there used to be graffitied metal shutters and piles of black bin bags and an overflowing builder's skip there is now a greengrocer's with fruits and vegetables arranged outside, another shop selling books and newspapers, a hairdresser's, a dry cleaner's and an Indian restaurant with delicious smells wafting from the open door.

I stop for a moment and take some pictures, and the greengrocer in a blue overall says to me, 'Cheer up, petal! Why the scowl on a day like today?' I realise that I am indeed scowling, and I rearrange my face. The man grins and says, 'There you go! Here – this'll give your face something to occupy it!' and he tosses me a banana. It surprises me, and I nearly miss the catch, which makes him laugh. He's still chuckling when I walk off, then he raises his hands to make a gesture: both thumbs joined at the tips, with the index fingers pointing upwards.

The last time I'd seen this gesture was when Alex – girl-Alex – had done it to me as shorthand for a bored *whatever*. I'm pretty sure the greengrocer doesn't mean that.

Why is everyone being so nice?

Alex and I come back through the main gate of the holiday park, and there are a few familiar faces. I see Josef, the guy on the gate, who's usually grumpy, but today gives me a comedy salute; Mick and Nick, the cleaners, say, 'Hi, Mina! Hi, Alex!' in unison from behind their trolley of stuff, and I'm sort of relieved that it's not floating or anything: it's their regular cleaning trolley, only painted orange, with great-grandad Roger's face on it.

And then they too each make the same gesture as the greengrocer did, clearly expecting me to return it, so I do, and they are delighted. So I do it to Alex, and he laughs.

'What does it mean?' I ask him as he raises his hands to gesture back.

'It's a letter W, isn't it? It stands for WWW Day. It caught on a few years ago and now everyone does it. Mass groovy, eh?'

'I see,' I say, but it comes out pretty glum. Alex had made a few gentle attempts to bring me out of my mood on the long walk back from Brown's Bay, but he gave up ages ago and stayed quiet.

Then he says, 'Come this way. There's something I want to check out.'

CHAPTER 35

Alex leads the way to Grandad Norman's bungalow, moving stealthily as if he doesn't want to be noticed.

It's still there, standing on the patch of scrubby grass outside: the deep pink flyke gleaming in the afternoon sunshine, its seat lifted up, revealing the motor inside, and a repair manual propped up on the steering bar.

His back to us, Grandad Norman is crouched over his workbench, tightening something with a spanner and humming to himself the song I'd heard Dad singing this morning.

'Dance to your daddy, my little laddie . . .
Dum diddle dum . . . when the boat comes in . . .'

Alex motions for me to stay quiet, and I say nothing. Then, when my brother beckons, we tiptoe away unseen.

'What was all that for?' I ask him, but he shakes his head, deep in thought.

*

By the time we get back to our house, I'm both terrified and exhausted.

I'm tired of everything being different. Most of all, I'm tired of being scared.

Without Manny, I can't get home, and if we miss this supermoon it'll be months till the next. How long is left until the window closes? How will I make it through without going crazy? Without being found out? And, by then, Mina and the other Manny will certainly have come out of the cave in my world with goodness-only-knows what results.

'The school will send a letter, you know. To Mam and Dad. About our absence,' says Alex when we're alone in the kitchen.

'*A letter?* That'll take a day or two.' Before I can stop myself, I say, 'Don't you have email?' Of course I know the answer.

'What's that then?'

'It's a letter that you send by computer. It arrives instantly. You should try it some time.'

I'm being mean. I can't even help it. I'm just so tired and scared.

'Tell me about this he-male thing,' he says.

'Alex. Please. I can't explain everything. Honestly, I can't. Emails, mobile phones, Kwik-e's, the internet, computers . . . I just want to go home, and I'm in real trouble, and so's Mina.'

I'm hit by another wave of fatigue. I hardly slept last night. 'I need to sleep. Just for a bit,' I tell him.

A couple of hours later, I'm woken from a deep, dreamless sleep by Alex knocking on my door. 'You hungry?' he says, putting his head round the door. 'Hungry' doesn't even begin to describe the ravenous, empty groaning in my stomach.

'Set the table, please, Mina!' Mam calls through to my bedroom. I glance over at the bedroom desk where there's a letter that I began to write before I slept. It's to Mina, my other self. It starts, *Dear me* . . . My hearts sinks when I remember I may have months to finish it.

The plates and stuff are all in the same place, and I manage not to make any mistakes till Dad comes over to the table with a pot of something delicious-smelling and says, 'Only four places, love? What about your grandad?'

'Hee hee! Something smells good!' comes a voice from the front hallway, and in walks Grandad Norman. He's taken his overalls off and has on a bright red sweater, his white hair slicked back like he's just come out of the shower.

'Hi, Grandad,' says Alex.

'Hello, son! And what about this one?' He jerks his thumb at me and grins. 'Still want to call me by my first name? It's that flinkin' school of yours! Wasn't like that when I was a kid.'

'I . . . I was just joking,' I say, quietly, trying to stay calm, and he laughs again.

'Course you were, love,' he chuckles, then he sings a song in a tuneless groan:

'I don't care what you call me
As long as you call me soon!'

Everyone laughs; everything's fine. We all sit down to eat, and I realise that I love my Grandad Norman instantly. It's like he's put a little fish-hook in my heart and is gently reeling me in, and I don't mind at all.

I lower my head to my plate and start checking my food, which Dad spots straight away.

'What's wrong, Mina?'

'Nothing!' I say brightly. 'Just, erm . . . there are no, er . . . no *ants* in it, are there?'

'Why would there be ants in it? It's a fish pie. Cream sauce and a flaky, lemon-scented pastry.'

I force a laugh. 'Just kidding! Ha ha.' I start eating. The fish in the pie is lovely: firm and fresh. Definitely no ants.

'Cor – fish pie!' exclaims Grandad Norman, tucking in. 'This is a rare treat, Ted! Haven't had real fish since my birthday! Where'd you get it?' He takes another huge mouthful and closes his eyes to appreciate the flavours even more.

Dad says, 'Oh, the usual. The boats came into Culvercot this morning, and they were selling it all on the seafront. Picked up some coley and some mackerel. Thought you'd like it! Looks like Mina does too. Slow down, pet – you'll give yourself stomach ache!'

'Like it? I love it, son! Eeh, it's the taste of my young days. Expensive, was it?'

Dad shrugs modestly. 'Aye. Twenty pounds, seventeen and six an ounce. But worth it now and then, eh?'

While we all eat, I think about what that means. 'Seventeen and six an ounce'? I know an ounce is an old measurement of weight, but how much I have no idea. I push that aside for the moment, and instead I ask, 'Erm . . . how often did you eat fish when you were young, Grandad? I mean Norman. Grandad Norman?'

He looks at me out of the corner of his eye. I clamp my mouth shut just in case he notices my wonky teeth and widen my eyes innocently. He puts his knife and fork down. I see Mam roll her eyes with amusement as if she's heard this story a dozen times.

'Here we go down memory lane,' she says affectionately. She turns to Dad. 'Can't you stop him?'

'You're kidding, love. At his age, he might not get started again!'

Grandad Norman laughs hard at this teasing, and I do too, although I'm a bit sorry to realise that we haven't done family banter like this for ages in my real life.

Do I really want to leave this warm, close family and go back to a world of bickering and tension?

The old man clears his throat. 'Well, Mina love. Wasn't just me. We all ate loads, all over the world. Not just fish – meat as well. Nearly every day, I'd say. Bacon at breakfast, ham in sandwiches, prawns and scallops dredged from the seabed, beef, pork – fried-chicken shops here, there and everywhere; lamb, fish and chips, sushi, tuna baguettes, sausages . . . you name it! And all so cheap. And, well . . . you know the rest, eh?'

I try this: 'Oh yes. Good job that doesn't happen any more.'

Dad has never been one to back away from the chance to teach a lesson, or to pass on some nugget of information that may come in handy during a quiz. 'So there you have it, Mina! Solid proof of what I was saying the other day.'

Dammit.

'Erm . . . remind me, Dad. What were you saying?'

'You remember! When the world stopped fighting, we put all that money and thought and energy into solving other problems. The fish thing? That was easy once LGF came along.'

Good old Alex helps me out by saying, 'Yeah! Laboratory-grown flesh means we don't overfarm, don't overfish! They reckon the sea is bluer now than it used to be because it's healthier.' Then he winks at me.

'Oh, but it definitely is!' I say, delighted to have this

puzzle solved, then I realise this sounds mad. 'I mean it definitely, probably is. I think.' *Definitely, probably?* I'm talking like Manny.

Grandad Norman is frowning at me, and I blush, knowing I must sound so strange. If I lower my head any more, I'll get fish pie up my nose.

Thankfully, my comments have diverted the conversation to the upcoming WWW celebrations. By keeping quiet, I learn more about the big parade tomorrow, including Grandad's exhibition of classic flykes, although everything kicks off tonight, with music, fireworks, speeches, dancing.

'I tell you,' he says. 'If I don't get the limiters fixed on that Chevy Sport, I'll be leading the flyke parade in an illegal vehicle. Don't you tell anyone, kids!' he adds with a big wink.

Mam says, 'Ee, I hope the weather holds off. The forecast's not looking so good . . .'

Then there's a loud jangling ringing from the hallway that makes me jump.

Dad says, 'Get the phone, will you, Mina pet? Anyone for more pie?'

Ring-ring. Pause. *Ring-ring.* Pause. I've left the table to 'get the phone', but I'm looking at this thing, and I can't say I'm completely certain what to do. Imagine – a single telephone in the house that you have to stand in the hallway to use!

Next to the telephone is a little replica of one of those old red-painted public call boxes with all the windows. (There's a full-sized one on the seafront in Culvercot, only now it has one of those heart-attack machines in it.) This little one on the hallway table has a slot in the top and is half full of coins. This is a strange, wonderful world all right, but why would you have a pot of money next to a telephone?

Ring-ring. Pause. *Ring-ring.* Pause.

'Are you gonna answer that or not, Mina?' Mam shouts.

I reach out and pick up the bit you hold and put it to my head. I don't know why, but I have a feeling that this may be a phone call that will change my life.

'Hello?'

CHAPTER 36

'Willa? Willa! Is that you? You're still here then!'

'Manny! Where are you? I'm so glad to hear your voice! Of course I'm still here.' I've closed the door to the kitchen, but I can hear that the conversation has gone a bit quiet, as if people are trying to listen to what I'm saying.

'Mina? Who is it?' says Mam from the kitchen.

'It's . . . it's a friend, Mam.'

'Tell her you'll call her back. Your supper's getting cold.'

'In a minute!' I wish I could take the phone into my room or something, but the whole thing's attached to the wall by a cord. I cup my hand over the phone part instead. 'Manny, what's up? You've found your mam! That's great but . . .'

'I know, it's amazing, and I want you to meet her, and they've been looking for her for years, and . . .' He is tripping over his words he's so excited. But there's fear in his voice as well.

I say, 'When are you getting back, Manny? I'm still here because it doesn't work without you.'

There's a pause.

'Manny?'

'I was hoping you wouldn't say that. I . . .' His voice is crackly and distant.

'What? Speak up. Whatever it is you feel, Manny, I need you to come back and feel it here, otherwise we're stuck in the Sideways World till the next supermoon.'

Long pause. I mean *loooooong* pause.

'Manny? Manny?'

'I'm here.' There's something he's not telling me. I'm not psychic or anything, but I can sense a change. It's in his voice. 'Listen, Willa. I'm in Edinburgh, right? I can't just *come back*. And besides . . . it may not work.'

'What do you mean it may not work? We've got to *try*!'

'I can't just leave my mam! We've done this "first meeting" thing with her, all arranged by the social services. I can't run away even if I wanted to! This is my mam, Willa. In our world, she might . . . she might even be . . .' He struggles to find the right words and says, 'Anyway, here she's definitely alive.'

'How did you get there?'

'The train. That's still the same, at least. More or less. The way they work is different, though. Did you know—'

I'm not interested, and I interrupt him. 'Can you get the train back?'

He sighs. 'No. How would I do that? Jakob never lets me out of his sight. How would I buy a ticket? Their money here is all different. Do you know what a "shilling" is? Besides, it's a public holiday tomorrow. WWW Day. Everything's shut: it's like Christmas Day. There are no trains. Everyone's on holiday.'

It's my turn for a long pause now. Eventually, I say, 'How long have we got, Manny? You know – till the thing doesn't work any more?'

He doesn't hesitate; he's thought about this. 'I honestly don't know, but . . . Probably one more high tide. I can feel it slipping away even now. I'm sorry.'

'And then we have to wait months? I can't do that! Anything could happen in that time.'

Manny doesn't reply.

'I've got to go, Willa. Jakob's calling me. I . . . I'm sorry. I'll see you soon.'

'But, Manny, there must be . . .' I'm talking to myself. The line's gone dead.

From the kitchen, I hear the scraping of chairs as people get up from the table and the clinking of dishes.

Grandad Norman says, 'Excellent fish pie, Ted. Can't believe that granddaughter of mine left hers unfinished! Anyone'd think she had fish every week!'

I lean against the wall and slide down it on to a little stool next to the phone.

I'm still sitting here when Alex comes through, carrying

a pile of towels. He says, 'I'll just put these in the airing cupboard for you, Mam!' then he bumps the door closed with his backside.

'Well?' he whispers.

I shake my head. 'It's no good. The call finished, and I don't know how to call him back, and even if I could I don't know what to say. He . . . he's in *Edinburgh*, Alex! I have to stay. Till the next supermoon.'

Alex stands there, thinking, still holding the stack of towels, when Mam calls, 'Mina – put the telly on to warm up, will you? News is on in five minutes.'

Alex flicks his eyes to the kitchen and chews his bottom lip. 'Listen, Willa. I saw the news earlier. I don't want to scare you, but I . . . I think you should prepare yourself for a bit of a shock.'

Oh, flinkin' groovy.

CHAPTER 37

'Shock? What sort of a shock?' I wail. 'Alex! I'm gonna be . . .'

'Shh,' he says, just as Mam shouts, 'Mina – you okay?'

'Yeah, Mam. It's all groovy!' Alex calls back. Then he says to me, 'I have an idea.'

His eyes are pleading with me to trust him. 'You do?' I say.

'It's probably not a very good one. But we have to act normally. You have to play along. Go and watch the TV with them and you'll see what I mean. Just . . . follow my lead.'

'Mina! The telly!' shouts Mam again.

Alex is off down the hallway, and I go into the living room, where I stand staring at the little TV with its bulbous screen.

'What are you doing?' says Grandad Norman, sounding very confused. He's making me nervous.

'Where's the remote?' I say.

'The remote what?'

I sigh a little bit inside. 'I just need to turn on the

TV.' He gives me a funny look, then presses a button on the front panel.

Mam and Dad come in and settle on the sofa, followed by Alex, who gives me a sly wink while the news starts on the TV.

'You watching, Mina? That's a nice change,' says Dad, and he pats the sofa next to him.

To begin with, it doesn't look much different from any other news programme, only there's no war to report on. So far as I'm concerned, a typical programme goes something like this:

'Good evening. Here is the news from the BBC. Lots of people were killed today as the war gets closer. We go live to our reporter next to a smoking building . . .

'The refugee crisis in a country you have probably heard of but couldn't point to on a map is getting worse . . .

'Climate scientists have warned that rising sea levels are provoking further tensions in East Asia . . .

'And, finally, something funny about a squirrel . . .'

This news programme, though, is not like that at all.

'Good evening. Here is the news from the BBC.'

At least that's the same. It might even be the same man doing it. Grey hair, gloomy voice? Anyway, that's where the similarities end. For a start, the presenter is smiling, and he is wearing a cheerful violet shirt with little yellow spots, and no tie.

'All around the world, people of all nations, religions and races have been working together on the final preparations for tonight's global WWW celebrations. We go live to our peace correspondent, Jamie Bates, who is in Western Dabbala, where, fifty years ago, the last shots were fired before humanity laid down its arms.'

I sit, transfixed, as the same man who was reporting on the appearance of the Whitley Cog appears on the screen. He had started it all; if I hadn't gone into the shop that day to buy sweets and seen the report about the cog on the TV behind the counter, I might not even be here, trapped in this other world.

Now the same reporter is dancing with grinning people as they erect a huge statue of someone with long grey hair and play raucous music and rev noisy car engines. The reporter has to raise his voice to be heard.

'. . . as these vintage gasoline-powered automobiles are brought out of storage for just one day to contribute to the noise of celebration here in Western Daballa! Back to you in the studio, Hamish!'

A smiling Hamish now introduces other reporters in other locations: Australia, Japan, Brazil, Germany . . . Everywhere has a similar story: happy people getting ready for a massive party. I keep flicking glances over to Alex. Where is the news that he says will change everything?

'. . . loudest party of all, Hamish, here in Times Square, New York, where America's youngest-ever president, Sasha Obama, will light the touchpaper to ignite this year's celebration display, which you can see here being lowered into position on Governors Island in New York Harbor, suspended from four US Peace Force helicopters. It is as tall as the Statue of Liberty and faces the mighty Manhattan skyline. The ceremony will honour the Englishwoman whose vision inspired former President John F. Kennedy to bring world leaders together in the big push for a World Without War.'

Hearing again the name of John F. Kennedy makes me sit up. The man who Maudie was shaking hands with in the photo on her wall? The president who was murdered in 1963?

I realise I must record this as part of my evidence-collecting. I leap up and get my camera, still in its cardboard disguise, from my schoolbag in the hall. Rushing back in, I say, 'Photo everyone!' and they all look at me like I've gone mad.

Dad says, 'Why now, Mina?' But I'm too late: the news programme has moved on to another story.

I just manage to snap a picture of Grandad Norman before he says, 'Ooh! That's an interesting camera, love? May I see?'

Alex to the rescue again. 'Look!' he yells, pointing at the screen. 'Erm . . . interesting story coming up! I've seen this!'

I dash out and get rid of the camera. I hear the newsreader say, *'**And finally . . .**'* and hurry back in. Alex jerks his head at the screen in a *watch this!* gesture to me.

I watch, and everything comes crashing down in an instant.

CHAPTER 38

I'm not sure if I can stand any more stress. But there's more heading my way.

> *'And finally this evening, the WWW anniversary is not the only special occasion being celebrated. If you look out of your window, especially if you have a telescope, you may notice something unique about the night sky – or you may even feel it! The author of* **Cosmic Resonance**, *Amara Kholi, reports on a very unusual planetary alignment.'*

Grandad Norman says, 'Oh aye. I've seen her programme. *Cosmos-whatsit*. Load of old donkey's, that is . . .'

'Shush, Norman! And mind your language!' says Mam.

The picture cuts to Amara Kholi, short and middle-aged in a colourful sari, standing in front of one of those massive satellite dishes in the desert somewhere – the ones that point out to space.

'It may seem unlikely, but if you think you can detect the movement of the planets and the stars without one of these contraptions behind me then you may not be alone. Thanks to the World Without War initiative, scientific resources have been devoted to investigating so-called "super-sensors" – they are people, and animals, who can detect the minute changes in gravitational forces caused by the moon and other space bodies.'

'I tell you – it's all donkey's!' says Grandad Norman, and he winks at Mam.

'Thanks to research by the Fry Foundation, it now appears that a small number of people really are able to feel changes in gravitational pull as tiny as 0.0002 newtons. To put it in perspective, that's a bit like being able to smell a single sweaty sock as far away as the moon!'

Grandad Norman laughs at this, and Mam says, 'That'll be one of your socks for sure, Ted!' and Dad laughs too, making my heart ache for the loving teasing between them all.

At the same time, I'm still trying to pay attention to the TV and take all this in. *So all that stuff Manny* said about 'feeling' the moon? And Maudie's super-complicated website by her friend who sends her birthday cards?

That friend who is now smiling at me from the grainy TV screen. 'We used to have grand old chats,' Maudie had said.

I look over at Alex. 'Oh my word! It's her!' I say. 'From your book!' and he nods. I feel as though I've got a huge half-made jigsaw, and people keep adding more pieces.

Dad is looking at me again. 'Are you all right, love? You've gone a bit pale.'

'She's just had a whiff of one of your socks, Ted, hee hee!' says Grandad Norman.

'Shush,' says Alex. Amara Kholi is still talking.

'**Super-sensors are reporting that the force of the moon is greater than at any time they can remember. And the reason for that is pretty simple. The moon is closer to the earth right now than it has been since the days of gasoline-powered cars and worldwide conflict. After tonight, such a close perigee will not occur for another sixty-eight years. That's plenty of time to get ready for it! This is Amara Kholi for the BBC News, wishing you a very happy WWW Day.**'

Mam stands up and pushes the button on the TV to turn it off. 'Well, that's a typically daft story to end on. Honestly, I don't know what the BBC's coming to . . . Are you sure you're all right, Mina?'

I haven't moved. The whole horror of what I'm facing is descending on me.

This super-sensor thing that brought us here won't happen again for sixty-eight years?

Did Manny know? Is that why he was being weird?

I look over at my brother. 'Alex!' I say, my voice straining with the anguish of what I've just worked out. 'There's no point in waiting for Manny to come back from Edinburgh. It'll be too late! Either I find a way to go back now, or I'm stuck here till I'm eighty!'

There's a kind of thick silence in the living room. It's Grandad Norman who speaks first. 'You've been acting strange all day, my love. What on earth has got into you?'

Then Mam says, 'What's all this about Manny and Edinburgh?'

This, I realise, is my last chance. I get up from the sofa and clear my throat. I feel like I'm doing a show-and-tell at school. I stand in front of the TV and say, 'Mam, Dad . . . Grandad Norman. I have something to tell you.'

Alex's face is rigid, his teeth clenched in a *no, don't do this* expression. But I don't care. I have no choice. I'm going to confess and beg for their help.

CHAPTER 39

It goes as well as you might imagine. In fact, it's pretty much like the last time I told my parents, back in what I still think of as the 'real world'.

Imagine standing in your front room and telling your family that you are from another dimension. That, owing to a once-in-a-century lunar event, you and your best friend (who can detect the pull of the moon's gravity) have been able to travel through some sort of hole in space-time and swap places with your interdimensional doubles.

Not only that, but unless you bring that best friend back tonight from a hundred miles away then you'll be stuck, unable to swap back. The next high tide is at twenty past midnight. It really is your only chance.

Here's how they react:

Grandad Norman has his arms folded, head on one side and smiling, as if he's thinking, *Hee hee, that granddaughter of mine has one heck of an imagination!*

Dad's face is scrunched up, like he's in pain.

Mam starts to cry.

'Oh, Mina love. What's this all about? You've been acting strange for ages. Is it to do with that dream you were talking about? Come here, eh? We'll sort this out, I promise you.' She holds out her arms for a hug, but this is not the time.

'No!' I say. 'I'm sorry, but you have to listen! I can put it right, but I need your help. We need to get Manny back from Edinburgh tonight, and . . .'

Dad gets up. He's trying to be sympathetic and firm at the same time. 'Mina, sweetheart. You've been like this for a few days. These . . . delusions you're having . . .'

'They're NOT delusions. It's true! You've just seen it on TV. Manny's a super-sensor, and Brown's Cave is where it happens . . .'

I dry up. I see the looks on their faces, and I can't bear it any longer.

'Alex!' I plead. 'Tell them it's true!'

Alex's brow is knitted in the sort of expression that means *What did you go and do that for?*

Dad stops me. 'Don't bring your brother into this, Mina. I think . . .'

There's only one thing for it. 'Look at my teeth!' I shout, and I pull my lips back with my fingers. '*Look!*'

Mam takes a quick glance and says, 'Aw, pet. Have you been in a fight? Did you injure yourself, Mina?'

'No! And I'm Willa, not Mina, and Willa hasn't been to the orthodontist yet because . . .'

It's all too late. I realise from the looks on their faces that I just seem completely crazy, and I sort of freeze there, pulling this horrible face. After a few seconds, I take my fingers out of my mouth, then I push past them out of the room and slam my bedroom door behind me.

There's a knock on my door. 'Go away!' I say. I have never felt worse.

'It's me,' says Alex, coming in. 'You shouldn't have done that.'

'I had to, Alex! I had to tell the truth.'

My brother purses his lips as if to say *no, you didn't*. He flicks his eyes along the hallway and closes the door. Then he whispers, 'I told you – I have an idea. A plan. Come with me.'

Alex and I have gone out for a walk to 'clear my head'.

When we left the house, Mam said, 'Look after her, Alex. Don't be back too late.'

I saw Grandad Norman setting out a chessboard. Alex said that he and Dad would be occupied for a while.

Alex has told me about his plan, and, if it's to work, I need to speak to Manny. I have to persuade him to do a totally crazy thing.

We've only gone as far as the main road, where there's a red public phone box. We both cram into it, and Alex finds out the number of the Royal Hotel by calling some other number where a real person looks it up for you. 'Directory Enquiries,' he calls it. Odd, if you ask me, but hey – it seems to work.

'Did you see the news?' I say to Manny as soon as I get through to him.

Alex has given me a handful of coins that he's taken from the little box in the hallway at home, and I have to put money into the slot every minute or two.

Manny didn't watch the news so I have to explain to him what I've just seen on the TV about the moon and super-sensors.

'Willa – I swear I didn't know. It was a *feeling*, that's all. Only . . . now I know where it's from. The feeling. The . . . the "thing". I had no idea there were people called "super-sensors". It's just . . . kind of always been there, you know? But I've felt it so much stronger this supermoon than ever before. This sixty-eight-year thing must be what's made us come here.'

'I have an idea, Manny – of how to get back. At least Alex has had an idea. It's crazy and it may not work.'

There's a long pause, during which the phone goes *beep-beep-beep*, which is a sign I need to put more money in. 'Manny? Manny? What's wrong? You there?'

'I'm here, Willa. And the thing is . . . I want to stay here.'

'But you can't! And I can't go without you. We need to go now! Otherwise . . .'

'You don't understand. I told you before – I've found my mam, Willa. I don't want to leave her now.'

My scream fills the tiny phone box.

'*Noooo!* Please, Manny!' I crouch down in the tiny space, clutching the telephone receiver as Alex taps anxiously on the glass.

Through the thick door of the phone box, I hear an amplified voice: '*Ladies and gentlemen! Boys and girls! Welcome to Whitley Bay's Fifty-year Anniversary of a World Without War!*'

The whole crowd outside starts to whoop with joy.

I straighten up again. 'Do you hear that, Manny?'

'Yeah. It's going mad here too.'

'But do you hear what it is *for*, Manny? A World Without War! We need to tell people in our world that it's possible! Otherwise, *my* dad's going to have to fight!'

The phone beeps again. I don't even know if Manny heard the last bit. I shove in my last coin.

I'm desperate, and it is desperation that makes me say what comes out of my mouth. As the words form, I know it sounds cruel, but I'm not sure I have any choice.

'She's not your mam, Manny! She's the *other* Manny's!'

Has he registered what I said?

I practically yell down the phone. 'Right now, Manny, there's another version of you and another me, and they're shivering in a cave on the other side of . . . of . . . the cosmos, and they're completely terrified. Imagine if that was you! Well, I mean, it *is* you, only it isn't, only . . . oh, I don't know!'

Poor Manny hasn't had the chance to work this out. He hasn't had the conversations I've had. This is all new to him, and he sounds stunned.

'Another version? Of us? You mean – *we swapped places*?'

'Yes! Definitely. Well . . . probably.'

Slowly, as if he's dragging the words out, Manny's voice crackles in my ear. 'Willa? Perhaps I could go with you and then . . . come back?'

Quickly, I say, 'Can you get anywhere outside your hotel unnoticed?'

'Are you kidding? The whole WWW thing has started already. They're in the streets now. Can you hear it? There's the Scottish National Cat-strangling Championships going on outside.'

'Manny! That's bagpipes I can hear . . . Oh, you were joking?'

'Look at it this way: chaos may be a good cover, if that's what we need. Do you know Arthur's Seat? That's where we're going.'

'Arthur's Seat? Of course I know it! It's the photograph in our toilet! Thank you, Manny. Oh, thank you!'

And so I tell him Alex's idea. And he listens. He says it's the stupidest idea he's ever heard of.

But this is Manny we're talking about; of course he'll give it a go. Although we're going to have to be quick.

'Whereabouts at Arthur's Seat?' I say. Before I can extract any more details, the phone starts beeping again. I have no more money, and the line goes dead.

CHAPTER 40

Alex and I hurry back through the crowd of people, young, old and very old, that has gathered on the Links in front of a huge video screen. It seems to be showing scenes of WWW preparations around the world, all set to music. It's a bit like the stuff we saw on the television news earlier. All around me, people are making the same W gesture with their fingers.

I'm nervous of wasting time, but I take out my phone, still in its disguise, to record some of it, and a shiver of realisation goes through me.

'My phone!' I say to Alex, waving it in front of him. 'Why didn't I show it to Mam and Dad? If that doesn't convince them that I'm from another dimension, then nothing will. I mean . . . it worked for you! Didn't it?'

Alex wobbles his head in a sort of *maybe-it-will-maybe-it-won't* way, but I don't care. I'm certain. Anything to stop us having to enact Alex's insane plan.

I turn it on, and my stomach flips in dismay. Two per cent battery left. I know that when it's that low it diminishes really quickly.

'You okay, Willa?' says Alex. 'You look horribad!'

My breathing is becoming more rapid, and my palms are damp. My finger hovers over the record button, and I hesitate over how to use that two per cent.

There's just no way on this earth – or any other earth, come to think of it – that the mam and dad who sat there as I bared my teeth at them like some deranged monster will *ever* believe my story. And, even if they do, they're not going to be able to get Manny back from Edinburgh in time.

It's a bit of a shock to realise that I no longer care whether they believe me or not. I know what the truth is, and that's all that matters. This is down to me. Unless I act on Alex's plan, I'm going to be stuck here for the rest of my life. Not only that, but Mina and the other Manny will emerge – somehow – from the cave where they found themselves and have to live in my world. And that world will be plunged into a third world war.

Thing is, I know the truth. And I can prove it to the people that matter: the people back in *my* world; a world heading into war, a war that my dad will have to fight in, because they think it's unavoidable. Because they think there's no alternative. So, with a sweaty finger, I tap record and point my phone at the crowds watching the big screen in front of me.

A few seconds later, the picture changes to a still caption, and a hush descends on the crowd. All their eyes are fixed on the screen, and nobody takes the slightest notice of me and my strange-looking 'camera'.

WWW
LIVE FROM NEW YORK
FORMER PRESIDENT OF THE USA
JOHN F. KENNEDY
FOUNDER OF WORLD WITHOUT WAR

The crowd bursts into applause. I look round at Alex. I'm still filming, my mouth hanging open in astonishment, and I mouth, 'John F. Kennedy?'

He nods and shrugs. 'So what?' he says.

'But . . . President Kennedy was . . . was killed?' I say.

Alex shakes his head with a baffled look on his face. 'No, he wasn't! He survived an assassination attempt. Is that what you're thinking of? Someone tried to shoot him when he was in a car in Dallas, oh . . . years ago. It was a mass close thing, but . . .'

'November the twenty-second 1963,' I say, 'and he . . . he . . .'

I tail off, shaking my head in wonder.

Was *that* what happened to change the Sideways World? An assassin's bullet that missed its target! Was that the point at which this world's history took a different direction?

There he is on the big screen on the Links in Whitley Bay. An old, old man walking stiffly to the podium in a crimson shirt and stylish sunglasses, acknowledging the cheers of the crowd with a wave.

'How old is he?' I say to Alex, who shrugs again.

'Dunno for sure. A hundred and ten, hundred and twenty?'

The camera cuts to a close-up of his face – craggy and old, but still handsome, topped with dove-white hair.

'My fellow Americans,' he begins. 'My fellow . . . human beings!'

This gets a cheer. People are already hugging one another in delight.

He continues, his American-accented voice raspy and slightly nasal, but still clear, despite his great age. 'Many years ago, when I was president of the USA, I said something that some of you may remember. I said, "Those who make peaceful revolution impossible will make violent revolution inevitable."'

People around me nod at one another in recognition of this phrase.

The old man continues. 'Then I met a woman who inspired a vision. A vision that led to that peaceful revolution – the greatest in our beautiful world's history. A movement we called the Rainbow Uprising.

'Yet it was neither she nor I who did this. It was you,

your parents, your grandparents and even your great-grandparents. One by one, we looked one another in the eye. We sought out the things that unite us, rather than those that divide us. We embraced our sisters and brothers in humanity and said no to hatred, no to conflict. No. To. War!'

He pauses while the cameras cut to scenes of cheering and applauding people all over the world, and close-ups of young and old moved by his words.

'Instead of fighting,' says John F. Kennedy, 'we talked. We argued – oh boy, did we argue, and still do!' He grins and lets his gaze sweep slowly over the people watching, until he takes off his sunglasses to stare straight down the camera lens, and I could swear he's talking directly to me. 'We abandoned nuclear weapons in favour of nuclear power. As the Bible advised, we turned our swords into ploughshares, and our spears to pruning hooks. We spread the word of peace worldwide. Because, when we talk, we don't fight. And, when we don't fight, we solve those other problems. Problems of health, inequality, pollution, energy. And that, my friends, is all down to you!'

The crowd are ecstatic now, shouting, 'Yes! Yes!' and I find, to my astonishment, that a tear is running down my own cheek as I continue to film this extraordinary event.

'My friends. We know the answer. We have *always*

known the answer. And that is to step back from fighting, step back from war, lay down our arms together and advance to a World Without War!'

He holds up his fingers to make a trembling W sign, and everybody around me does it too, smiling at one another as they do so. It is breathtaking. And what comes next is the most amazing thing of all.

'My friends, on this, the fiftieth anniversary of the very first day in world history without armed conflict, I'd like to welcome on to the podium with me the young Englishwoman who inspired this movement with a simple conversation all those years ago. She's not so young any more – but then which of us is? People of the world, please welcome . . .

'Lady Maud Fry!'

And there she is: Maudie. Maudie! No doubt at all. Our gardener! I watch, dumbfounded.

Instead of the grimy overalls and tie-dyed hippie T-shirts, she's wearing a smart shirt and jacket. Her long white hair is washed and styled like an ageing movie star's, and she is slimmer, with a suntan, round glasses and dazzling Hollywood teeth. This is the same woman as in the picture in the foyer at school! Now, though, she's not stiff and formal like she seemed in the photo, but unmistakably Maudie: relaxed and smiling her impish grin, ascending the steps with the ease of someone half her age.

The crowd around me go absolutely wild seeing her on the screen, even more so when the caption comes up saying:

**MAUD FRY FROM
WHITLEY BAY, ENGLAND,
INSPIRER OF THE WWW**

A *huge* cheer erupts from the crowd when they see the name of their town being beamed all over the world, and their local hero, Maudie Fry, waving modestly at the hordes before her.

I try to listen, but someone has tapped my shoulder. I look round to see Deena Malik smiling at me.

'Hey, Mina!' she says. 'Nice to see you! Isn't this great? Our school sponsor! She's looking well, isn't she? She went to school with my great-aunt, you know.'

'Really, Deena? If only you'd mentioned it before,' says her dad sarcastically, and Deena playfully slaps his arm. 'Now, shush. Hey – she's lost her Geordie accent, hasn't she?'

Maudie is telling us, almost word for word, the same story she told me, most recently as we sat by her wood-burner, sipping hot chocolate.

'. . . so, there I was, sitting with President Kennedy and telling him how I joined the navy instead of continuing my education, and I told him about the dream

I had of a world where people would talk instead of fight, and settle their disputes without violence . . .'

I'm grinning and shouting and cheering, and I don't even notice at all that my phone is completely dead now.

Then Alex nudges me. 'Come on!' he shouts over the din. 'We have to go!'

And I know he's right. I know I can't hang around any longer, so reluctantly I back out of the crowd, unable to take my eyes off the vision of Maudie on the huge screen, waving at the adoring masses.

CHAPTER 41

The spring evening sunshine breaks through the gathering storm clouds and dazzles off Grandad Norman's Chevrolet Super Flyke Sport 212.

Alex and I are standing in Grandad's workshop, talking in low voices, both of us staring at the restored flyke, pink and gleaming, preparing to enact the plan that will get me and Manny back home.

I stroke my hand over the smooth double seat that's just like a motorbike's.

'He won't even know I've borrowed it, will he?' I say – more to convince myself than anything else. I think of Manny 'borrowing' Jakob's camera and swallow nervously.

Alex doesn't disagree, which is kind of him because he almost certainly does. Instead, he says, 'We. We've borrowed it, you mean. We're in this together.' He goes on. 'Listen, Willa. I've thought about this a lot – ever since seeing that thing on the news tonight. We've got about five hours till the next high tide – you do understand that? What we are doing is, well . . . it's illegal. And dangerous. But I still think we can do it.'

'What about the police?'

'The police? That's all a bit twentieth-century, isn't it? People in uniforms going around with guns?'

I think about this for a moment and say, 'I don't think our police have guns. Most of them don't anyway. Besides, what about the army? Alex, I don't want to be arrested.'

He lets out a small chuckle. 'No police, Willa. We have Community Order Volunteers and they're all busy with the WWW parade. And as for armies, well – in a World Without War, there's not so much need for them any more.'

'Yeah, I get it.' I sit down on an upturned wooden box, just like I used to do with Maudie. It's almost as if I'm trying to find reasons for *not* doing what I know I *have* to do. 'Why are you doing this, Alex? I mean . . .'

'I told you, Willa. I want Mina back. You're great and all that – don't get me wrong. But you're not my *real* sister. Right now, my real sister is terrified in the back of a cave. I have to help get her back. Besides, it's just not right. The world, the universe, the . . . the multiverse, whatever you call it, shouldn't *be* this messed up. Perhaps in sixty-eight years we'll be able to deal with it better, but right now I can't see any good coming of it, and it's down to you and me to put it right.'

'But you'll have to stay in Edinburgh. What will you tell everyone?'

He looks at me steadily. 'The truth, obviously.

Whether they believe me or not is up to them. If this crazy plan works, it won't matter much anyway. Everyone will be back where they belong, and there's no way of proving otherwise for sixty-eight years. Chances are we'll still be around!'

This was quite a speech from Alex, but he hasn't finished. 'There is one more reason,' he says, and a half-smile creeps on to his face. 'No one ever breaks the rules here. Everything is ordered, everything works, and it's wonderful. Perfect, even. But, you know . . . sometimes perfect is a bit, well . . .'

'Boring?' I say, and he laughs as if he's happier to let me say it than actually utter the word himself. I look up and his face looks so like my sister's that for a fleeting, lovely second I allow myself to imagine that everything's all right again.

I know that this is my only chance.

'Has Grandad done it? You know – the speed thing and height thing that he had to install?'

Alex looks over the vehicle and turns a key that lights up the dials on the front panel and a bright headlamp. 'Nope. He hasn't yet. I reckon this thing'll fly like a bird.' He sounds totally confident, apart from a big swallow he tries to hide, which tells me he's more nervous than he wants to show.

I realise at that moment that I love my brother with a feeling that reaches across dimensions and binds my heart to his. Though I'm still not sure I have the courage to go through with this. I mean, it is a more-than-slightly crazy plan.

Alex and I are going to steal this flyke, fly it to Edinburgh, and bring Manny back in time to catch the last high tide of this perigee.

Slightly crazy? Make that totally flinkin' mad. Unfortunately, it's the only plan I have.

'Are you sure it's safe?' I say, and his answer isn't encouraging.

'No. Not really.'

He sees my anguished expression and tries to sound reassuring. 'Look, Willa, this is old technology. It's a vintage flyke. Nineteen nineties or something. There's a reason they were discontinued. But, when you're very near the ground, they're fine. And, when you're high enough for the emergency wing to be deployed, that's fine too.' He taps a panel on the rear of the flyke, which he says contains the parachute or 'emergency wing'.

'The danger zone is between the ground and, say, a hundred feet up. We'll make a rapid ascent and then plot a course over the water so there's a chance of a softer landing if, erm . . . well, you know . . .'

'If we suddenly plummet earthwards?'

'Yeah.'

'And we find ourselves in the sea.'

'Well, yeah. But that's better than hitting the ground.

And, besides, you'll be wearing one of these.' He holds up two yellow vests that are exactly like the ones you see being demonstrated by cabin crew on an aeroplane. 'They inflate automatically when they hit water. You'll be fine!'

I'm not sure I want to ask the next question, but I find myself saying, 'Did it happen often? You know – accidents?'

'No. But often enough for flykes to be banned other than in special displays and stuff. It was all before I was born. Now, like Grandad says, they've got to have speed and height limiters on them.'

I swallow hard, and a wave of uncertainty washes over me when I think about what we're going to do. 'I need a moment,' I murmur to Alex, and I push past him. 'I'll be right back.'

'Hey!' he protests. 'We haven't got lo—' But I'm gone, running already.

I don't even know where I'm going, but I find my feet moving faster and faster until I'm running through the holiday park in the twilight, past the wooden cabins with soft lights in the little windows, and past the wildlife reserve till I'm on the path with the sea view, and I don't stop till I'm at the seat where, not long ago, I sat with Maudie and watched the boats, and I collapse on to it, panting, expecting to cry (again), but finding to my surprise that I am dry-eyed and clear-headed.

Above me, the clouds have cleared again, but they're

still forming to the north, big towers of fluffy purple in the distance. To the south, the moon has begun to rise over the mouth of the Tyne.

Where am I, I wonder? If I think too much about the whole dimension thing, I just get upset and confused, and so I don't. Instead I think about Mam and Dad, and my grumpy sister, and Maudie and even stupid Deena Malik, and I know that even though it *looks* as though I have a choice I really don't.

Option one: I do nothing. That means I stay here, forever out of place in a perfect world, while my own world destroys itself.

Option two: I do everything I can to get back home.

I do Maudie's breathing exercise:

In, two, three, four . . .

Out, two three, four, five, six . . .

I close my eyes again and rest my hands on my knees, palms up. *If only I could stay like this*, I think.

'Well, fancy seeing you here.' My eyes snap open.

Grandad Norman.

CHAPTER 42

He stands in front of me, looking friendly enough, but I find myself thinking, *Has he come to stop me? Does he know what I'm about to do?*

'Have you been waiting for me? Just beaten your dad with the old Sicilian Defence. He was so mad, hee hee! Hey, budge up, love. Thought we might have a chat about all that business you were telling us about.'

As Grandad Norman sits down heavily on the bench, I spring to my feet as though his weight has bounced me up.

'No! That is, erm, no thanks . . . I was just leaving.'

Oh no, oh no. This is just the worst thing. I have only just got to know Grandad Norman, and already I think he's sweet and kind and clever and all those things you want a grandad to be, but, if this plan is to work, I'm going to have to be really horrible to him.

'Ah, righto.' He sounds slightly hurt. 'I'll, er . . . I'll walk up with you then? I need to tinker a bit more with that old flyke.'

'Oh really?' I'm trying to keep the panic from my voice. 'It, erm . . . it goes, doesn't it?'

'Oh aye,' Grandad chuckles. 'It goes like stink! Haven't got the limiters working yet so it's still not legal. Shouldn't take me long now.'

'Oh good,' I sigh. 'I mean . . . bad luck.'

'I've taken the emergency wing out, obviously. With the height limiter on, there's no need for it, really. Means the whole thing's a bit lighter as well.'

'Oh yeah, obviously!' I'm desperate to get back to Alex before Grandad gets there. 'Is there anything else I should know? That is, if I was going to buy it, for example?'

I'm talking rubbish, but I still haven't worked out what to do.

'Buy it? Why on earth . . .'

Think, Willa. Anything!

'A . . . a friend of mine, erm . . . Deena's dad is into old flykes. He might be interested!'

Grandad grunts. 'Well, I'm not sure how safe it is, to be honest. At the moment, that is. Until I've . . .'

'But it is safe? I mean, basically? It goes, yes?'

'Oh aye, it goes all right. What is this, young Mina?'

I stop on the path in front of him and look up at the kindly old face of the grandad who died when I was little and who I can barely remember. 'Grandad Norman. I'm really sorry for what I'm about to do, but it's not me, all right? I'm not the Mina you think I am. All that stuff I said before? It was the truth. You know when I showed you my teeth and everything?'

He giggles again. 'To be honest, pet, I didn't pay you much mind. You look great to me, whatever your teeth are doing. I thought it was one of your stories. You're full of them, you know!'

I part my lips again, and this time he looks properly. He furrows his brow, leaning in close to get a good look. 'Well, goodness me. How on earth did that happen? You had lovely straight teeth, pet. Sorted out ages ago, they were. That looks like a badly kept graveyard.'

Gee, thanks, Grandad. I didn't think they were THAT bad . . .

'Like I said, I'm not really Mina. Mina will be back if what I'm about to do goes to plan. When you see her again, please don't blame her for this.'

'You're talking in riddles, pet. None of this makes any sense to me.'

'Nor me, either, to be honest, Grandad. But like I say – sorry.'

I step forward and give him a big hug, which surprises him, and he hugs me back so that I get the briefest flash of a memory from when I was very little, but it may well be just my imagination. Then I turn and run back up the path, knowing he's too slow to follow me.

'Hey! Hey, hang on! What's this all about!' he calls

after me, and he sounds so sad and confused that I have to clench my teeth to stop me getting too sad or I might change my mind.

Back at the workshop, Alex is stretched out on a battered sofa, reading a magazine called *What Classic Flyke?*, when I run in, yelling, 'Quick, quick, Grandad's coming! Get the flyke ready!'

Good for Alex. He doesn't ask questions; he leaps up and starts pushing the flyke on its tiny little undercarriage wheels. He calls back over his shoulder.

'You'll need more clothes. I should have told you earlier. It gets cold up there. Be quick.'

Alex points behind me, where, hanging on nails, are some oily work overalls belonging to Grandad. There's a tatty sweater, a knitted woollen cap and a pair of gardening gloves. They're going to have to do. He tosses me a pair of welding goggles as well. I clamber into Grandad's massive old sweater and overalls, rolling the trouser legs up so I don't trip on them. I grab *What Classic Flyke?* and shove it down my front for added insulation. The gloves go on last.

What must I look like?

'We're running late,' Alex says. 'We'll have to fly over land for some of the journey to save time.'

He's already astride the flyke and fastening the safety belt round his waist when we hear Grandad calling,

'Mina! Mina! Where are you, sweetheart?' from down the path.

Good job I took those deep breaths before because now I can hardly breathe at all.

I jump on the seat behind Alex as he turns the key. The front panel lights up, and the motor beneath us starts to whir.

'Right, Willa – start pedalling as though your life depends on it. Because it more or less does.'

Both of us place our feet on the pedals, just like on a bicycle, and start pushing, slowly at first, but getting faster and faster, and as we do the whirring pitch of the motor gets higher and higher.

'Harder!' says Alex.

'What the blazes are you two doing? Get off that thing right now!'

Grandad Norman has come round the screen of trees and starts to run towards us as soon as he sees us. Just as he's about to grab Alex, the flyke rears up like a frightened horse, and I'm nearly tipped off the back. Grandad grabs for the sleeve of my overalls, and his fingers connect with the fabric, but I wriggle my arm hard, and he doesn't get a proper grip.

'You little devils! This is dangerous!' He is shouting with anger and fear – and I can't say I blame him.

He makes another lunge for the flyke at the exact moment that the front rears up again, and I'm tossed back in my seat, further toppling Grandad's balance, and he lands heavily on the grass.

'I'm so sorry, Grandad. You're lovely, really!' I yell, and I mean it.

Then the flyke swoops forwards and upwards, just clipping the tops of the bushes. If my safety belt was any looser, I'd have definitely fallen off.

'Come back right now! You'll kill yourselves!' shouts Grandad, shaking a fist and rubbing his bruised bottom. But his voice is way below us now. The cool wind is in my face, and I'm astonished at how fast we gain height. When I look down, my stomach seems to turn over. Before I screw my eyes tight shut, I see the grass roof of the big cow byre, and the black-and-white cows with their calves munching on the grass below – and then I bury my face in Alex's back, gripping his waist with my arms.

'Did we make it?' I squeak after a moment, but he can't hear me for the rush of wind. I dare myself to open my eyes. Far below is the sea and ahead a bright light: St Mary's Lighthouse, beaming out to sea, its long white tower bathed in multicoloured spotlights for the WWW celebrations.

Alex tips the control bar to the right, and we bank gently, steering the flyke in a huge arc round the lighthouse and through its blinding light. When we've past it, I breathe properly for what seems like the first time. I can't cheer, or go 'Wa-heeyyy!' or anything like that, mainly because I'm panting with terror, and also because I feel dreadful about poor Grandad Norman, who definitely doesn't deserve to have his classic flyke stolen by his grandchildren.

'We're on our way,' I say, but Alex still can't hear me. So I say it again, just for myself, as if I'm feeling good about it. 'We're on our way.'

CHAPTER 43

In front of me, Alex grips the big horizontal steering bar. We both have goggles. The strap on mine is keeping my oversized hat in place. The wind whips past us. In fact, the flapping of the creases and folds in my overalls is the loudest noise of the journey.

We're going terrifyingly fast, the flyke's motor converting every push of my feet on the pedals into the much greater power needed to keep us airborne.

'Edinburgh,' says Alex, 'is one hundred miles, as the crow flies.' Even I can work out how long that will take if we're doing fifty miles an hour.

We're flying over the sea, but only a few hundred metres from land. On the water close to the shore are countless boats with their lights on, some anchored in little clusters, others alone – from big pleasure cruisers and fishing boats down to small yachts and speedboats. Alex has turned off the front and rear lights so that we're less visible from the ground. Far below us and to the left, I can make out a silvery strip of road lit up by both the setting sun in the west and the moon, which is higher in the sky now and directly behind us.

The red rear lights of the vehicles heading north are matched by the white lights of the vehicles on the other side of the road heading south. Most seem to be ci-kars. On the other side of the road, the grey-green of the rolling Northumberland hills and moorland stretches away to the vivid orange and pink horizon.

For a few exhilarating seconds, a seagull flies alongside us, but we're too fast for it, and it swoops off to the side and out of sight below.

I can't say that I relax, but my legs settle into a neat motion. The pedalling is not so difficult once we have the rhythm. It's far too windy and the flyke's old motor is too noisy for Alex to speak to me. Despite my gloves, my hands are freezing cold. At one point, Alex reaches back and taps my knee to get my attention, and points down. Far below us is an undulating grey line crossing the inky countryside. We're flying over land now, as Alex said we would, and that is Hadrian's Wall – the vast construction built nearly 2,000 years ago, which marked the northern limit of the Roman Empire. We'll soon be flying into Scotland and then over Edinburgh.

It's now dark, but I hadn't noticed the moon getting darker too as a huge cloud blankets it. Soon the lights below us go hazy as we enter low cloud, and the temperature drops still further. Suddenly a flash of light illuminates the whole sky, followed a few seconds later by a crack of thunder, and I scream and clutch Alex tighter.

The rain starts immediately. Not so much drops of rain as huge sheets of it that fill my mouth when I breathe and soak me through. The rain jacket I'm wearing turns out to be useless, and everywhere water can get in it does: the neck opening, the cuffs, it even gets in through the zip and the bottom. My legs and feet and hat are saturated in seconds. At times, it's like we're flying underwater.

We are in a cloud so thick that I can't even see the land below us and, when the next flash of lightning comes, it seems like it's right next to us: a thick band of blinding bluish light forking to the ground, hurting my ears with a crackling boom, and throwing the flyke violently to one side so that I have to stop pedalling and grip the seat with my legs to stop myself falling. The wind is buffeting us hard, bringing with it further great bursts of rain.

The next flash of lightning is behind us.

Then the cold really kicks in. A shiver to begin with, then a creeping, all-consuming chill that gets worse as we come out of the raincloud ten minutes later and the night air penetrates my soaking clothes. Still, my feet press down on the pedals, as if they're doing it automatically. Alex reaches back, finds my hand and squeezes it reassuringly. I squeeze back – at least I think

I do, but I have so little feeling in my fingers that it's hard to tell. Alex descends closer to the ground, where the air is a tiny bit warmer, but it doesn't make much difference. My ears throb with agony, and I feel like I'm going to pass out with the cold.

Over his shoulder, I can see my brother raise his wrist and look at his watch.

It's 9.30 p.m.

'We're not going to make it,' I groan to myself.

And then Alex lifts his other arm to point, and I see a faint glow in the distance, a sort of shimmering dome of light miles ahead of us, and a long way down.

Edinburgh.

As we get closer, the lights grow brighter, and I can make out the shapes of districts spreading out like stumpy tentacles along the roads that feed into the city. Soon we're directly above houses and streets, and the sounds of a massive party drift up to us: loud, drum-heavy music, thrashing guitars, bagpipes, clanging church bells and the amplified vocals from high in a mosque's minaret. The swirls of sound come and go on the wind, and I almost forget how bone-chillingly freezing I am. My teeth have stopped chattering; instead, my jaw is just clamped shut and aching.

Then, far below us, I see the shape we're looking for. A roughly circular gap in the city lights. I tap Alex, and he gives me a thumbs up: he's seen it as well. He dips down further, further, till my ears pop, and we can make out the tiny figures of people on the ground. Little pinpricks of light accompany them – everyone seems to be holding a torch of some sort, but I'm way too high to make out any more details.

This, then, is Arthur's Seat – the steep-sided hill in Edinburgh with a lake on one side, where I came with my family two years ago and took the picture that's hanging in the downstairs toilet.

People and their torches form lines going up pathways; they are dotted round the wide, sloping fields: dozens, hundreds . . . *thousands* of people, and my heart sinks. There's no way at all of spotting Manny.

What was he thinking of?

He probably didn't know. How would he? He just thought of a place that might be easy to find. He had no idea that what looks like *every single person* in Scotland would be gathering at Arthur's Seat for the WWW celebrations.

Or worse – perhaps he hasn't come at all. He definitely *said* he would. But what if something's happened to prevent him?

We've slowed down now. I can tell because the wind is not whipping against me with the same painful force. Alex turns his head, and I move forward as he yells in my ear.

'I'M GOING TO GO LOW SO HE SEES US! WE HAVE NO CHOICE!'

I've been trying to watch Alex's handling of the controls, and I'm relieved that they're not at all complicated. I'm going to have to do this myself soon.

He flicks on the headlights, pushes the steering bar forward, and the flyke starts to descend further and further towards the heads of the crowds on the hill. People turn and look up, and from now on there's no chance that we will go unnoticed. Our only hope is that no one tries to stop us.

What we're doing is not allowed: I understand that. It even makes sense. But 'good sense' sometimes has to take second place to 'what is necessary', and right now the essential thing is to find Manny amid this throng of people. I look down and see figures waving at us. Perhaps it's not so bad, after all.

'THEY'RE WAVING!' I shout into Alex's ear. 'IT'S OKAY!'

He says something in reply, but I don't hear it properly because at that moment there's a high-pitched *whoosh*, followed by a shower of sparks that misses us by only a few metres before bursting into brilliant light far above.

A firework! Is someone firing at us? Who on earth would be reckless enough to launch a rocket straight at us? Unless . . .

Manny would!

CHAPTER 44

Seconds later, there's another firework, followed by a piercing whistle.

'Over there!' I shout, pointing in the direction of where both the fireworks and the whistling are coming from and, sure enough, as we bank round – earning an 'Oooh!' from the crowd – I can see Manny, tiny but unmistakable, waving a huge sparkler in each hand, a referee's whistle clamped between his teeth, and blowing with all his might. We get lower and lower till we're only a house's height above him.

'Out of the way! Out of the way!' yells Alex, flapping his arm, and the crowd scatters as, hovering, we make a wobbly descent to the grass.

If I thought we'd get a round of applause or something as we touched the earth, I'm about to be disappointed. What I'd taken to be people waving happily turns out to be shaking fists. They are furious, and shouts of 'That's dangerous!' and 'Where are the marshals?' come from the crowd.

I hear someone say, 'It was him! Stop that boy!' But

they're still maintaining a distance – a wide, misshapen ring of people surrounding us on a bit of levelish ground, curious and angry.

There's an eerie silence as the flyke's whining motor powers down without turning off completely. I can still feel it buzzing beneath my bottom. My legs stop pedalling and – oh my! – the relief is immense.

Manny stands with two adults, a man and a woman. The man's holding a chill box and a rug, like they're going for some midnight picnic.

They do not look friendly, I have to say.

Alex murmurs to me, 'Get in the front seat. Don't touch the off button. Remember, pull back on the steering bar to gain height; right-hand lever is forward speed. Oh and good luck – sis!'

Sis! What can I respond but, 'Thanks . . . bro!'

There's a couple of seconds between us that feel like a lifetime – the lifetime together that we never had – as the boy from our mantelpiece shrine reaches forward and lifts the goggles from my eyes so we can look at each other for what will be the last time. My frozen face manages a smile.

'Really, thank you,' I say, and he nods. As he turns, I grab his sleeve. 'Have this,' I say, and I press into his hand the bar of Fry's Chocolate Cream that has been in my pocket all day. He looks puzzled. 'It's not much, I know, but it's from my world. I'd like to leave something behind.'

Alex smiles as he takes it and steps away from the flyke. I slide my bottom into position. I look up and see that the crowd surrounding us have edged a little closer, and their murmuring sounds more hostile.

Manny is gripping the hand of the woman beside him in both of his. 'You'll see me again, Mam – I promise, promise, *promise*. But, right now, you know . . .'

There is no doubt it's his mam – the same woman that I saw on the printed sheet in Winston Churchill House. She's fragile-looking, with big eyes and a nervous movement about her, like a baby deer. It's almost enough to make me change my mind. How will she react to Manny suddenly leaving her?

The man says, 'Manny, what is going on? I hope you don't think you're going to get on that thing! What on earth has got into you?'

'Jakob, I don't have a choice! If I don't do this, then . . .'

'No way! As one of the responsible adults here, I shall be in huge trouble. Come on, mate – let us talk about this, eh? We can sit down and have a proper conversation. I realise this has all been very challenging for you.'

I've now put my hands on the steering bar, watching the two of them as Alex stands by. I've said nothing, but I'm *very* aware that the curious and angry-looking crowd will soon be so close that I won't be able to take off. Manny bends down to the picnic box and lifts the lid off it.

'Manny – what are you doing?' says Jakob. 'No, no, no, Manny – that's my last tin. It is for our picnic! Put that back!'

I recognise it straight away. Manny is holding a swollen tin of *surströmming* and a tin-opener. 'I'm sorry, Jakob,' he says. 'But this is all this stuff's good for anyway.'

'No, Manny. Please. Let us talk about this, eh?'

'No! Right now, Jakob, you just have to listen. Brown's Bay, between Culvercot and Whitley Bay. That's where I'll be, just after high tide. Make a phone call to the coastguard.' He turns to his mam. 'It'll be the real me, Mam! I promise!'

Manny's mam is on her knees now and reaching out to grab his legs to stop him, but he dodges her hands.

'Please, Manny!' she moans.

There are tears streaking their cheeks. I can tell that Manny is longing to step forward to hug her, but, if he does, he surely won't be able to let go.

'Brown's Bay, Mam! I promise!'

And, with that, Manny stabs the tin hard and sprays the jet of stinking fish juice at the advancing crowd.

The effect is instantaneous. With grunts and cries of 'Och, that's flinkin' rank, that is!' and 'What on earth is that?' the crowd stops, retching and holding their noses.

Suddenly a large man wearing a hi-vis jacket and a kilt, holding his arm over his face, pushes to the front and booms in a loud – if slightly muffled – Scots voice,

'A'right, a'right, stand back, everyone! I'm a WWW marshal, and I demand to know what's goin' on here! This is a *massive* health an' safety breach. Who's responsible?' His radio, attached to his marshal's vest, crackles. He says, 'Aye, Bob – back-up requested, please. I've got an unauthorised flinkin' *flyke* here, for heaven's sake. Just landed in the middle of a crowd. Seems like kids. And they've got stink bombs. Over.'

He turns his attention back to Alex. 'You the owner of this thing? You, wee man, are in *big* trouble!'

'You ready?' murmurs Alex to me under his breath. 'It's been good knowing you, Willa!'

And, with that, he turns to the marshal and shouts, 'You're going to have to catch me first, you great fat haggis!'

The crowd gasps – maybe at Alex's insult, or, more likely, because he runs, head down, into the marshal so hard that the man topples backwards down the hill. He lands with a painful-sounding thump on his backside, his kilt flapping up over his waist, making everyone gasp again. Then Alex runs off in the other direction, pushing through the astonished crowd.

Manny has leaped on to the flyke behind me, wriggling to release his hand from his mam's grip. 'Let go, Mam!'

'Manny! Don't go! Please! I want my son, Manny. I want my son! Someone stop him!' begs his mam, and I feel a twist in my heart at the depth of her pleading.

'Stand back!' I yell and start pedalling hard as a few brave members of the crowd step forward, but they're too late. With a lurch to the left, a spin to the right and a screech of the motor, the flyke is on the move.

I hear Manny go '*Whoaaaah!*' and grab my shoulders as he tips out of his seat, and for a moment I think I've lost him, but somehow he has his legs tangled in the safety harness, and *that* is how we make our getaway: me screaming incoherent vowels like '*Aaah!*' and '*Eeee!*' and '*Ohhh!*' as Manny dangles upside down from an almost-out-of-control flying jet ski, shouting, 'Brown's Bay! I love you, Mam!'

Back to gain height, right lever forward . . . Is that right?

Without Manny's pedal-power, the flyke can't gain very much height, and suddenly I'm dive-bombing the crowd, still with Manny hanging below me. People scream, and many of them flatten themselves on the ground; then, with an extra huge effort, I'm swooping upwards again. As I do, I feel a sickening tug from behind, and looking back I see that Manny's foot has come free of the straps, leaving him hanging by one ankle only.

I level the flyke at around twenty metres high. It's flying in a straight line, and I punch the button marked AUTO, not knowing what it'll do. Cautiously, I take my hands off the wheel and it stays steady. Still pedalling, I reach down and behind me, making the flyke lean alarmingly.

'Manny! Manny! Take my hand!'

Using all his strength, he heaves himself up from the waist, but he can't reach my hand, and flops back down again, swinging beneath the flyke, which lurches horribly again. I'm dimly aware of screams from the crowd below, although there are one or two 'oohs' as though people think they're watching some stunt exhibition.

The weight of Manny's fall has put a huge strain on his safety strap. My own strap seems secure, but Manny's is beginning to fray against the sharp steel base of the flyke. With every swing to and fro, a few more strands of the webbing come apart, and I have no choice: I'm going to have to land and face the consequences or Manny will plunge to his death.

I reposition myself in the driver's seat, and it's only then that I see that I'm flying over a huge pond and *I can't land*! Can I make it to the edge of the lake before Manny's strap breaks?

Manny's desperate scream from underneath the flyke spurs me to one last effort. Thanks to the slope of the hill, I have actually gained some height. I figure if I stop pedalling for a few seconds, I can reach round and underneath, haul Manny up and get my feet in the pedals again before we hit the water.

It's my only chance. As soon as I stop pedalling, the flyke starts to fall. His fingers touch mine and, with a desperate heave, he hauls himself up, grabbing my sleeve and pulling himself towards me bit by agonising bit, grabbing the fabric in clumps. Neither of us says anything, not wanting to waste our energy even on things like, 'Come on, you can make it!'

But I *think* it. I think it so hard that I feel he must hear me. He reaches out his left hand and grabs the seat at the exact second that the final strands of the safety strap snap, and he's on, lying crossways over the rear seat of the flyke and then wriggling himself upright. We start to pedal together. The bottom of the flyke skims the water, but . . .

We've made it! We gain height rapidly as a massive explosion sounds in my ears.

It's followed by a flash of blinding light in brilliant colours, then more bangs, and I realise we have flown straight into the middle of a massive WWW fireworks display.

Rockets whizz by. One hits the underside of the flyke and makes us wobble, and Manny yells in terror, but he's safe now, although he's unsecured by any safety strap. Me? I barely flinch – after all, what are a few fireworks compared with a lightning storm? I steer the flyke away from the rockets and the deafening explosions and crackles, and a shower of pink sparks bursts all around us.

We follow the main road that winds south out of the city and, in only a few minutes, the lights of Edinburgh are retreating behind us, and I feel I can sigh with relief.

We . . .

Are . . .

Safe.

That's when I hear the unmistakable sound of a helicopter flying above us, and a search beam picks us out in the dark.

Seconds later, I can feel the downdraught of the chopper, and a voice says, '*Descend immediately. That is an order.*'

CHAPTER 45

The message is repeated: '*Descend now. Proceed immediately to the ground. That is an order.*'

I risk a look upwards. At first I can see nothing at all, my eyes dazzled by the beam of the searchlight. Then, when it sweeps round, I can make out a woman wearing some sort of harness, leaning far out of the open-sided helicopter and holding a megaphone to her face.

'*You are in breach of Scottish transport laws. Make your way safely and immediately to the ground.*'

The helicopter has been descending above us, and I realise I've been getting much lower too, to avoid colliding with it. I can see the tops of some tall pine trees rushing by below us.

'*Thank you for complying with our instruction. There is a safe landing spot in one thousand yards.*'

'What are you doing?' screams Manny in my ear.

'I can't help it!' I shout back. 'It's forcing me down . . .'

I've hardly finished speaking when Manny reaches over my shoulder and grabs the flyke's steering bar, pulling it hard to the left. Immediately, the flyke banks, turning sharply out of the downdraught of the helicopter. Then, with a sharp tug, we start to gain height, missing the helicopter's rotor blades by much less distance than I'd like – but it's all happening too fast for me to worry because, seconds later, we're above the chopper and leaving it far behind.

'Faster!' yells Manny.

'I can't!' We're both pedalling as hard as we can, but it seems that, above a certain speed, it's down to the mechanics of the flyke to increase the speed. I'm so terrified that I don't feel cold any more, and I remember that Manny doesn't even have a thick coat or hat. It doesn't seem to bother him, though.

Then, from the west, which is on our right, two massive drones appear out of the darkness, both with flashing blue lights. They're on us in seconds, and the crackly, amplified voices start again, a man's this time, and he sounds angry.

'*This is Chief Inspector Macbeth of the Scottish Security and Safety Authority. You are instructed to land your vehicle! Now, do you understand? We are authorised to fire a magnetic hook for your own safety!*'

'Get lost!' shouts Manny, and he makes a rude gesture with his hand.

'*This is your final warning!*'

There is no way I'm going to obey now. I am steeped so far in trouble that, even if I did what this Inspector

Macbeth said, I'd be no better off than if I carried on. The two drones and the helicopter are above and beside us, and they're trying again to force us to the ground.

With a pull on the power lever, I shout to Manny, 'Stop pedalling!' and we do.

Instantly, the wind in our faces lessens. We start to plunge to the ground at the exact moment that there's a bang from behind us: they've fired out the magnetic hook. Seconds later, our pursuers whizz over us at high speed, dangling a steel cable with a huge metal disc attached to the end. It misses us by metres. I look down, and the tops of the trees are approaching faster and faster.

'Pedal now!' I yell, and we both pump our legs, but it's like trying to start a bicycle on a steep hill. Harder and harder, I press on the pedals, and slowly they get easier; yet the treetops are still getting nearer.

'Pull up! Pull up!' shouts Manny and, as the tip of a huge pine scrapes the bottom of the flyke, we start to gain height again, and the two giant drones bank round . . .

And fly away. Their blue lights get more and more distant, and I hear Manny whooping with joy behind me. As the flyke climbs into the sky, I can see the silvery glint of the Tweed River passing underneath us.

'The border!' shouts Manny. 'They had to turn back at the English border!'

I think I actually laugh with relief. The cold I felt

before has gone, replaced by a kind of numbness as the flyke settles into a straight line, following the river towards the sea. We are above the height that fireworks go; now and then, we look down on coloured fountains of sparks and hear distant booms and crackles as people all over the countryside and up and down the coast celebrate the WWW anniversary.

The moon has risen fully now, the clouds almost all gone, and I feel a growing sense of relief. I don't need to ask Manny: I've already calculated that we have an hour to get to Brown's Cave when the tide will be at its height. We have already passed Lindisfarne Castle on our left – the old island lit up like a Christmas tree for the celebrations – and then there's Bamburgh Castle, people on the ramparts still setting off some late fireworks . . .

We'll make it, Willa. We'll make it!

Ahead, on the slightly curved edge of the horizon, I can just make out the city glow of Newcastle. I pedal a little harder, not caring about the ache in my calves and my ankles and my bottom and lower back . . . In fact, everywhere that isn't numb is aching, and some bits seem to be both, which is a new and completely unpleasant sensation.

Still, I let myself dream of getting back home to my family and telling of our wonderful adventure, and the amazing reality of a World Without War. I even allow myself to imagine that I'm already there, and that everything has happened smoothly.

There's an unfamiliar shudder from the body of the flyke. Just a little one: a sort of fizzing feeling underneath me that lasts a few seconds and then stops. I feel my ears pop again, and I know we're losing height far too quickly.

Manny yells from behind me, 'What was that?'

CHAPTER 46

A few minutes later, the flyke has done its fizzing cough four more times. The instrument panel in front of the steering bar flickers, and the light goes out. We're now flying in the dark, with only the moon and stars providing any illumination.

With each cough, we lurch downwards and lose another two or three metres of height. I steer us away from the land, and we chug along above the water – slower than before, although it's hard to tell without a working instrument panel – following the coastline exactly.

With a trembling, numb hand, I unbuckle my safety belt. If we hit the water, I'm pretty sure the flyke will sink like a stone, despite its resemblance to a jet ski. I don't want to be strapped into it if that happens.

And so we fly-chug on, losing a few more metres in height every kilometre or so. I've been pedalling hard for four hours now, and every extra push by my feet sends pain coursing through each leg in turn from my ankle to my thigh. I'm panting hard and sweating.

Soon we are low enough for me to make out details on the houses that line the shore. I can detect the movement of the ocean beneath us, which has gone from being a smooth black mirror to an undulating silk scarf, and now we're close enough to see little whitecaps on the waves. Because the flyke is slower, I'm worried that we'll miss high tide, so when I see St Mary's Lighthouse in the distance, lit up for the celebrations, I gasp with relief and pedal even harder. Still we get lower.

I'm exhausted; I can hear Manny panting and groaning with every turn of the pedals. Any idea that I may have had of performing a show-off victory circuit of the holiday park – you know, waving down to Mam and Dad and the crowds – is forgotten as we sail past it, the beam of the lighthouse now higher than the flyke.

Then I see lights on the water ahead of us, and I groan out loud. The fishing boats of Culvercot, dozens of them, plus yachts and pleasure boats of all kinds, are gathered in Brown's Bay for the celebrations: an illuminated mini-navy seemingly guarding the cave entrance. By the time we get there, we'll be hardly any higher above the water than the boats. Manny has spotted them too.

'They'll see us,' he gasps in my ear.

Too late. One of the boats has already picked us out with a searchlight.

'You ready, Manny? We're going to have to ditch the flyke in the water and swim!'

He pats my shoulder to say yes. I think he's too exhausted to reply.

To the right, the Whitley Bay seafront is lit up with a fairground and a big wheel and night-time celebrations. Multicoloured lights are beaming on to the huge white dome of the Spanish City, and in front of it a band is playing to a huge crowd.

By now, we're only about four metres above the surface of the water, and I turn sharply towards the land. The tide is right up the beach, leaving only a tiny strip of sand before the cliff – which we'll surely crash into with full force.

The boat's searchlight still has us in its beam: everyone can see us now. We're a hundred metres from the shore, heading straight for the concrete promenade wall, and we miss a tall yacht's mast by millimetres. Below us, the people on the boats are yelling and waving at us.

'Ready . . . ready . . . ready . . . stop pedalling!'

The water is just three metres, two metres underneath us, and the promenade wall looms closer and closer . . .

'Jump!'

And we both do. I land face down, fully submerged in the shallow water, my chin grazing the sand painfully. My self-inflating life jacket does not self-inflate, and a strong wave tips me over again before I struggle to my feet just in time to see poor Grandad Norman's Chevrolet Super Flyke Sport 212 hit the sand and flip over, crashing into the base of the promenade with a crunch of metal, rubber and wood and a loud, impactful bang.

'Manny! Manny!' I spin round, knee-deep in the waves. 'Where are you? Manny?'

He surfaces right next to me, staggering to his knees and clutching my legs, coughing and then vomiting a huge bellyful of seawater. He says nothing, but strides through the little breakers to the strip of sand, where he collapses, wheezing.

'I can't . . . I can't . . .' he gasps.

'You can, Manny!' I say. 'The cave's just there! We've come this far. You can't give up!' I kneel next to him on the narrow beach, clutching his shoulder and pleading.

'I can't . . . I can't *feel* it,' he says, and forces himself up on to one elbow. His hair is plastered to his forehead, and sand clings to his face, and even his green eyes have lost their intensity. 'The moon, the . . . *thing*, Willa. It's so weak.' He shakes his head sadly, then coughs again. '*I'm* so weak. I think it's the flying, the pedalling, you know?'

'No. No, Manny. What do you mean? We've come so far! Come on, on your feet!' I pull him with all my strength, and he staggers upright, dripping seawater. 'That's it now . . . Come with me. Look – the cave's so near.'

Its entrance is already blocked by the tide, but we're wet anyway.

I spot a small rowing boat heading towards us, and people have come to the steps at the top of the promenade, alerted by the crash of the flyke. Someone calls, 'Are you okay? What's going on?'

I wave back, shouting, 'Yeah, yeah – fine,' but it doesn't stop them. Three or four people are now coming down the concrete steps, keen to give us help that we just don't want.

'Come on, Manny, faster! We have to at least try!' I'm dragging him along. He takes a deep breath, straightens up and starts an agonising jog along the coarse sand towards the cave opening.

But we are pursued by a man and a woman holding torches, shouting, 'Stop! You can't go in there! It's not safe!'

The water is up to our thighs as we go into the cave, the shouts of our would-be rescuers echoing in the dark opening. Manny and I push forward through the water, further into the darkness, and I smell the familiar scent of seaweed and lichen and dead fish. The tide is strong: every time a wave retreats from the cave, it threatens to pull us over, but metre by metre it gets shallower till it's only ankle-deep. In the blackness, I can just about make out the wall ahead of us, and I drag Manny towards it.

The shouts of the people on the promenade have faded away. No one seems to be pursuing us. Manny and I are on our own in the dark cave.

We've made it!

'Are you ready, Manny? We go back together, then you return here on your own like we agreed. Right? To . . . to be with your mam?'

He says nothing, he's so exhausted. Without waiting for a reply, I grab Manny's wrist and slap the back wall.

Then I await the grey fuzziness to surround us.

CHAPTER 47

Nothing happens. Well – not *nothing*, exactly. A sort of grey cloud half appears and then retreats. Which is something, but not what we want.

I slap again.

The same thing happens. Grasping my hand in his, Manny puts his hand on the back wall too. We try different places: up, down, to the left and right, till we're hitting the rock desperately, randomly, again and again in a desperate semi-dark percussion. Harder and harder, faster and faster become Manny's blows on the rock till he's hitting the stone with his whole body, moaning in despair.

'No! No! No!' he cries, his voice choking with tears.

In the half-light, I see him pull his arm back and ball up his fist, and I grab on to his arm and stop him or he'll surely break his knuckles.

'Manny! Stop!'

Slowly, he sinks to his knees, sobbing, then sits with his back to the rock as the encroaching waves lap at our feet.

I hardly dare ask, but I do. 'What's going on, Manny? You can come with me now, and then come back, surely?'

He pulls his hand away from mine. My eyes are getting used to the dark now, and I can see his outline clearly, his eyes glinting with tears.

'Don't you see, Willa? I can't come back, not after you explained it. I'd love to stay here, but it's not my world. You were right. She's not *my* mam, is she?' His voice is raised over the swirling, sloshing seawater at our feet. 'Did you hear her? When she shouted, "I want my son"?'

I had heard. It was heartbreaking.

'It came to me after we spoke on the phone, and you told me about the *other* us – the you and me who have been trapped in this cave. They're there – here – right now, Willa. It's like . . . I can feel them.'

I look around, and I try my hardest to feel them too, a ghostly sensation of two terrified children in a dark cave.

Manny sniffs. 'I felt like a fraud, Willa. I felt like I was stealing from my mam. Stealing her *real* son, replacing him with me. Do you see? And leaving the other one here, in this cave.

'He's scared to death, probably. Thinking he's having some nightmare, or maybe trying to escape and risking being drowned. It's *his* mam, not mine.'

Through sobs, he says, 'But it's . . . it's not strong enough. I told you.'

'It is! It has to be, Manny! We just have to wait. It's coming – I saw it. Did you? It was there, the greyness. It was—'

He cuts me off with a wave of his hand. 'It's not. I *know*, Willa. I can feel it. There's not enough . . . whatever it is to take us through. I'm . . . I'm sorry. We're too late.'

I am so panicked that I can't think straight, and I stand in front of him, trying to yank him to his feet. 'What do you mean, Manny?'

I take a second or two to digest the full meaning of what he's just said. 'But – we're going to be stuck here. Forever!'

He laughs mirthlessly, but I don't think he's being mean, just realistic.

'Yep. You'll be stuck here with Mina's mam, Mina's dad, Mina's brother. And I'll be stuck with someone else's mam, and he – me – both of us – will be miserable forever in a world we don't understand.' I hear his head fall back to hit the rock behind him with a thud. 'The moon's leaving its perigee now, but I always felt there was something else. Do you remember how exhausted we were after travelling this way? Well, that was it, the "something else". We're just too weak, Willa. It's the journey we've just done – it's exhausted us. I'm sorry – I'm truly sorry – but . . .'

He doesn't finish his sentence. Instead, he gets to his feet and walks towards the water.

A strong wave surges in through the cave and washes over his feet first and then mine. I hardly notice any more. I take a step towards him on the sand, despair and exhaustion coursing through me.

'Oh, please, no, there must be a way,' I moan. 'Where are you going?'

From the mouth of the cave come voices and the creaking sound of a boat's oars.

'Hello? Are you all right?' someone shouts. I can spot flashlights flicking over the cave roof, and I cling on to Manny as I sink to my knees in the waves.

All of this for nothing.

I think of everything we did, everything we risked. I think of the other Manny and Mina living in our world – the world of conflict, of war. Of my mam and dad and girl-Alex, and not seeing them any more, and I start to sob uncontrollably. Great lungfuls of sadness and fear make me tremble and moan, and I screw my eyes shut, hoping that when I open them I'll be in my bed at home, recovering from a vivid nightmare, even though I know that's not going to happen.

There's a splash in the dark water beside me, but I don't raise my head as it'll be someone from the rowing boat, and I just don't want to face them.

Then comes a soft crunch on the sand and a gentle nudge on my hunched shoulder, and I slowly uncurl myself, expecting to see one of our rescuers.

And definitely *not* expecting to see what I do.

CHAPTER 48

The cog's low growl purrs in my ear, and then it nudges me again, harder this time, as if to say, *Get up!* I uncurl my arms and raise my head, at which point the cog moves its face right next to mine, as though it wants to peer deep into my soul. Its own amber-tinted eyes seem to be lit from within, and its fish-scented breath is strangely comforting.

'Manny,' I say slowly, unable to take my eyes off the creature. He stops his advance into the water and turns. His face is grey, all life drained from his eyes as though he's already given up.

The sound of the rowing boat's oars is very close now, and the flashlights are more intense. 'Hello? Anyone else in there? Stay put – we're coming to get you.' Thing is, they seem like a million miles away – almost from another world.

As though in a trance, I scramble to my feet, and the cog gets behind me, rising up on its hind legs, stiffening its huge triangular ears, and seeming to push us both towards the back of the cave with its little paws. In a flash, I get it.

'The cog can pass through the dimensions as well!' I yell to Manny. 'The cog will take us back! It's like it wants to! It *knows*!'

Is it doing this deliberately?

I don't wait to find out.

'Come on! Hold my hand, Manny. Now!' I yell.

It's me this time – all me. Manny brought us here, but I'm bringing us back. I grip Manny's clammy, half-dead hand in mine.

As the torch beams flash closer, I grab the tiny human-like paw of the cog in my other hand and place both our hands on the seam of dark sandstone. The cog doesn't struggle but waits patiently as in seconds the grey fuzz gets thicker and thicker and fills the cave and my head and my mouth and my heart . . .

It's working! The cog's power is taking us back through!

Suddenly, with the grey mist swirling round us, the creature wriggles weakly away from me, as if all of its energy, all of its life, is spent.

'No!' I shout in desperation. 'No, please – not now!'

It limps into the channel that leads to the cave mouth and flops on to the surface of the water with a soft splosh, sinking slowly beneath the surface. I realise that it has given its life for me and Manny, but to no avail. It tried but failed to take us across the dimensional barrier and back to our own world. The flashlights are right upon us now.

A man's voice calls with a tone of impatience, 'What are you *doing*, Willa?'

Another voice goes, 'Whoa! What was that? Did you see that, Del?'

'What? Aarggh, I felt something on my leg? Oh – I see it! There! Is that a dog?'

'God almighty, it's a shark! Look at the fin! There it goes – man, it's fast. What the flamin' heck?'

I'm glad the cog got away, I suppose, and now I wearily straighten up again, and I wait, exhausted and drained and numb with cold, for the people who saw me go into the cave with Manny to guide me out.

A torch beam flashes in my eyes.

'Aye, Del. It's her.'

A man in yellow waders who I recognise from somewhere steps forward out of the shallows.

'Willa Shafto. What the blazes is it with you and this cave? Hold on to me.'

Del? As if emerging from a deep well, a memory drifts back. Del. Del Malik. Deena's dad. The man who rescued me before?

Del's voice booms around the cave as he yells to his companions, 'Got them. They're here!'

'Are you . . . is this . . . ?' I can't even formulate the right question. 'Is this the . . . *real* world?' I say.

'Flippin' "real world". What are you on about? I'll give you "real world", miss. How come you've done this again?'

He grabs me round the waist and lifts me up, not roughly, but not at all gently, either. It's like he's lifting a sack of something. He mutters, as if to himself, but it isn't, 'You, my love, have got some serious explaining to do. Should have flamin' left you. A few hours in there would have brought you to your senses. Archie – you grab the lad.'

Del is striding angrily through the water to the entrance of the cave, flashlight beams flicking all around us. We emerge, and Del dumps me down in knee-deep water. I stare up at the concrete promenade and the seafront, where there's no music, no lights, no fireworks, no people . . .

No WWW celebrations.

Bravo Foxtrot Delta one nine two. We've got them. Boy and a girl. Yep, same ones.

'Someone call their parents. Again. Tell them they're okay. Although one of them's in fancy dress of some sort.'

I stand on the prom in Grandad Norman's overalls, the welding goggles hanging round my chin. The gloves and cap have been lost somewhere. I'm shivering with cold and confusion and fear.

I still have my phone. My frozen fingers clamp round it, and I pull it from my damp pocket.

A police officer gently tries to take the phone out of my fist. 'Come on, love, I'll take this.'

I snatch my hand back, tightening my grip still further. 'No! Get off!'

'All right, all right, it's okay. Here – put this on.'

Something heavy is draped round my shoulders: a police uniform jacket. I allow myself to be led up the stone steps that go from the promenade to the seafront. I gaze around, speechless, and everything's normal again: the cars passing on the road, the broken sign of the tatty Culvercot Hotel.

Manny and I sit on the open tailgate of a police car. Someone puts a bottle of water in my hand, and I take a shaky sip.

I have hardly said a word since being hauled out of the cave. Around me, people are gathered, staring at me, until a stern voice says, 'Oi! That's enough, knock it off, folks – give the kids some space.'

My teeth are no longer chattering, and I take another gulp of water. I'm vaguely aware that someone has been stroking my back in a comforting gesture. I turn my head, and there is a woman in a yellow jacket with NORTHUMBRIA POLICE on it and a hat with a chequered black-and-white band.

She jerks her head at another officer, who starts ushering people away, saying things like, 'Come on, move along, please – we're still working here.'

Once a bit of quiet has been restored, it seems as though it's just me and the policewoman sitting in the rear of the car. She has a kind face, and she says quietly, 'You all right, love?' and I nod – although more from reflex than any sense that I really am 'all right'.

And then I feel my shoulders slump, and I'm crying – sobbing, in fact. The policewoman puts both her arms round me, and I don't know how long I'm there, but afterwards I'm being driven in the police car back to Mam and Dad.

I still haven't let go of my phone. My knuckles have turned white, I'm gripping it so hard. Because my phone contains the proof.

The proof of where I have been. The proof that the Other World is real.

No one's going to believe me, I can tell that already. Because, if I thought this was the end, it is in some ways just the beginning . . .

PART FIVE

CHAPTER 49

I wake up in my bed. I don't dare to open my eyes, so instead I lie there for a few seconds, trying to work out if everything is all right.

It's very quiet. Eyes still shut, I smell the duvet under my nose. It smells right, and so I risk opening my eyes. The first thing I see is the poster of Felina on my wall. That's good. I dare to look around a bit more.

My strange multicoloured school clothes are on the chair. But – hang on – they're soaking wet. I was wearing them when I came home last night, dazed and tired, in Mam's car. A proper car. One with wheels . . . There are overalls there as well, and a pair of welding goggles on the floor.

I don't remember much about coming in the house, although fragments of memory are returning. A hug from Dad. Alex saying something. Girl-Alex, that is . . . I remember undressing and getting into bed . . .

I slept as though as I was dead, but I'm properly awake now. I think. The rest of my room is as it should be. The walls are the right colour. I'm in my usual pyjamas.

My clock says it's 6.30 a.m. Too early for the rest of the house to be up.

My phone is still gripped in my hand.

Finger by finger, I release my grip and turn it over in my hand. It's out of juice. Has been since . . .

Since I recorded the speech by John F. Kennedy.

Did that really happen?

Still feeling slightly dazed, I place my phone on the charging pad by my bed and wait. I find I can hardly swallow with nerves so I get up and get a drink from my bedroom sink and see that my toothbrush and toothpaste are back to normal.

A few seconds later, my heart leaps at the phone's little tinkling chime as it comes to life.

With a trembling finger, I start the phone, opening up the camera app first.

There it is: a tiny thumbnail picture of the giant video screen with a one-hundred-and-something-year-old man. The last thing I recorded. I press play. I can hardly breathe.

'My fellow Americans, my fellow . . . human beings!'

Frantically, I swipe through the rest of the camera's memory. It's all there. All the pictures I took. All the videos I recorded. They're all there!

Now I can breathe! In fact, I'm breathing too fast, and I try to slow down.

In, two three, four . . .

Oh, forget it.

'Mam! Dad! Alex! *ALEEEEEEX!*' I'm screaming at the top of my voice. '*Maaaaam!*' I run out of my bedroom and into the hallway, screaming, shouting, laughing like a maniac, thumping on their bedroom doors. *I have the proof!*

'It's worked! It worked! It flinkin' well WOOORKED!'

CHAPTER 50

I call Manny straight away. It rings and rings and rings, and with each ring I'm getting more and more anxious until after what seems like an age he answers.

'You made it,' we both say together, then, 'Yes!'

'How are you feeling?' he asks.

I have to think about this. 'Strange.'

'Me too. Oh my word!'

'What, Manny, what?'

'Nothing. It's just . . . it's all coming back. That smell. Hang on.' There's a pause, and I hear bedclothes rustle. Then a mad laugh. 'Thought so. I trod in cog poo in the cave. It's still on my shoe!'

The memory of the cave and the cog floods back. 'The cog,' I say. 'Do you think he made it?'

'He helped us, Willa. I hope he did, but he seemed very . . . weak, I guess. Did it work, by the way? The camera?'

'Come round when you can, Manny,' I say. 'It totally worked!'

*

We sit and watch it – me, Mam, Dad, Alex and Manny – with my phone plugged into Alex's laptop. Manny and I talk them through it all – the photos of the holiday park and the sign with Great-grandad Roger looking like the man on the KFC logo, the video clips of the ci-kars in the street and everyone's colourful clothes. The cog peeing in the bushes. Everything, in other words, that I have just been telling you about.

As you'd expect, it takes ages. I have to keep stopping and telling them stuff, and I wish I'd taken even more pictures and recorded more video. I filmed nothing in school, for example. I didn't even *go* to school the second time. (Perhaps it's just as well. If anyone in my class saw it, it would completely freak them out.)

Mam and Dad are being extra-nice to Manny. You know, 'More toast, Manny, pet?' – that sort of thing. I think they're feeling a bit guilty since it's now clear we were telling the truth, and he wasn't the bad new kid leading me astray after all.

Mam, who's quite practical with fixing things and all that, keeps wanting to see the flying vehicles again and again. She marvels at them, zooming in and pausing and asking questions about how they work, which I just can't answer.

Dad is fascinated with the pictures of the holiday park, saying things like, 'I never imagined it could be like this.'

Alex is just stunned into complete silence, her jaw

hanging open. It really is as if she cannot believe what she's seeing before her eyes, yet she has no choice.

I kind of flick past the picture of Mam and Dad kissing by the fridge. Alex sees it and goes back. 'Oh, *gross*!' she groans. Mam and Dad pretend to laugh, but I can tell they're a bit embarrassed. They haven't done much in the way of kissing lately.

And then comes a part that I haven't seen before.

I hit pause as soon as I see boy-Alex's face on the screen. In the background is a red telephone box with me in it. He must have done this when I was on the phone to Manny. I'd given him my phone to hold while I fed coins into the box underneath the telephone. I didn't even know he'd worked out how to use it.

'Mam. Dad. Alex?' I say. My heart is hammering. 'I haven't seen this bit before. I'm not sure if . . . that is . . . this may be a bit, well . . . put it this way . . .'

'Oh, for goodness' sake,' says Alex, and she thumps the space bar on her laptop to play it.

'Mam, Dad, Alex – girl-Alex that is, ha ha! That's ripped! You don't know me, and you might never meet me. But I'm Alex Shafto. In your world, I left you when I was a baby. Mina – or Willa to you – told me about, erm . . . me.' He laughs a bit sadly and looks away from the camera while he thinks of what to say next.

I glance at Mam, and there's already a tear rolling down her cheek.

'Erm . . . this is so weird that I don't really know what to tell you. Only that, if all this works out, then you'll know that Willa's telling the truth. All of this really did happen. I wish I could meet you because in my world my mam and dad are pretty groovy, and they love each other, and just like everyone else here they talk instead of fight. So I'll probably never see you, but . . . Uh-oh, here's Mina coming now. Gotta go! Love ya!'

Mam sniffs and wipes her eyes. She gets up from the sofa and goes over to the mantelpiece, where she takes down the little framed picture of baby Alexander. I see her shoulders shaking as she cries softly. Then Dad joins her and puts his arm round her and kisses the top of her head.

For the rest of the morning, the five of us sit there, hunched over Alex's laptop, and we watch the lot. Mam calls our schools to say Alex and I aren't coming in, then Dad calls Winston Churchill House to reassure Jakob that Manny is safe. Then we watch it all again, especially the stuff with Maudie and the ancient President Kennedy.

It turns out there is a limit to how often people can say, 'Oh my God,' or, 'Wow!' or, 'I can't believe it,' and Mam and Dad and Alex reach it fairly quickly. Eventually, we're all sitting in silence in our little front room. Mam hasn't stopped hugging me, as if loosening her grip will make me disappear into the other world again. Alex is just shaking her head in what seems like disbelief, but obviously isn't. It's the opposite. She's shaking her head in stunned *belief*.

Manny has gone really quiet – like, silent. I say, 'What's up?'

He swallows hard and then grins. 'Nothing,' he says. But his kiwi eyes are glistening. I think he's just moved by the whole thing. Mam lifts her arm as though she's going to give him a hug, but he gets up from the sofa and moves away to stare at nothing out of the window.

Mam, Dad, Alex and I exchange looks. It's all a bit awkward.

It's Alex of all people who gets up and stands next to him – Alex, who falls in and out of love every other week, who spots Manny's heartache.

'It's your mam, isn't it?' she says, and Manny nods.

Without turning, he says, 'We've got pictures of everything and everyone but her.'

He's right, of course. For all the proof of the Sideways World on my phone, there's nothing for Manny to remember his mam by. Unless . . .

Seconds later, I'm upstairs, rummaging through the pockets of the wet clothes on my bedroom floor. I kept it, didn't I? I must have.

There is the soaking, swollen magazine, *What Classic Flyke?*, that had been shoved down my front, but that's not what I'm searching for.

Then my fingers close round a soggy piece of folded paper, which I carefully unpeel. I'm so nervous, so absorbed, that I haven't noticed that Manny is standing over me.

Manny's scrawly handwriting is smudged and almost unreadable; the ink on the back has washed away to practically nothing, but there, on the page that Manny used to write his letter to me, is the unmistakable face of his mam. Carefully, I pull the paper straight and lay it on my desk to dry out.

Manny's never been much of a hugger, really, but right now his skinny arms encircle me, and he squeezes his thanks as a tear drops from his chin on to the page.

'Hey, careful,' I say. 'It's wet enough already.'

CHAPTER 51

Back in the living room, Dad stands up, puffs his cheeks out and shakes his head. 'Blimey,' he says. 'If I hadn't seen all that with my own eyes, I think I'd call it a load of old codswallop. As it is, though, I need to see this cave for myself.' He holds his hands up defensively. 'I'm not going in. I just . . . need to see it, okay? Who's coming?'

Once again, I make the journey along the seafront, only this time in our car. Was it really just last night that there were scenes of wild partying, and music and fireworks? Now it's all eerily quiet.

Almost no one is about. From the car's telescreen comes a newsreader's voice.

'*This is the BBC news. According to senior government sources, war is now unavoidable, and stay-at-home orders are . . .*'

Dad hits the off button. No one says anything.

We're all crammed into our car, and very quiet on the journey towards Brown's Bay. The day is misty and cool.

Through the swish of the windscreen wipers, the Culvercot Hotel appears ahead of us like a huge broken tooth.

'What's going on there?' says Dad.

We drive past a collection of vehicles that have stopped by the steps down to the promenade. There are two police cars, an ambulance, at least three motorcycles, a big car with blacked-out windows and about a dozen people, men and women in assorted uniforms: police, army, others that I don't recognise. Dad stops the car a few metres further on, and we all spill out, although we don't get far.

Two young soldiers in green berets and jumpers are erecting a barrier across the pavement. 'Stop right there,' one says. 'No further, please.'

'What's happening?' Dad says.

'Sorry, sir,' says one of the soldiers. 'Classified. Don't even know meself. Move along, please.'

But we don't move, and they seem okay if we stay where we are. A woman with white hair and big round glasses comes and joins us.

'It's all go round here, innit?' she says to no one in particular. 'It was the lifeboats last night and them two kids. And now this!' She takes out her phone and starts filming. 'My Terry'll never believe me. He says nothing goes on around—'

"Hang on," I say, interrupting her. I recognise her, and Manny is blinking in surprise as well. "Sorry – but . . . are you Bonnie?"

She smiles. "Aye, I am, hinny. Do I know you?"

"You work at Winston Churchill House!"

Manny is shaking his head and Bonnie says, "Eeh no, hinny. You're mistaken." Then she chuckles and adds, "We must've met in another life, eh? Still how'd you know my name?"

Thankfully, I don't have to answer, because at that moment a voice barks, 'Put that away, please, madam! *Now!*' A large man in uniform strides towards us, pointing at the camera phone, which Bonnie hastily pockets. He barks at the soldier, 'What did I tell you, corporal?'

The other man mutters, 'Sorry, sir,' and they both turn to face us.

'Flamin' cheek,' mutters Bonnie. 'It was old Paula at the hotel that raised the alarm, you know. She was down with her dog on the bay this morning first thing. Poor creature starts whining, Paula goes to look and there's a dead *bear*, for heaven's sake! Just inside the cave there. Well, she didn't know what it was, to be honest. All fur it was. With a tail. She reckons . . .'

I don't really hear the rest. It's like there's a buzzing in my ears, and Manny and I look at each other in horror as, between the cars and the motorcycles, we see a group coming up the steps from the promenade. Two police officers are carrying a stretcher and on it, covered with a sheet, is something large and rounded.

They are about to load it into the ambulance when

someone shouts, 'Hold it there!' and the rear door of the car with the blacked-out windows opens.

A woman in camouflage uniform with short grey hair beneath a maroon beret gets out, and someone calls, 'This way, General.' From the other rear door comes a small woman with untidy grey-streaked hair and a grey anorak zipped up to her throat.

'Ooh, "General", eh? That's important!' murmurs Bonnie.

I'm straining to look between the shield of bodies and vehicles, but I'm not even sure I want to see what it is. The general has her broad back to us and lifts up the sheet to look beneath. When she does, a long black tail flops off the stretcher and hangs down, brushing the damp ground, then the stretcher is loaded into the ambulance. The general and her small companion huddle together to talk.

In seconds, it seems, everyone is getting back into the vehicles, ready to leave. Three or four soldiers remain, guarding the entrance to the promenade, and that's it.

'Well I never,' says Bonnie. 'What on earth was *that* all about? Any ideas?'

We all say nothing. She'd never believe it anyway. I hear a sniff and, when I look across at him, Manny is wiping his eyes on his sleeve. Bonnie, meanwhile, is still chuntering on.

'Did you see her on the news this morning? Her in the anorak talking to boss-lady? You know, the government scientist? Reckons the war's gonna go chemical, she says, God help us all. What on earth's she doing here?'

No one's listening to her. Manny's leaning on the rusty railings above the promenade, and I go over to him.

'I'm sorry about the cog,' I say.

'I thought . . .' he says hesitantly. 'Oh, I don't know. It's like that cog gave his life for us, you know? My mam loved molphins, as she called them. She reckoned they were magical.'

A chill passes through me when I realise how insensitive I have been. I'm back with my family and, although it's not perfect, at least I *have* a family. Manny has no one. He gave up his only chance to be with his mam because she wasn't his 'real' mother.

'I'm sorry,' I say again. 'About your mam, I mean. And she might have been right about the molphins being magic.'

He sighs. 'Yeah.'

'I bet you'll find her in this world, Manny,' I reassure him. 'I . . . oh my word!'

The realisation hits me like a powerful punch in the gut, and I spin round to where the vehicles are starting to pull away. The government scientist from the news – I recognise her. 'Manny! That's Dr Amara Kholi!'

'Who? What?'

I need to speak to Dr Kholi. I can't think of anything else – certainly not the soldiers who have sprung to life as I rush at the huge car with the black windows.

'Dr Kholi! Dr Kholi!' I shout, and I jump out in front of the vehicle.

CHAPTER 52

Everything happens at once.

Dad shouts, 'Willa? What on earth are you playing at?'

Alex rushes forward to grab me but is grabbed by the arm in turn by a police officer who says, 'Oh no you don't, miss!'

She wriggles. 'Get off me!'

I'm slapping the bonnet of the car, shouting, 'Dr Kholi! Listen to me! Listen to me!'

The driver of the car stops abruptly and gets out, shielding himself with the car door and holding a pistol with both hands, pointing it in the air. Mam squeals.

From inside the car, I hear a booming voice: 'Stop!'

And everyone does. The driver lowers his gun.

Instantly, everything is silent and still, apart from the small voice of Bonnie going, 'Ee, wait till I tell my Terry . . .'

I can just make out the figures in the car through the tinted windows.

'You've got to listen, Dr Kholi! I'm a friend of Maudie! Maudie, erm . . . Fry? Except she's not called that here.

She's called Lawson. You know her son, Callum. You wrote that thing – you know – *A Quantum-thingy* . . . *Approach . . . Thingy to Lunar Thing*?' I can't think straight, and I'm so flustered. 'You know! Oh, please! I know what that animal is! You have to let me explain.'

The rear window descends, and an arm in a camouflage uniform sleeve comes out, beckoning me towards the car.

When I peer in the window, the general and Dr Kholi look at me with intense curiosity.

'This had better be good,' says the general, sternly. 'And I mean . . . *very* good.'

So, while Mam and Dad and Alex wait outside, Manny and I sit in the back of the car with Britain's top general and leading scientist, and I play them the film on my phone. I can't help wondering if, just as Maudie Fry changed the Sideways World in the back of the car with President Kennedy, we might be doing the same thing.

It's a very small and discreet group that drives into the Whitley Bay HappyLand half an hour later. The general has swapped her big car for an unmarked one so as not to attract attention, and we all gather in Maudie's sitooterie beneath the faded BAN THE BOMB banner.

Dr Kholi smiles. 'It's nice to see you again, Maudie! This is a clever girl – she remembered my *Quantum and Multidimensional Approach to Hypersensory Lunar Perception*. Not my *snappiest* title, I admit.' She snuffles a tiny laugh as if that was the nearest she ever came to making a joke.

Then she peers at Manny, staring into his eyes – looking for what, I can't tell. 'And as for this young man . . .' She nods, as if satisfied about something, but doesn't finish her sentence.

Suddenly this small woman seems taller. 'This is a matter of the most profound national and international security. We – and by "we" I mean a network of scientists from around the world who advise governments on highly controversial issues – have been using satellites to monitor a "grey hole" near here for some time.'

Mam and Dad have each pulled up a wooden box to sit on, but Dad gets up again. 'Hang on, a grey hole . . .'

'You might call it a "cosmic corridor". I know, I know: all terribly hard to comprehend. But, given the dangerous state of international relations at the moment, it is essential that all information is strictly controlled. I'm sure you agree.'

She seems very confident. Dad sits down heavily.

'And now,' says Dr Kholi, turning her attention to me, 'kindly show me the film you took with your phone.'

And so we watch it yet again. This time Mam doesn't cry at the bit with boy-Alex, but watches it with a sad smile instead. It's Maudie's turn to be astonished.

Actually, I don't think 'astonished' is really a big enough word to describe seeing yourself on film being greeted by a long-dead American president. Stunned? Gobsmacked? All of those, and more. She shakes her head and repeats, 'Maudie Fry . . . That was my name before I married Callum's dad.' She nods to the ancient advertisement on her shed wall for Fry's Superior Chocolate. 'Family connection, you remember? My great-great-great-grandfather Joseph Storrs Fry invented chocolate bars, you see . . .'

'This animal,' says Dr Kholi, interrupting Maudie's trip down memory lane, and pointing at the picture of the cog on my phone. 'Is it the same individual we just found by the cave?'

I look at Manny, and we both nod. 'I think so,' I say. 'It's a semi-feral hybrid mammal. Created in a lab, originally, but something went wrong . . .'

Dr Kholi's shaggy eyebrows shoot up.

I say, 'I don't know what happened. But there aren't many left. And this one was able to pass through the dimensional barrier. It brought us back.'

The general clears her throat. 'Does this make any sense to you, Dr Kholi? Is it possible?' she says.

Dr Kholi pauses before replying. 'Yes. In theory, at any rate. Put it this way, it's not necessarily *im*possible.'

The general runs her hand through her short hair. 'I'm not sure I can believe this, you know.'

Dr Kholi says, 'The thing is, General, if it's the truth, then it doesn't really matter whether or not you believe it.'

We play the rest of the film. At the end, Dr Kholi says, 'Kindly disable the passcode for this device, Willa.'

I look across at Mam and Dad. They look at the general, whose face is unmoving and stern. Dad nods at me, and I log in to the phone to switch off the security functions.

'Thank you,' says the doctor, taking back the phone and handing it to the general.

'Hey, hey! You can't do that,' says Dad quickly.

'I am afraid I can, Mr Shafto,' says the general with an apologetic smile. 'I have the authority under the Emergency Wartime Act of 2030 Section 20. Impounding of private property. You can take my word for it or look it up. I'll wait.'

Dad looks at Mam. They both look at me and Manny. Eventually, Dad gives a tiny nod.

'Thank you,' says the general. 'Now, have any copies been made of this? Have you shown any of this film to anyone outside your family?'

We shake our heads. The general says, 'Good. The activity of this phone will be checked, and someone will be sent to your home to double-check all your other devices too. Willa, you can consider your adventure over. Manny –' the general nods to Dr Kholi, who takes a tiny plastic tub out of her fleece pocket – 'please lick the stick inside this pot and seal it up again. I need a sample of your DNA.'

Manny does this and hands it back to Dr Kholi with a single word: 'Why?'

'Ongoing and vital research into hypersensory lunar perception. If we discover anything, you'll be the first to know.' The general gets to her feet and replaces the beret on her head.

'Wait!' I say. 'Stop! What about the war?'

A wintry smile slowly spreads across her face. She looks at me with a sort of gentle pity. 'What war is that, Willa?'

'Our war?' I say, nervously. 'The war that's about to happen here? I mean . . . what about that whole thing I saw and filmed? The speech. The World Without War. It can happen here too!'

The general is still smiling, and I hate it.

'Can't it?' I say.

She gives a little chuckle, as if I've just said something funny or cute. 'Willa. Wars cannot just be turned off and on like a light switch. You'll understand that one day. When you're a bit older.'

Manny's on his feet now, knocking his stool over. I'm surprised to see his face is suddenly flushed and his eyes are blazing. 'When she's older? What if, thanks to this war, she never *gets* older, eh? That could be any of us! You'll be all right, won't you, in your stupid bunker and your stupid uniform?'

The smile has vanished from the general's face, and she glares, thin-lipped, at Manny's insolence.

He goes on, his voice hissing with anger, 'You don't care, do you? None of you care. Well, *they* cared,' he says, pointing at my phone. 'Those people cared enough to try – and look what happened!'

Now that he has everyone's attention, Manny lowers his voice almost to a whisper. 'I admit it,' he says, looking at all of us in turn. 'I admit I never even wanted to think about the war. I thought I'd stick to worrying about things I could change. But you know what? I was just being lazy. That was before I realised we *can* change things. It's not always easy, and it's not always quick, but you heard what the old president said: "No problem of human destiny is beyond human beings."'

'That's quite enough from you, young man . . .' the general begins, but it's too late.

Manny has already left.

CHAPTER 53

There's an embarrassed silence that ends when Dr Kholi murmurs to me, 'I'll do my best to make sure this film is seen in the right quarters.'

I'm not hopeful.

Manny stays with us that day. I don't think he can face answering yet more questions at Winston Churchill House. We're in the kitchen when the news comes on the screen and this time no one turns it off. World leaders are saying that further talks are pointless. A passenger ship has been sunk in the Indian Ocean. Commercial aeroplanes have been grounded worldwide and all international travel suspended. Schools will be shut and reserve military personnel put on stand-by.

The prime minister will be making a statement at 8 p.m. When her name is mentioned, Dad growls like an angry terrier.

We have come back to a world that's about to go to war. Manny still has no family. It occurs to me that it might all have been a massive risk for nothing.

*

Mam, Dad, Manny, Alex and I are all watching the TV at 8 p.m. when the front doorbell goes.

It's Maudie. She's changed out of her dungarees into a long patterned skirt and a colourful patchwork waistcoat. Her greasy old beret has gone, and her hair is in a long plait, with real daisies woven into it.

'You know I don't have a TV,' she says as we squash together on the sofa to make room for her. 'But Amara Kholi's just phoned me. She says this might be worth watching.'

It's as if she knows something: I certainly don't feel like getting dressed up to hear that we're going to war.

The screen goes black, and the first few bars of the national anthem play before the picture fades up on the prime minister in her London office.

A STATEMENT BY
THE RT HON. FREYA BOATENG
PRIME MINISTER OF THE
UNITED KINGDOM OF GREAT BRITAIN
AND NORTHERN IRELAND

'My fellow British citizens. My fellow human beings . . .'

Manny and I exchange a glance. He has recognised these phrases too.

'Oh, for heaven's sake,' says Dad. 'Listen to her. She makes me sick.'

'*Shh,*' we all say in unison.

The prime minister says, 'I had a very different speech prepared until a little earlier today. It was a speech in which, with the heaviest of hearts, I was to warn you all of the catastrophe that was coming our way. For today we are all facing a very grave situation. Probably the gravest danger in the history of our planet. The forces of freedom and the forces of tyranny are poised for the greatest battle that will ever be fought on this beautiful planet that we call our home. A battle that will rage and rage and have no winner, for a war on this scale has only losers. A destructive inferno that will cause more misery than has ever been known and from which our earth, and the life upon it, may never, ever recover.'

Our eyes are fixed on the screen. I don't think any of us has breathed. The prime minister pauses, her mouth turned down, her eyes moist with emotion.

'Instead, I am here to tell you that this may not happen, after all. Today I was inspired by two children who had a vision of an ideal world. I saw this world as they saw it. It is a world in which we look one another in the eye with honesty, love and forgiveness. A world in which we seek out the things that unite us, rather than those that divide us. A world in which we embrace our sisters and brothers in humanity and say no to hatred, no to conflict. No. To. War.'

It is electrifying. We are all hearing the words of a long-dead president echoed by a living leader.

'I have now spoken to some of my fellow world leaders, including many of those considered to be our most obstinate enemies. I have shared this vision with them. We have agreed to a temporary suspension of hostilities.

'The situation remains very grave. Yet, for now at least, instead of fighting, we will talk. We will argue. Oh boy, will we argue!' She allows the hint of a smile to cross her face. 'Meanwhile, however, we will endeavour to spread the word of peace worldwide. Because when we talk we don't fight. And, when we don't fight, we can devote our energies to solving the other problems that face our world, our planet and our glorious, ever-inventive human race. Problems of disease, of inequality, pollution, energy and climate change.

'Make no mistake, however. Peace and war cannot be turned off and on like a light switch. It has taken many months – some would say years – for the international situation to become as dangerous as it is today. It may take that long – or longer – to achieve a lasting peace. But, with dedication, discussion and faith, such a peace is, I truly believe, possible – for I have seen it.

'My friends, let us go forward together, firmly resolved to keep our commitment to world harmony and to live in love and peace with all.'

It takes a little while for it to sink in. I whisper to Dad, 'So the world war isn't happening?'

In a kind of daze, he nods and says, 'Looks like it.'

Then Alex is shouting to a friend down her phone, 'OhmiGOD, ohmiGOD!' and I'm on my feet, cheering with Manny, then I trip and tumble on to a laughing Maudie. From outside, I can hear the sound of car horns honking, and a ship's hooter out at sea, and a firework, until the rest of the prime minister's words are lost in a riotous cacophony of celebration.

I see Mam and Dad kissing each other, and it's actually not gross at all.

CHAPTER 54

A Few Days Later

Everything, down to the last detail, has been planned so as to attract the very minimum of attention.

For example, the car that was sent to collect me, Mam, Dad and Alex looked just like a regular local taxi. When powerful people wish to conceal something, there seems to be almost no limit to what they can do.

It is 10 a.m., Tuesday, 4 June. School tomorrow. I think They wanted to get this all sorted out, tied up, sealed down and brushed away before I start to tell anyone what really happened this past week.

By the way, you'll see I write 'They' with a capital T. 'They' is just my term for the collection of people who seem have taken charge of all this. We've had days of it: people turning up at the house, usually in unwashed, unremarkable cars, and none of them in any sort of uniform – not even suits and ties. The American ambassador, a tall man with silver hair who smelt of expensive cologne, came to our house in bikers' leathers on a delivery scooter.

To all of them, I repeat my story. Again and again and again.

And now Mam, Dad, Alex and I are being driven north, up the A1 into Scotland, with a stony-faced driver at the wheel who has said nothing but, 'Good morning.'

Dad's in the front passenger seat, and he shifts round to try to engage the driver a bit more, but he just keeps staring ahead at the road.

'Come on, mate. Who do you work for? Who's your boss?'

The driver sighs and shakes his head a little sadly as he indicates to overtake a truck. He puts his foot on the accelerator, and the car surges with power. The road ahead is empty, and I watch as the needle on the speedometer creeps to 75, 80, then 90 miles per hour. Whoever the driver is, he's keen to get us to our destination quickly.

(Dad has shaved his beard off, by the way. I think he saw the other version of him and realised he looked younger. I'm getting used to it. Mam is pleased, at least.)

An hour or so after we got into the car, we pass a sign saying WELCOME TO SCOTLAND. Our driver slows down and turns the vehicle off the main road and then, a little further, up a stony track past an empty farmhouse until we can see the blue sea ahead of us.

I say 'blue'. No sea will be as blue as the sea in . . .

Where was it? I guess the Sideways World will have to do. That's what Manny and I call it anyhow.

The thought of Manny fills my heart with a strange combination of sadness and fear and happiness. I wish he was with us now. I know that, wherever the driver is taking us, Manny will be part of the conversation.

We drive past another sign:

HM GOVERNMENT
STRICTLY NO VEHICLES

Then we come to a gentle stop near a clifftop path. As we do, another taxi identical to ours pulls up alongside us, and Manny gives me a nervous wave from the back seat, where he's sitting with Jakob.

Two cars are already parked a little further away. Two men get out of one car, and a woman from the other. All three are wearing sunglasses. The men – large, blank-faced in zip-up jackets and jeans – walk part of the way towards us, then stop. One of them touches his ear, and I see his lips moving, but he's too far away and it's too windy to hear what he says.

'Blimey,' murmurs Dad. 'If they're trying their best to look like undercover government agents, they're doing a brilliant job.' I swear I see the flicker of a smirk on the face of our driver.

The woman continues to walk towards our car,

attempting a warm smile, one hand deep in the pocket of her long coat, the other holding a small backpack. She seems familiar. She motions to Mam to lower the rear window, and she leans in towards us, taking off her dark glasses. She is tall and long-necked with short white hair and narrow eyes the same brown as her smooth skin.

'Hello. Thank you for coming. Shall we walk a little way? This won't take long, I promise.'

'Do we have a choice?' says Dad, coldly. 'Prime minister?'

CHAPTER 55

'I'm sorry,' says the prime minister. 'This is just routine. Would you mind, erm . . .'

She indicates our driver, who says, 'Mobile phones, smartwatches, please.' Mam and Dad and Alex hand over their phones, Dad his smartwatch. 'Raise your arms, please.' He then thoroughly frisks all four of us, feeling his way expertly up our arms and legs. He mutters a polite, 'Excuse me, madam. Excuse me, miss,' then he looks in our ears.

'All clear, ma'am,' he says to the PM.

Manny gets out and is subjected to the same routine. I see Jakob open his passenger door, but it is firmly but politely shut by the driver, who indicates that he should stay where he is.

There's a weathered picnic table about thirty metres along the path. The prime minister leads the way, and we all sit down, a little awkwardly. Mrs Boateng takes a deep breath, which she holds for a moment before starting her monologue. She has a soft northern accent that seems to be more noticeable than when she speaks on TV, and it somehow makes her sound like a friendly librarian.

She's opposite me on the picnic table, and she focuses her sharp eyes on me, resting her chin on her clasped hands.

'Willa.'

'Yeah? I mean yes?'

The PM smiles again. 'You may already know that your film has inspired a significant change in international relations.'

'Yeah?' I say again, and she chuckles slightly.

'It's a good thing, Willa. A very good thing. Your story about what happened has been very consistent. Very consistent indeed. The footage is impressive. Convincing, even.'

She pauses and takes a deep breath. 'It all means I believe you. *We* believe you.'

Dad says, 'Who's this "we"?' He sounds a bit aggressive, but I suppose he's just worried and exhausted. The prime minister doesn't seem to mind.

'Good question, Mr Shafto.' She pauses. 'And one that I can't really answer. Not without compromising our situation.'

'So how do we know we can trust you?' says Dad.

'*Dad!*' Alex is as embarrassed as it's possible to be.

'You don't.'

The prime minister says this so matter-of-factly that Dad just says, 'Oh,' and then shuts up.

'The fact is, Willa,' she continues, redirecting her attention to me, 'your story is utterly, completely and undeniably *un*believable.'

'But I thought you just said . . .' I begin.

'I did. I said *I* believe you. *We* believe you. Dr Kholi, whom you met, also believes you. Almost no one else will. Especially without evidence.'

'But there is evidence! I took photos, video: you have them. You have my phone,' I say.

She nods. 'We do. And we won't be returning any of it.' She reaches into the backpack and brings out a white box with the Apple logo on it. She hands it to me. 'Top-of-the-range, brand-new smartphone, Willa. Five years' unlimited calls and data all prepaid.'

'Whoa!' breathes Alex, quite impressed.

'Hey, hang on . . .' starts Dad, but Mrs Boateng holds up her hand to stop him. She looks round the table at us, then makes eye contact with Mam and Dad. 'You will also find there is substantial new investment available via special government grants for developing your leisure park. All quite legal and no need to involve SunSeasons Corporation or to evict Maudie Lawson.'

'Hey! How do you know about that?' asks Mam.

The prime minister arches an eyebrow in reply. 'Listen carefully. We have suspected the existence of "grey holes" for some time now. You can look it up. They are linked to some frankly poorly regulated experiments involving

353

the Large Hadron Collider at the CERN institute in Geneva, Switzerland, some years ago. Have you heard of this?'

I nod.

Mam says, 'I think we've *heard* of it, haven't we, Ted?'

'Yeah. Some sort of nuclear-test thingy?'

The prime minister gives a tight smile. 'In a way. Several scientists warned way back in 2016 that simply switching on the LHC at CERN might produce unpredictable results. Well, they were right. Until now, "grey holes" have existed only in mathematical theory. We now believe that there are at least four of them around the world, and they've been growing in size since 2016. These allow for near-instant physical travel between an infinite number of universes, many almost identical to our own. Until now, there had been no evidence that this had yet occurred.'

It sounds as though she's memorised this. She stops talking, allowing me to process what she's said.

'Until now,' I repeat.

'Quite. I think you can all imagine the sheer terror, the inconceivable global chaos that might ensue if it became widely known that such a cosmic corridor existed, whether or not its existence depended on the position of the moon. It would undoubtedly threaten the very fragile peace that we seem to have recently achieved.'

Mrs Boateng gets up from the picnic table and walks

a couple of metres towards the cliff edge, where she stands, the strong northerly breeze billowing out her coat.

'There is nothing that I or anyone else can do to stop you from telling your story, Willa. You can tell as many people as you like. You can write a blog, a book or a film script, host a podcast. Without evidence, it will be just that, though. A story.'

'But it's true!'

She comes back and leans on the table with outstretched arms. 'I know it is. And the truth may be the most powerful thing in the universe. But sometimes it's too powerful. It has the awkward habit of just *being*.

'That is why your phone and its data will be kept locked away until long after we're all dead. No digital copies have been made nor will they be. Whatever story – if any – you choose to tell will be denied at every official level. This meeting, for example, is unrecorded and never took place. You will never meet me or anyone connected to me again. And as for you, Manny Weaver . . .'

She looks behind us to where yet another taxi is coming up the path. 'I wanted to be here for this. I wanted to tell you personally.'

From the taxi steps Dr Kholi, who thrusts her hands in her anorak pockets and comes towards us, her head bowed against the strong sea breeze. She looks up when she is near our table.

'Manny?'

She takes out a phone from her anorak pocket, turns it on and hands it to him. He doesn't seem to mind that I watch over his shoulder as a slight woman with a long blonde fringe appears on the screen.

'Emanuel?' she says, her nervous eyes blinking and darting from side to side before her gaze settles on Manny. 'Is that really you? My baby boy! I can't wait to see you.'

Manny mouths the word *Mam*.

He glances around and moves away from the table, staring at the screen as his mam talks to him. I think he wants this moment with her to be private, and I don't really blame him. Mrs Boateng has watched all of this and brushes a tear from her eye.

A few minutes later, Manny comes back, his expression a mixture of amazement and joy.

'Your mum has been unwell,' says the prime minister. 'She's still a patient at a hospital near Edinburgh, but she's making an excellent recovery. We are very confident that you can be reunited permanently in a matter of days.'

'But . . . how did you find her?'

Dr Kholi says, 'She too is a "super-sensor", Manny – sensitive to the tides and the pull of the moon. She was part of an international research programme that I conducted several years ago. The matching of your DNA was a fairly routine task. We've known for a long time that some rare people have this gift.'

The prime minister straightens up again and claps her hands together. 'Now, if you'll forgive me, I have a number of things to attend to, and I daresay you want to get back to your normal lives. Lewis will drive you home. And, Willa and Manny?'

She holds out both her hands, and we each take one. 'I don't want you running away with the idea that international peace can be turned on and off like a tap. It's going to take a lot of work, but we have made the first important step. Thank you.' She squeezes our hands. 'The whole world thanks you.'

CHAPTER 56

Six Months Later

There has been no World War Three – at least not yet. In fact, at home we don't really put the news on much any more. Dad's RAF medals have gone from the mantelpiece. I guess he doesn't like being reminded of just how close he came to fighting again.

It's a cold, still night and the noisy building work at HappyLand stopped hours ago. It's all going to be finished by next spring. There'll be a covered, heated pool and a new, expanded wildlife sanctuary. There'll be brand-new bunga-lodges too, all painted different colours, of course. It's like I can see a new, perfect world being built before my eyes.

Mam and Dad haven't had a row in ages and have started running a weekly charity quiz night together at the Beehive Pub in Earsdon. I came into the kitchen earlier when he was practising with a wooden-spoon microphone.

'Complete this quote, history girl,' Dad said, stroking

his chin. (I don't really mind the nickname now.) 'Ask not what your country can do for you . . .'

'But what you can do for your country! John F. Kennedy. Easy-peasy!' I said, and Dad grinned with satisfaction.

Once a month, when the moon is full, Manny and I have taken to remembering our strange adventures by getting together with Alex and sometimes Maudie. Usually we go down to the promenade above Brown's Bay.

Tonight, though, Manny and I have come to sit in one of the new bird-watching hides that are nearly finished. Maudie reckons she's seen a long-eared owl. Really, though, Manny and I just like looking at the moon.

In any case, the entrance to the cave where it all happened is completely blocked off now. A load of construction workers spent weeks filling the entire cave with rubble and concrete. The locals were furious. The local council were apologetic but said they had received the instruction from national government. It was, apparently, a 'health-and-safety' hazard and the whole cliff might collapse otherwise. It's kind of sad to look at it now.

I often bring a Fry's Chocolate Cream to share, but I don't have one tonight on account of having split my last one with . . . guess who? Well, we moved up a year in September, and there's a new head who changed all

the classes around, and I ended up sitting next to . . .
Deena Malik!

It's odd: we were both furious at first, but we kind of got used to each other. We ended up talking more, and, well . . . I don't think we'll ever be *best* friends, but she's okay.

'Are the others coming?' says Manny, his breath forming clouds in front of him. He has a big pair of binoculars for owl-spotting. I haven't asked where he got them.

'They said they would.' I check the time on my phone. 'Alex told me she'd come after she'd finished telling Finlay McQueen that she was now in love with Gino Angelis instead. Maudie's probably still studying. They'll be here soon.'

I saw Maudie earlier. She had a new delivery of chocolate. 'You'll like this,' she said. 'Costa Rica toasted blend.' Then she got into the taxi that takes her to the university in Newcastle three mornings a week. She's studying for a degree in astrophysics and is their oldest-ever student.

'Eighty-five is nothing, Willa,' she said. 'Not when you've seen a hundred-and-twenty-year-old president give a speech.'

Tonight the sky is clear and the moon seems brighter than ever. It's another supermoon, but it'll be decades before it's as close as it was last spring.

Manny brings out the wrinkled copy of *What Classic Flyke?* and opens it on the newly cut wooden floor. (Our favourite article is headlined 'Queen Anne: "My Horses and my Classic Flykes"'.) It's pretty much all we have left as evidence of our adventures, and we're careful to keep it to ourselves. There's a picture in there of a Chevrolet Super Flyke Sport 212, just like Grandad Norman's. I still feel bad that his got smashed up, and I worry sometimes that Mina and Alex will get the blame. I hope that – eventually – Alex will convince them of the truth.

'How's your mam?' I ask, and Manny smiles shyly.

'She's doing okay. Pretty well, in fact. I'll be living with her four days a week from next week, and Jakob reckons it'll be permanent by Christmas. Can you imagine – Christmas with me mam? Jakob says he's going to come for Christmas dinner, and he'll bring some traditional Swedish food.'

'Yeah. I've already told him you love *surströmming*,' I say with a straight face, then we both look at each other and burst out laughing.

'Can you feel it?' I say to Manny after a while as we look at the creamy-yellow moon. 'Tell me again what the moon feels like.' I'm still getting used to talking with braces on my teeth, but Manny never mentions it.

He grins and pushes his long fringe back and tells me again that it's a warm feeling, mainly in his head and his stomach, but sometimes tingling elsewhere as well, like in his feet. It's exactly how Alex describes being in love.

He takes my hand, just like he did when we went through the grey hole, and I'm convinced I feel it too. And for a while we just sit there, watching the moon, and I wonder yet again if one day – not now, perhaps not even soon – but *one day* we might celebrate a World Without War here.

From behind the hide, I can hear the swishing of footsteps through grass, and I turn to see two approaching figures silhouetted in the dark. One moves easily and smoothly, effortlessly texting as she walks, the glow of the phone's screen half lighting her face; the other is rounder and stiffer, carrying something that I hope is a large flask of hot chocolate. About five metres behind them are two more figures, hand in hand.

'They're here,' I say. 'And Mam and Dad have come too.'

Manny lets go of my hand and raises his fingers in the W sign to me. I do it back to him and say, 'Do you guys want to spend Christmas with us?'

'That, my friend,' he grins, 'will be flinkin' groovy!'

THE END

Acknowledgements

I am grateful to everyone at HarperCollins without whose patient advice this book would be very different and quite probably unreadable.

I owe particular thanks to the utterly brilliant editorial team who steer me through the fraught process of creation. Nick Lake, Julia Sanderson, Jane Tait and Samantha Stewart are a boundless source of suggestions, judicious cutting, accuracy and tact.

Apart from the publishing team, there are so many other people who play a part in your enjoyment of this book, including printers, wonderful booksellers and, if you're reading this in a language other than English, the very clever translators.

Thank you, all!

RW

The Real Maudie

I'm occasionally asked if I base characters on real people, and the answer is 'sometimes'.

This is me, aged about three, with the real Maudie Fry. Not an old woman, as you see, but an elderly gent, Mordant 'Mordy' Fry, who lived next door when I was little. He and his wife, my 'Aunty Fry', were a sweet, childless and rather old-fashioned couple who were endlessly kind to our family and were like an extra set of grandparents.

Aunty Fry died when I was five; Mordy a few years later.

This book is dedicated to their memory.